Jean

COAST-TO-COAST ACCLAIM FOR JOHN DUNNING AND HIS NATIONAL BESTSELLER

THE BOOKMAN'S WAKE

"*The Bookman's Wake* not only kept me up far too late one night, but got me up two hours early the next morning."
—*Boston Globe*

"*The Bookman's Wake* is the book we've all been hoping it would be. . . . Even more memorable than the plot are Dunning's characters and the harsh secrets they keep. . . . Nail-biting suspense."

—*Denver Post*

"Bless us all, Dunning and Janeway are back. As before, Dunning's text is enlivened with fascinating tidbits. . . . Nothing bookishly sedentary here."
—*Los Angeles Times Book Review*

"A stunning book. . . ."

—*Associated Press*

"The author . . . immerses the reader in this intriguing, little-known milieu without losing sight of the page-turning yarn he's spinning. In the end you may be disappointed that the last plot twist has finally played itself out."

—*People*

"Mad, fantastical, and darkly original. Bookbinding has never been so spellbinding. . . ."
—*Kirkus Reviews*

Books by John Dunning

FICTION

The Holland Suggestions
Looking for Ginger North
Denver
Deadline*
Booked to Die
The Bookman's Wake*

NONFICTION

Tune in Yesterday

*Published by POCKET BOOKS

DEADLINE

JOHN DUNNING

POCKET STAR BOOKS

New York London Toronto Sydney Tokyo Singapore

This book is a work of fiction. Names, characters, places and incidents are products of the author's imagination or are used fictitiously. Any resemblance to actual events or locales or persons, living or dead, is entirely coincidental.

 A Pocket Star Book published by
POCKET BOOKS, a division of Simon & Schuster Inc.
1230 Avenue of the Americas, New York, NY 10020

Copyright © 1981 by John Dunning

Published by arrangement with the author

ISBN: 0-671-00352-6

First Pocket Books printing February 1997

10 9 8 7 6 5 4 3 2 1

POCKET STAR BOOKS and colophon are registered trademarks of Simon & Schuster Inc.

Cover art by Danilo Ducak

Printed in the U.S.A.

Introduction

A fellow I knew once asked how long it takes to write a book. I thought he was kidding but I told him anyway.

It takes as long as it takes.

The Holland Suggestions and *Looking for Ginger North* took about six months each. But that was long ago and they were first novels. I didn't fret much then about the stuff I didn't know, being happily unaware how much of that stuff there was in the world.

Denver took eighteen months. This was a multi-layered historical novel with fifty characters and two major false starts. One of these snipe hunts ate up 300 pages. Once it got rolling, the book was written in 139 consecutive workdays—Saturdays, Sundays and Allegheny River Days all included.

Booked to Die took two years. Even then it didn't want to work until I sank all the way into despair, threw out the central idea and took up with a second-string plot.

The Bookman's Wake was three years on the fire. This was a trek through hell, full of false middles and bogus characters who appeared suddenly to muddy it up and were ruthlessly cut in later drafts. There were long interruptions, and the ending seemed to hang forever out of reach.

And then there was *Deadline*, the sweet little thing you hold in your hands.

Forget literary vanity—this isn't conceit talking. *Deadline* was a sweetheart because it was so free and easy, so author-friendly, that it was almost indecent. There was no struggle: it started in the right place and unfolded like a roadmap, leading straight to what then seemed like the inevitable conclusion. There were no fits and starts, no dips into hell, no groping around for True North. It took six weeks, start to finish, and remained for years the only book its author ever sold straight out of the typewriter, without having to suffer the agony-of-defeat known in the writing business as Rejection.

If I could do it again, and teach myself to do it on demand, I could maybe get rich. As a radio comic once said, you could bottle that and sell it to Rexall. It arrived like a new girlfriend comes to a teenager, unexpected and gone before he can stop and figure out what happened. Today, fourteen years later, I know how it happened. But I still don't know how to do it again.

A writer whose process has evolved into what can only be called slugging it out in the trenches cannot help being suspicious of a gift like that. I've always felt a little like a thief when I thought of *Deadline*. I want to hand it over with an apology, though I still run into readers who remember it as my best book. I have not re-read it in all these years, though I think of it often. There is always a temptation with a reissue to make changes. I know that, for starters, I'd be tempted to change the name of the heroine. I'd probably make her a Mary or a Rachel the way everyone else does when they write about the Amish. I know (and knew then) that Amish fathers do not name their daughters

Diana. Amish daughters do not do what this one does. But I also know that the surest thing about people is that they are wonderfully unpredictable. Individuals will always rise up and counter the flow of the tribe, no matter how hidebound and pious that particular tribe may look to an outsider. Jacob Yoder is, first of all, a man. And yes, there are runaways from that closed society, and a few do find what they're looking for and never return to that world they came from.

John Gardner once wrote that to change a character's name from Jane to Cynthia is to make the fictional ground shudder beneath her. Touch even this one thing, and I would have a different book: I would have turned this happy novel into a pit of snakes. So I'll tell you a few things about the process, then I'll let it go and be happy that this new edition is finally here.

A book needs hot fuel to propel it. Books written out of anger are sometimes the easiest to write and can be—if the author avoids heavy-handed preachiness—potent and effective work. *Deadline* and its predecessor, *Denver,* were written with the same bile-dipped pen. Both grew out of my experience at the Denver *Post,* where I arrived in 1966 on a wave of idealistic excitement. I soaked up the reporter's life: I was always turned on, it was like food and water, and I ate it up. Journalism is a marvelous career for a young man, and the *Post* was in every way my university. But it's a young man's game, and those who let themselves grow old in it risk becoming the cynical reporters of movies and books. Their salaries lock them in bondage and their alternatives are few. They can behave themselves, make friends of the right people and move up in management, where they quickly become—in the eyes of their former friends—part of the problem. They can move on to public relations, cheerfully promoting the interests of the villains they once tried to get indicted. They can wake up at forty simply dreading the prospects of another St. Patrick's Day Parade, another rubber-chicken luncheon speaker with a Ph.D. in boredom, another lady with a two-headed peacock. A few drop out and write books, a career that (I'm here to tell you) is not for the fainthearted or the guy with an addiction to regular paychecks.

This is all well and good but where, you ask me, did the anger come from? Without belaboring the point, let's say that there were one or two people in management at this otherwise fine newspaper who thought they had the right to kill investigative or critical stories when the controversy involved their friends. Angry? You bet. I still carry it a quarter of a century later.

But they were boss and I was not. I was gone.

Still, it was an experience. Henry James said that a young writer should try to be one of those people on whom nothing is lost, and here was a rich caldron of life simmering on the front burner. I was ready to write it, and I settled on an historical framework first for various reasons. In the 1920's the *Post* was steeped in yellow journalism. Its owners, Frederick Bonfils and Harry Tammen, were full of hell and willing to do most anything to sell newspapers or ad copy. The central focus of my novel *Denver* was to be the takeover of the state by the Ku Klux Klan, but the hero was a reporter for the *Post* who struggles against this evil stupidity and in the process must overcome a raft of personal problems and professional obstacles. It should be noted that, historically, Bonfils and Tammen were minor heroes in the Klan controversy. Bonfils crusaded editorially against the hooded bigots, and it was largely through his efforts that Mayor Ben Stapleton was exposed as a Klansman and subjected to a recall election, which failed. But it's easy to crusade against politicians and bad government. It's a different story when your advertising interests are on the line, and if history teaches us nothing else about Bonfils and Tammen, it tells us this: whatever else they did, they always operated with the economic health of their newspaper foremost in their minds. They would kill a reporter's Klan story, not for political reasons but because he had uncovered a membership roster that revealed most of their advertisers as Klan sympathizers.

Fair game, I decided. But when I wrote the finished scenes, the picture playing in my head was not of Tom Hastings, my hero, sitting in that *Post* newsroom in 1923. It was myself I saw, bucking the same brand of odious management in 1969. One scene in particular unfolded almost literally from life, exactly as it happened to a friend of mine and was later described to me. Instead of Chamber of Commerce kleagles from the 1920's, the villains were auto dealers of the 1960's, white-collar grafters who had been caught rolling back the odometers on their used cars. In fiction and life the results were the same: neither story saw the light of day, but by then my newspaper days were over.

Denver was a tough book to write. I say it took eighteen months, but in a sense I had been at it for the entire five years I worked on the newspaper and I'd been thinking about the newspaper parts of it during all the years since then. Now it was finished. I shipped it to my agent, Phyllis Westberg, in New York, and settled in for the uneasy wait. The next morning I came down to my workroom because this is what I do. I get up at 4:30 and if there's nothing to write, I sit at my desk. I was deep in the clutches of postpartum blues, at loose ends but full of restless energy. Suddenly, without idea or direction, without a character named or developed, I began to write a sketch for *Deadline*.

I still had the anger, the hot fuel to drive it. Even a book as big as *Denver* had barely skimmed the foam off the top of that volcanic kettle.

The following month, to my great amazement, I had a second book virtually ready to send to New York.

There's a principle that writers sometimes talk about when they gather in pubs or mingle with each other at cocktail parties. John Williams, who won a National Book Award for his novel *Augustus,* described it to me this way. You break the book's back. Call it what you will—getting a bead on it, seeing it at last for what it really is, finding the path to True North and having it all slip into place—whatever you call it, there's not a writer on earth who has not had that experience. You struggle with concepts big and small for weeks, months, years, and then it breaks and you see so clearly how it needs to go. How long it takes to reach this point is what determines the answer to the question that started this essay a few pages ago. The silliest inconsistencies hang you up forever. The smallest obstacle creates a ripple effect when you tinker with it, and the more you tinker with it the bigger the impact on material already written and yet to come. It can cascade back through the book with the power of a tidal wave, washing away your underpinnings and eroding your foundations. When this happens, you do what people along the Mississippi do every other year or so—you pick up your soggy stuff, rebuild your house and go on with it. If Jane simply must become Cynthia, with devastating consequences for Robert, you suck it up and let her do it. If Robert then jumps off a bridge, you follow that line and see where it goes. You follow your people into their various scenes knowing that every incident has its opposite possibility. The same thing could happen in another place, or between different characters, or with different results. Indecision and doubt ride with you day and night. The alternate worlds that can rise up in any one novel are terrifying as you contemplate working up yet another one. Your hero takes a turn and you can't know if it's right until sixty pages have passed and the trail has petered out in a box canyon. John Fowles, in *The French Lieutenant's Woman,* wanted Charles to turn left and go back to town; Charles went right instead, down to the dairy to meet Sarah. Charles is motivated by something Fowles can't yet understand, but it works. If it had not, I believe Fowles would tinker until it did.

On a far more common level, I can tell you that none of these acts of literary tightrope walking occurred in *Deadline.* Maybe I was wrong but I was never in doubt. The book came to life in a few hours and I broke its back that first morning. I quickly saw where it needed to go and what had to happen. I had little to lose—I still thought of it as a time-killer, an amusement to relieve my anxiety over *Denver.* I knew it would crap out against the big blank wall, probably by the weekend, so I could have my way with it for now.

I devised the plot from a clip file I kept, newspaper and magazine stories I had found interesting. I sat at my desk and began to deal out these articles like a poker player. I was attracted to items with no obvious links to the others—since this was for my own entertainment, I could make the long reach and take the big risk and the consequences would be a few wasted hours. I had a *Christian Science Monitor* wire story on the Amish. I clipped it out because people who cling to tradition in the midst of unrelenting "progress" interest me. I had a feature article from *Dance* magazine, of all places, on the Rockettes of Radio City

Music Hall. It was mainly a profile of Russ Markert, the man who created, recruited and trained this celebrated dance group. I don't remember if I laughed as I shoved the Rockettes and the Amish into the same little pile. What the hell, I was having fun.

I had a *Rocky Mountain News* piece about a young woman who had been killed by an unknown assailant. The woman herself was never identified and was buried in an unmarked potter's field grave. Other bits of business filtered in. The Patty Hearst kidnapping was still a hot topic. Student radicals hadn't yet been relegated to history. Daniel Ellsberg and the Pentagon Papers would play into it. And I knew I'd need some FBI people, who in their opposite extremes would represent good and evil.

Now I needed a hero, a man of the press to tap in to that hot fuel and drive the book.

Enter Dalton Walker, a guy I still think of as a close personal friend. Walker would be, first of all, a strong writer with all the national awards to back him up. Nothing impresses certain people in management as much as awards. I remember the day Bob Jackson visited the *Post*. Bob had taken the picture of Jack Ruby shooting Lee Harvey Oswald and had won a Pulitzer for that millisecond of glory. The story was laughingly told that a *Post* editor almost broke a leg chasing him down the hall to offer him a job, without first finding out if he knew a Brownie from a box lunch (he did, by the way, but he never blended in, and his *Post* tenure was brief). Like Jackson in real life, my fictional reporter had won the Pulitzer. To newspaper people, this is the equivalent of ascending the steps to the throne and sitting at the right hand of God. He is loved by management but secretly resented by the rank and file. His presence pisses them off mightily, and he becomes, of necessity, a loner. Walker would be so good that he could write his own ticket at the newspaper. He would do only the assignments that interested him. He'd be frequently on the outs with the city editor and would not be afraid to jump the bones of the bigger brass if he felt strongly about a point of contention. In other words, everything I'd like to be.

There was still something lacking somewhere. I looked again at the clippings about the unknown woman in potter's field and it sparked a memory of a much older case, similar, yet strikingly different. A few years earlier I had been struggling to make a living as a freelance magazine writer. I read the instructional books of one Max Gunther, a highly successful nonfiction writer whose work in the *Saturday Evening Post* and other periodicals I had admired. In one of his books (I'm going by memory here) Gunther had told a story that he had carried around for years and now knew he would never write. In the early 1940's, a circus tent had caught fire and some people had died. A small girl was among the victims, but her remains were never identified or claimed. The story haunted him. Who would bring a kid to the circus and not show up to identify her?

I opened my file of newspaper clippings and the answer stared up at me. There was an article about the FBI hunt for Katherine Ann Power, last of the fugitives from that 1970 Boston bank robbery. The FBI couldn't find her and they never did, until she came in under her own steam in 1993.

Kathy Power walked into the room, touched me on the shoulder and said I'm your gal. I'll play the role of Joanne Sayers.

What did I know about Katherine Ann Power? I had no way of knowing what her life was like, where she was hiding or what kind of person she might be. From nothing more than her situation Joanne Sayers grew, providing the counter-drive that carried the book to a finish in forty-two workdays.

Bang, it was done.

Deadline was published in 1981 as a Fawcett Gold Medal paperback original. A hardback was published the following year by Gollancz in England. The book was a runner-up for the Edgar award, if that means anything. Some people think it was filmed under the title *Witness,* but that 1985 Harrison Ford movie was wrought by other hands. It must've been a good idea whose time had come.

John Dunning
Denver, Colorado
April 1995

DEADLINE

One

Walker thought of himself as a hardened man. He had seen enough death in his time—riots, executions and later Vietnam—but now, coming suddenly upon death on a busy New Jersey street, he was shocked. On a dirt lot behind a shopping center, a circus tent was on fire. There wasn't anything to be done. If there were still people inside, they were goners, plain and simple. Still, he pulled the car to the curb and wrenched open the door, taking himself with long strides toward the burning canvas. The first of the fire trucks had arrived, but the tent already had crumbled in around its two main poles. It went up like a sheet of paper, reminding him of those old *Hindenburg* pictures with the people rushing out of the flames looking like ants scurrying away from something they couldn't quite understand. Rescue units came past; another large pumper came by in a shock wave of sirens. So much death, so much pain, and all in the few moments it took him to stop and cross the street.

It drew him until he could feel the heat on his face and arms. He was a kid again, covering his first fire, with a young man's fascination for the wailing siren. He had been around the world ten times over, had won a Pulitzer Prize and a National Book Award, and still he was drawn by sirens and smoke.

The tent belonged to one of those tiny traveling circuses, the kind his dad had known when the world was younger—the kind of circus kids used to run away to join. They didn't have many like that these days. The big tent had held three thousand people, no more, and now many of them lay moaning and writhing on the brown grass at the fringe of the parking lot. Two firemen brushed past, and one of them thrust the head of a stretcher at Walker. "Here, buddy, take this." Walker gripped the poles and looked at the man on the other end. A sad face by nature, infinitely sadder now over the tiny burden he carried. Walker looked down and saw a small body covered by a sheet. A kid; five, maybe six years old. Some poor little kid, here with his dad to see the circus. Walker wasn't a crying man, but he wanted to cry for that kid. He looked up as the sad fireman, with a nod of the head, directed him out of the lot to a small circle of rescue vehicles. They laid the stretcher on the ground and almost immediately a coroner came and peeled back the sheet and worked over the kid for a few minutes. It was a little girl, Walker now saw, a lovely child with dark hair and pale, almost milky skin. Her face was unmarked: it was so often smoke or the feet of the mob that did the damage. Her hand hung limply over the edge of the stretcher, the fingers dangling in the mud. Her other hand was folded across her middle, clutching a tiny bear, the kind you win at the booths. The coroner tried to pry the bear loose, then gave up and covered the pale face with the sheet.

Walker picked up the loose hand and folded it across the stretcher. He stood over the little body, feeling helpless and very much alone.

* * *

Her face haunted him. Maybe it was a quirk of the trade, but Walker always thought in terms of story. If a thing moved him, he assumed it would move his readers as well. Sometimes you got rid of something by simply letting enough time go by, and sometimes writing about it was easier and faster.

He remembered a story the Des Moines *Register* had done some years before about a fatal car accident. Some reporter had reconstructed the lives of all those kids, right up to the moment when their cars came together in that crossroad. Helluva story. His kind of piece. Driving through the Jersey streets, he thought of the little girl in those terms. Interview some survivors, maybe take them through their day. Not many, just four or five. No, three. Three was perfect. Probably have to interview twenty just to get the ones he wanted. Start tomorrow with the little girl: her father, mother, whoever had brought her to the circus. Make a few calls, see if they would be willing to talk about it. People were funny that way. Sometimes, just when you thought they were about to clam up, something would come out that was so incredible, so great, that it lifted the piece and made it sail.

It all depended on how you asked the questions.

Such arrogance. Walker was on his way to a job interview, with no guarantee that there would even be a newspaper to write for tomorrow. But he would get the job. He always did.

He walked into the *Tribune,* and into chaos. A guard directed him to the newsroom, and the first person he saw as he opened the door was some gruff-looking bird right out of MacArthur and Hecht, sitting in the slot on city desk and passing copy to a kid. Jesus. It made him want to laugh, but it was an emotional laugh filled with nostalgia. The *Tribune* was in an old building less than an hour out of New York. It was big and cumbersome. The lights were bad and the floor creaked; the desks were wooden antiques and the typewriters were old Royals with all their insides showing. Walker had come in on the tail end of the fire story. People were breaking their asses to get from here to there. Hot copy flowed along the chain of command, and all of it seemed to be funneled through a single rewrite man named Woodford. Walker sat at an empty desk and watched Woodford work. He recognized at once the hustle of an old wire service man. Woodford had surely done time in some AP or UPI bureau in the middle of nowhere, some dead-end place where speed is what counts and you might rewrite fifty little stories in a single eight-hour day. Nobody wrote as fast as old wire service men. Across the room, a young lady called, "Frank, I've got another survivor on Two."

Woodford strapped on his headset and talked to the survivor. While he talked, his fingers kept pounding out finished copy, which was ripped from his machine and sent along the chain to the backshop. Walker looked at the clock. He knew the *Tribune,* an afternoon paper, would be a good forty minutes over deadline now, holding the page open for everything that could be fit in. Walker looked up the chain and saw, standing at the head of the room, a graying man who was probably the editor, Hiram Byrnes, reading each pink dupe as it passed across his desk. Occasionally Byrnes got up and asked somebody a question. The question traveled backward along the entire chain of command, and eventually reached a reporter in the field, who either answered it or hurried away to find another source.

Walker found himself thinking of other newspapers and other breaking stories, and of the dead who were always the unknown elements in those stories. And suddenly the chaos ended. Across town they might still be counting the bodies, but for Hiram Byrnes and his staff of *Tribune* wordsmiths, the day was done. The backshop could hold no longer; the paper was put to bed for another day. Byrnes had seen Walker come in. He motioned Walker back to his office, a private inner sanctum, carpeted, paneled and decorated with journalistic awards. They shook hands. Byrnes said he had read his stuff and liked it.

"We've been going crazy around here," Byrnes said. "Circus tent caught fire about an hour ago."

Walker didn't say anything. He didn't want to start out by being interviewed as witness to a breaking story. Who needed that?

"Well." Byrnes sat behind the desk and lit a cigar. "I want you to meet our city editor, Joe Kanin. He'll be in as soon as he gets the loose ends tied up. What do you think of our plant?"

"So far I like it fine."

But Byrnes was laughing. "Don't bite your tongue on my account. I bet I know the first thing you thought when you opened that door. Jesus God, *The Front Page*. Tell me the truth."

"The thought did cross my mind."

Byrnes was still laughing. "That's all going to change in another year. We'll be getting new furniture, and we're converting to cold type now. I can't wait to get those old Royals out of here."

Walker didn't tell him, but the idea saddened him. He liked the newsroom the way it was, and he had always loved *The Front Page*. The thought of steel filing cabinets and steel desks and computer terminals depressed him.

Byrnes launched into the interview, and it went about as expected. Byrnes talked mainly about the *Tribune,* as though the paper—not Walker—were the interviewee. In a sense, that was true enough. Walker hadn't exactly been looking for work when Hiram Byrnes called from out of the blue and asked him to come in. Managing editors never asked about him. They knew all they needed to know about Dalton Michael Walker. They knew he had won the Pulitzer at *Newsday* while still in his mid-twenties. If they knew about the dozen-odd newspaper jobs he had had since then, it didn't seem to bother them, because if the Prize wasn't enough, he had won the National Book Award five years later for an investigation of labor union corruption. The Book Award was for distinguished achievement in contemporary affairs, the Pulitzer for what was strictly a writer's piece, his sensitive penetration of a dying woman's emotions. A woman he thought he would never forget, a woman of rare beauty and courage, a woman he never thought about any more.

The *Tribune* seemed hot to get him, and he needed the job. It had been six months since he had worked anywhere, and the novel he had planned to write just hadn't worked out. Maybe he was only a reporter after all; maybe fiction was a step or two above him. So when Hiram Byrnes called, Dalton Walker jumped. The *Tribune* had been a smallish daily covering the mundane happenings of the Jersey outback, but last year it was absorbed into the Knapp newspaper chain, and now it had national pretensions. Knapp wanted to do in New Jersey what *Newsday* had done on Long Island: hard-hitting features of national interest that would go on the wire to Knapp's ten other papers around the country. Hiram Byrnes had been hired away from the Los Angeles *Times* to oversee the frantic growth that followed.

That much Walker knew about the *Tribune*.

Byrnes told him more. "People in this business get defensive about what they do. Sometimes it takes a load of dynamite to blast away those old ideas. You'll see who the problems are for yourself before long. When Knapp took over, they swept out some good people along with the bad and brought in some bad people along with the good. Some in fairly strategic positions. My job is to get them the hell out of the way and make this thing a newspaper. You're the first of my handpicked men. Walker, I'm telling you this because I want you here. I mean, I *really* want you here."

Walker just looked at him.

"I don't want you getting pissed off and quitting in the first ten minutes," Byrnes said. "I know how many places you've worked and why you quit each one. I can't tell you you won't have those frustrations here too. I wish I could. All I'm saying is, if things start to get to you, take it up with me before you jump ship. Don't feel that you were hired to win us a Pulitzer. I don't want you working under that kind of pressure. You're here to get good stuff in the paper, and that's all you're here to do. I want stuff that reads like a bastard, stuff that tears their goddamn hearts out."

Walker stared into a dark corner and saw a tiny white face there.

"Stuff we'll be proud to send down the wire to the chain," Byrnes said. "That's the only way I can make my case to old man Knapp when the chips are down."

"I hear you," Walker said.

"Great. The job's yours. It was yours before you ever walked in. Any questions?"

"Who do I answer to?"

"The city editor is Joe Kanin, but I've told them to leave you alone. I asked Kanin to help get your legs under you, funnel a few good stories your way till you get used to working in the city again." He picked up the telephone. "Margie, is Joe free yet?" A few moments later Kanin came in. He was a bald man of medium height and build. Walker sized him up at once as an enemy. Kanin's attitude was one Walker had seen before, a coldness that telegraphed trouble. *All right, pal, you won the Prize, but I run the newsroom.* Walker had bucked that tide before.

Kanin ushered him out into the newsroom. Walker waited at city desk while Kanin dispatched a reporter-photographer team to interview more survivors for the second-day fire story. When they had gone, Kanin stood off and gave him a dose of the icy eye. Walker gave it back to him.

"What do they call you?" Kanin said. "Do you want to be called Dalton?"

"Walker's fine."

They made the rounds quickly. Kanin introduced him to everyone in the room, then gave him a desk in a far corner near a row of filing cabinets. It looked like a good place to be—out of the firing line, yet still in the newsroom. Close enough to pick up scuttlebutt, yet not so close that every assistant city editor with a two-headed dog would dump it on him. Byrnes could talk all day about leaving him alone, but Walker knew better.

He wasn't in the newsroom long before that judgment was partly confirmed. He had just settled into his desk when Kanin came over with his first assignment. He sat on the edge of Walker's desk, a scrap of paper in his hand. "Here's one that'll make a real *reader.* And it'll get you down into the city."

"I've been down in the city."

Kanin ignored him. "How much do you know about the Amish, Walker?"

"They're like Mennonites, aren't they?"

Kanin smiled crookedly. "Not quite. The Mennonites are less strict than the Amish. The Amish are religious fundamentalists, but they're also isolationists. They believe the old ways are better, in every facet of their lives. Their religion prohibits any kind of modern technology. Old World Amish can't have cars. They're mostly farmers, but they can't use tractors—nothing powered by fuel, nothing with rubber wheels. They can't have electricity in their homes. Dancing is prohibited, so is makeup. There is no interchange with other churches. What we have, in other words, is a horse-and-buggy society in the middle of the machine age. You follow me so far?"

Walker squinted. But he said, "I think so."

"Hiram said you like stories with natural conflict, so try this one for size. At Radio City Music Hall there's a girl dancing with the Rockettes who comes from an Old World Amish family. Maybe you don't see the story in that, but believe me, it's there. You have to understand about these people and how they raise their kids. Obedience to parents is like a commandment. To do what this girl has done would mean a total break from her family, excommunication from her church."

"Lots of kids break from their families."

"You haven't been listening to me, Walker. Amish kids aren't like other kids. They're raised in such isolation that they don't know how to cope with the real world. The parents won't even let them go to school beyond the eighth grade, for fear they'll be tempted by worldly pleasures. I want to know how this girl made the break. What kind of emotional hurdles she went through. How does she feel now? And how the hell did she learn to dance like that, after spending her first eighteen years milking cows and sewing quilts? You tell me, Walker, does that story have natural conflict?"

Walker had to admit that it did.

"It's got another element, as I'm sure you know," Kanin said. "Radio City is still glamour. It's a national showplace. All this talk about closing it down has brought it into the limelight again. People want to read about it. They're especially hungry for backstage

9

stuff, because there's a feeling afoot that it won't be with us much longer. Combine the glamour, nostalgia and the girl with a Stone Age background and you'll have a feature that any editor in the country would use. Helluva piece." Kanin dropped a paper on Walker's desk. On it was a name, which he read upside down as Diana Yoder.

"What's the girl say?" Walker asked. "I can't imagine she'd want to be interviewed about this."

Again Kanin flashed that crooked smile. "If it were easy, I'd give it to one of the kids. See you later, Walker."

He watched Kanin walk away, then took up the paper and looked at the name. Diana Yoder. Amish girl. Rockette.

It was a story, all right. No doubt about that, but it left Walker with the taste of salt on his tongue. The girl would tell him soon enough that her religion was her own business, and he would find himself agreeing with her. But he would do it anyway because he was a pro, and to some extent he lived by the code of the old-style reporter. You didn't turn down assignments unless you had an understanding somewhere. His understanding included a certain up-front period of city desk hassle, so he would start on the Yoder thing tomorrow. He settled into his desk, filling the rest of the afternoon with calls to old friends: cops, politicians, contacts from his fiery youth. Some of them he had known at *Newsday,* long years before. He tried Al Donovan four times during the afternoon without success. Of all the cops he had known then, he had always liked Donovan best. Donovan had been with the FBI since 1939. Walker hadn't talked with him in years, but he knew he would still find Donovan in that tiny FBI office in Brooklyn. Donovan had been there since the Red scare days, and they weren't about to start moving him around now.

Deadline

But Donovan was tied up for the day. When Walker tried his number the fourth time, the day was over. He would get Donovan another day. A few reporters dropped by to welcome him aboard; one or two came over just to size him up. One of the last to go was Frank Woodford, the old wire service man. He was plump and in his late forties, and he wore loud clothes.

Woodford said he was glad Walker was there, and he seemed to mean it. "This paper's so gray it's goddamn pathetic. We could use some bright stuff around here. Want to go for a beer?"

"Let me take a rain check. I've got a few more calls to make."

"What'll you be working on?" Woodford said.

"Whatever comes up."

Woodford leaned close. "Listen, let me plant a bug in your ear." He looked at Kanin, still busy across the room. "Don't let Kanin stick you with that goddamn Radio City thing. He's been trying to unload that for almost a year now. Gives it to every new hand who comes in."

"What is it, some initiation joke?"

"Hell no, he's as serious as a heart attack." Woodford made a wry face. "Oh, hell, it's a story all right, or would be if the girl would talk to anybody. If she even smells a reporter coming her way, she runs like hell. Kanin's made her totally gun-shy. It's one of them ungettable mothers."

Walker didn't believe in ungettable mothers. But he didn't say anything.

"Kanin's flipped on the girl," Woodford said. "Ever since he first heard about her—must be ten, twelve months now. The funny part is, he's never even laid eyes on her. Real strange. One time I got drunk with him and I just flat asked him about it. Turns out he's from Amish country himself. He was born and raised

11

on a farm in Indiana. When he was twenty he fell like a ton of bricks for this Amish girl. There was no way it could ever work out. Their religion forbids it, so the girl ups and marries someone else, some guy in her church. And old Joe winds up bald-headed and sour, pushing papers on city desk and giving people a bad time."

"How'd he hear about her in the first place?"

"Same way you hear about everything. Knew somebody who knows somebody at Radio City. Um, here he comes."

"How's it going?" Kanin said. He looked at Woodford suspiciously.

"Fine," Walker said. "I'm pretty well settled in. I can get started in the morning."

Kanin nodded and looked at Woodford. "How you hanging on the fire story?"

Woodford shrugged. "Two more people died about an hour ago. That makes seventeen for tomorrow's piece."

"You coming in early tomorrow to put it together?"

"What else?" Woodford said. "Pretty cut-and-dried stuff," he said to Walker. Then, to both of them, "There is one funny angle. One little girl. They haven't identified her yet."

Walker met Woodford's eyes.

"They got all the adults named?" Kanin asked.

"Yeah, that's the odd part. This kid must have come in with somebody who survived the fire."

"How could that happen?" Kanin's tone was short, impatient.

"Hey, don't ask me, Joe. I just put 'em together, I don't make 'em up."

"Well, why hasn't the mother turned up to claim the body?"

"That's what the coroner wants to know." Woodford shrugged. "People. Jesus, you never know what they'll do."

Walker leaned across the desk on a propped-up arm. "That's a pretty strange angle, don't you think?"

"It's interesting," Woodford agreed. "We'll keep after it till they find the mother."

"What if they don't?"

"They will. Hell, they've got to."

Walker looked at them for almost a full minute. "Well, I can't imagine anything more important to a woman than claiming her dead daughter's body. Any way you cut it, it's a helluva story."

"Maybe the mother doesn't know yet. Maybe there isn't any mother."

"Everybody in town knows by now. And if there isn't any mother, then what's the rest of it? Who brought the kid to the circus and left her there dead?"

Woodford shrugged. "Look, all I do is put 'em together. I'll let you guys play Hollywood dick."

"Walker's already got a story," Kanin said.

"This one's better," Walker said.

"Believe me," Kanin said. "They'll find the kid's mother by tomorrow morning. It'll be an old-fashioned sob story, routine and quite ordinary."

"If it is, I'll buy you a lunch," Walker said. "And I'll get on over to Radio City."

Kanin glared at Woodford, daring him to say anything. "I'd like you to get on over to Radio City anyway."

Walker met his eyes. "We'll see," he said.

Two

Sometimes there are cases that no one can solve. Any coroner with a few years' experience will tell you that. Depending on the size of his case load, there will usually be, in a year's time, three or four or eight or ten bodies for which there are no easy answers. There is no identity, no past. Occasionally not even a cause of death.

Somehow Walker knew, from the moment Woodford opened his mouth, that the little girl's case was going to be one of those strange ones. When there were still no leads on the little girl by noon of the next day, he knew he was right. The story slipped off the front page and became another tragedy soon forgotten, and Woodford went on to other things. But it hung there like a ripe plum. Walker thought about it at night, alone in his apartment, sipping bourbon and listening to Bach. The bare facts of the case made no sense at all. Even if there was no mother, seven-year-old kids do not lose themselves in the society. There are records, foster homes, places for kids like that; they do not exist independent of the society. In many ways, it would have been easier to trace an orphan than to locate a natural mother. The coroner tried. He was determined that he would not bury a seven-year-old Jane Doe. But he did, almost three months later, in the public graveyard where he had put so many faceless, nameless men.

Walker was there for the burial. He brought along a photographer from the *Trib,* and they covered the funeral just as if the little girl had been someone important. They were the only press there. It had long since become Walker's story, worked in around his other assignments in brief ten-minute snatches of his day. Kanin kept him busy, and Walker on his own had turned up some good stuff. But the little girl was always with him. He had made daily phone checks with the coroner for three months, and now called the man by his Christian name. Walker knew the progress of the case as he knew few other things on this earth. Huge blocks of story, still unwritten but formed whole in his mind, were dammed up just under the surface. They needed only a lead to bring them out. Now Walker had his lead. It was a sad story, a crier, not the kind of thing he had envisioned when he had adopted it three months earlier, but a good tale nonetheless. Anything with that much mystery and pathos had to, as Hiram Byrnes put it, read like a bastard.

Walker gave it his best shot. The afternoon of the funeral he stayed late in the newsroom, working and reworking the paragraphs for just the right effect. He was writing for one reader only: the lady or man who had brought a kid to see the circus, then disappeared as if the kid had never existed. That person was out there somewhere, watching the paper for his stuff. Walker was sure of that. One day about a week after the fire he had written a short piece, not really worth a byline, but they had given him one anyway. They were so anxious to get his name in the paper that they would have put it on the little girl's obit if he had written that. As if anyone outside the news business gave a damn. But it served a purpose, got him established in *someone's* mind as the guy covering the little girl thing. Late that afternoon a call came in for him through city desk. Kanin transferred it, but when Walker turned on his phone, no one answered. He was about to flip off the switch when he realized that someone was there. He heard breathing, then a squeaking noise like a phone booth door being opened. A car horn blew and the person hung up. He took off his headset and went over to the desk.

"That caller I just had. Did they say anything?"

"Just asked for you," Kanin said.

"Didn't give any name?"

"Just yours."

"Was it a man or a woman?"

Kanin blinked as if, in the heat of a busy day, he was having trouble remembering a call that had come through less than three minutes ago. Finally he said, "Woman."

"What'd she sound like? Young or old?"

"How am I supposed to know?"

"Was her voice soft or hard?"

"Jesus, Walker." Kanin sat back in his swivel chair and studied him. "It was soft, I guess. Sounded young, but how can you tell from just two words? I mean, Christ, that's all she said to me. Just your name."

Late that night, he had gotten another call at home. It was a transfer from the *Tribune* switchboard, coming in about ten o'clock. This time there was no background noise at all, just a hint that someone was there, like the scent of old perfume on pages of a book. "Is this about the little girl in the fire?" he said. Immediately the phone went dead.

In all these weeks the caller hadn't contacted him again, but he knew she was there, watching the paper.

He had written two more little girl pieces, each briefer than the one before, each containing fewer facts and less hope. On both pieces, in what must have been taken up front as incredible arrogance and conceit, he had typed in his own byline, removing what was normally the editor's prerogative. They had let them go through that way, though the last story had quickly become a newsroom joke. Containing a scant six graphs of copy, it looked top-heavy and ridiculous with his name perched above it. Some of the young turks had joked about it in the halls after work, and some of their words had reached his ears. *This is a prizewinner? Holy Christ, what a sham.* The newsroom hardass, a young defector from the *Daily News* named Grainger, had taken to calling him Hiram's Folly. But he still had his admirers. One kid named Jerry Wayne still thought he was God warmed over.

And he had to admit it: he really hadn't set the world on fire in his first few months. He had had a few good things, but nothing that anyone else couldn't have done. The Radio City piece had been a waste of time; he simply didn't have the stomach for it. Diana Yoder was a gem, a lovely creature who wanted nothing more than to dance and be left alone. Walker could dig that. But an ugly confrontation with Kanin had followed.

"The girl doesn't want to do it, Joe. She can't understand why you keep persecuting her. And I've got to tell you, I don't understand that either. You keep sending people after her and she keeps telling you no."

"Shit," Kanin said. "For this I send my top reporter. Tell me something I don't know yet."

Walker sat in the chair facing Kanin and ran his fingers through his hair. "Look," he said. "We've been going around and around on this piece. I keep trying to sidestep it and you keep getting in my way. So let's

17

get our cards right on the table, okay? You will never get that story in your newspaper if you wait around for me to do it."

"Like I said, tell me something I don't know."

"It's not my meat."

"So where does that leave us? I want that story."

"Then send somebody else. Go yourself if it's all that important."

"Very funny, Walker."

"I wasn't trying to be."

"There are ways of getting this story," Kanin said. "Ways other than talking to the girl herself. But I never thought I'd have to tell you that. I mean, you're the famous Dalton Walker, investigative reporter . . ."

"Oh, can the shit. This isn't some goddamn labor union, it's a sensitive, moving piece, or should be. It's worth absolutely nothing without the girl's cooperation. You can send any jack-off out on the streets to get the facts, but it takes somebody who gives a damn to write it. And I wouldn't touch it the way you want it done."

"We'll see about that." Kanin slammed his desk drawer, pushed back his chair and stalked away to Hiram Byrnes' office.

Later that afternoon, Byrnes called Walker in for a chat. Briefly Walker ran through the facts of the dispute with Kanin. "Don't worry," Byrnes said. "I'll get him off the Yoder girl's back. But what about you? You got anything going yet?"

"A few things. Mostly renewing old ties." He shrugged. "Sometimes these things take a while."

"Don't worry about it. I told you when you came here, you don't have any deadlines on this paper."

It sounded ideal. For a while he pretended it was, ignoring the talk floating around the office, ignoring Kanin's deadly glare, which could freeze water across a crowded room. The hell with them. He worked into things at his own pace. Tidbits on the circus fire, all filed into a fattening folder in his cabinet. Lunch with Al Donovan, who had gotten slightly heavier and a little whiter of hair in the years since Walker had last seen him. Donovan took him to a classy joint in Brooklyn, but Walker paid the tab, knowing that the FBI never paid for lunches. Later he turned in an expense account, which Kanin scowled at for a long time before signing. The hell with them. Let the *Tribune* buy Donovan's lunch.

Often, at night, he sat alone in the newsroom and thought about the little girl, and a tent burning, and a lady with a soft voice who wasn't there.

But now, after all these weeks, he had it. He had something anyway. He stood at the edge of the tiny grave and watched the coffin being lowered, and he had a yarn that would tear their goddamn hearts out. Two men descended on the grave and filled it in with shovels and spades. The minister, one of six retired preachers who rotated on the coroner's list, had said a few words over the grave, then went away with the caretaker of the cemetery, leaving only Walker, his photographer and the men with the shovels to stay to the end. When the men were finished, a bulldozer moved in and leveled off the earth, leaving not as much as a mound to show that someone was buried here. Walker sent the photog back to the paper alone. He wanted some time at graveside. He sat on the brown grass and watched the wind blow the clouds across the sky. He took note of that: what kind of day it was, how far down the hill the grave was placed, how far away the trees were. It would all go in, and woe to any editor who messed with it. This was one he would have to baby-sit all the way through the back-shop and onto Page One.

There was never any doubt in his mind that it was

front-page stuff. He put in everything he had learned in six interviews with the coroner. All the weeks of checking and hoping. The false leads, the one trail that had led to Cincinnati before petering out. The chemical analysis, the fingerprints taken from the unburned hand, the long waits between agencies while reports were compiled and sent back. All negative. Walker wrote it like a short story, beginning with a soft description of the graveyard, then backing into the eulogy by the minister. He flashed back from the graveyard to the coroner's office, and told about the long fruitless search for the little girl's identity. Then he moved back to the present, to graveside and the end of the minister's speech. He finished up in four or five quick lines, giving it a hollow, haunting ending as the men moved in and covered up the hole. He typed in his byline and in big, bold letters wrote the words NO CUTS across the top of the first take. It would drive them crazy on the desk, but they wouldn't touch it. They wouldn't dare.

Kanin edited the piece. The words NO CUTS hit him like a slap. His eyes, reflecting anger and insult, held Walker's for a long time before he began to read. Quite deliberately, he pushed aside his copy pencil. When he was finished, he hand-delivered the copy to the news desk and talked briefly with the news editor. When all that was done, he came to Walker's desk.

"As long as you're telling us how great you are, why not write Page One on it too?"

Walker smiled but Kanin's face was cold.

"I've told them to banner it across the top of One, just above the main news lead. Does that satisfy you?"

"That's fine, Joe."

"It's a hell of a reader."

Walker didn't say anything. He didn't think Kanin expected thanks.

"No use pretending I like you, Walker. I think you're undisciplined and arrogant and have no respect for anybody else. But I know good work when I get it. We'll be putting a copyright on your piece and sending it along to the chain. See, Walker, I can do something right. Even for you."

Walker went up to the cafeteria and sat unwinding over coffee. When he came back, there were two messages on his spike. Donovan had called, and Diana Yoder had left a New York number. The Yoder girl was a real surprise. But he couldn't reach either Yoder or Donovan with return calls, so he settled in to await the paper's arrival from the press room. When the proof came up, he read through every word in the story, chasing in a correction where the typesetter had typoed the coroner's name.

It was done and on the street. But if his hunch was right, it was just bait for the real story. Walker put on his coat and stalked out of the newsroom. The day was just half finished, but he wouldn't be back. Everyone watched him go. No one said a word.

He tried his calls again from his apartment. Donovan was still out, but Diana Yoder answered at once. "Yes, Mr. Walker, thank you for returning my call. This morning I got a call from a Mr. Hiram Byrnes, who I believe is one of your editors."

"He is our editor."

She paused, not understanding the difference. "Mr. Byrnes was very generous. He apologized for having that man harass me all these months. He said it wouldn't happen again. He mentioned your name, so I feel I have you to thank for that."

"You were right and we were wrong. It's as simple as that."

"I felt I had to call you. I was terrible to you when you came to see me."

"Ah, the infamous thirty-second meeting." He laughed, thinking about it. Thirty seconds of frustration, before she had slammed a door in his face. "I'm sorry if the *Tribune* caused you any embarrassment."

"You're very gracious, Mr. Walker."

He had been called many things in his life, but never that. It brought out the worst in him. He asked her for a date.

She paused, actually considering it. Then she said, "I don't think so. I really don't think it's a good idea."

"Okay, I won't press you."

"You are a gracious man. Not my image of reporters at all."

"You're not my image of Rockettes either."

There was another moment of silence.

"Goodbye, Mr. Walker. And thanks again."

He found himself thinking, as he always did when he had just been turned down by a woman he found especially interesting, it's just as well. Women had a way of complicating his life, right when he needed it least. The Marilyn Jacksons of the world. Jesus, there was a name from the dim past. The Anne Rinkers. A girl named Lois Berman, whose parents fussed so much about her dating a non-Jew that they drove her crazy. And that crazy blond kid he had married a lifetime ago, her face now a pale white blur in his mind. Elena. The ghosts of a slow Thursday, spent as usual alone, with too much time on his hands.

Pushing Diana Yoder aside with the rest of them, he began to change his clothes. After he got into old jeans and a flannel shirt, he put on a heavy jacket against the cool night and walked to the cemetery. Black clouds formed over the sun as it settled in the west. In another hour it would be dark. He walked quickly, past paper racks displaying his morning's work. It was letter-perfect, the story, the play, everything. Even the headline was perfect. Streamed across the top of the page, just above the political crap from Washington, it said, IN THE COLD DARKNESS OF PLOT 33, A LITTLE GIRL SLEEPS. He couldn't have asked for a better shot.

Now, if this didn't work, he faced two choices equally grim. He could abandon the story or keep checking school rosters as Donovan had suggested. At first that had seemed his best choice: check the schools in a given radius, find out how many little girls had suddenly dropped out for whatever reason, then go through them in a slow process of elimination. He had expected a big job, but even so he wasn't prepared for what he got: 112 names, all kids between first and third grades, all attending schools in the densely populated Jersey suburbs, all transferred for one reason or another. He had worked through five names before understanding the full scope of the nightmare he had carved out for himself. One mother had remarried and moved to California, taking her kid with her. Another family had moved to Maine. A third little girl had had an accident, falling from a horse on a vacation in upstate New York. She was still in a coma. The fourth had transferred to Brooklyn. The fifth belonged to a State Department family, and the father was on his way to Belgium. It had taken Walker seven days to check out those five names to his own satisfaction. Then, as the funeral story came to a head, he formed his grand plan.

He walked through the cemetery gates, past the caretaker's cottage and along the tree-lined road where the respectable people were buried. At the far end of the cemetery proper, he left the trees and came out along a barren hillside that dipped gradually toward the river. In the distance he could see New York. Lights were coming on and people were coming out to play. In the west, the sun was nothing more than a streaking white memory behind the clouds. Walker cursed as a light rain began falling.

There was a scrubby group of trees at the very bottom of the hill, about thirty yards from the damp earth where the little girl was buried. Walker reached it as the last trace of daylight snuffed itself out. The dark shadows engulfed him as he sank back against a gnarled tree trunk. He waited.

Three

———

She came but it was hours later. Though Walker hadn't brought a watch, he thought midnight must have come and gone before he saw the first movement in the trees above the hill. She came quickly, surely, as though she knew the way well. She reached the rim and started down the hill, walking down the dirt road toward him without once breaking stride. She stopped near the bottom, her first moment of confusion. A tiny penlight came out of the cloth bag she carried, and she played it first along the ground and then at a copy of that day's *Tribune*. It took her perhaps five minutes, feeling her way along with the tiny light, to find the place where the little girl lay. In the dark the grave was almost indistinguishable from the earth around it. The dirt had sunk in slightly and was softer there, wet. The woman dropped to her knees in the mud and Walker heard a long sigh, breaking up at the end into a moan of raw grief. She began to sob, then cried violently over the grave for perhaps five minutes. Walker, watching from the trees, felt sad and a little sick. He was an interloper in a drama intended to remain very private. Something he would now make very public, because that's what he did for a living and it was that kind of story. Real front-page stuff, wherever features were valued as much as hard news, and it didn't matter much what the woman's reasons were.

It had the same taste as the Diana Yoder thing, only with this one there was no question of the public's right to know. It was a police case, an unsolved coroner's case, and possibly a court case as well. And if this sobbing woman was in fact the little girl's mother, it was the best possible angle for his story. A hell of a reader. But suddenly, for no good reason other than the woman's tears, he didn't want to do the goddamned thing. He was getting soft in his old age. He pushed away from the tree and was about to confront her, when she opened her bag and took out a small but unmistakable gun. She put the gun in her jacket pocket, took out what looked like wire cutters, then reached deeper in the bag and found what she wanted. A cluster of flowers. This she put on the grave, in the center of the pool of water, since she had no way of knowing the head from the foot. She put the wire cutters back in the bag, then the gun, drawing the strings tight and holding it against her legs. For perhaps five minutes she sat like that, soundless, absolutely still. Then, again, she broke down and cried.

Walker didn't move. He hardly breathed. The gun added a new element. The possibility that the woman was deranged now loomed large and real. Suddenly she stood and came toward him, swinging the cloth bag at her side. He heard her sniff as she came close. He couldn't see much about her in the moonless sky, other than the fact that she was slim and of medium height. She turned away and started up the long hill. He waited until she was almost to the top before he moved. At the top, he hurried along under cover of trees, leaving the road and cutting through the main graveyard, moving carefully between the tombstones toward the street.

She was just a shadow ahead of him as she neared the caretaker's cottage and the locked main gate, where she left the road. She skirted the fence until she reached a far corner. There she disappeared for a moment, and Walker had to hurry to avoid losing her. He did lose her, for more than a minute, but then she appeared outside the fence, walking along the street in the general direction of Newark.

He found her escape hatch. She had cut a piece out of the wire fence, just big enough to let her through. He wiggled through and into a ditch. When he stood, he saw her about a hundred yards ahead, getting into an old car that was parked under a streetlight—a Ford of some late 1950s vintage, green he thought, with a white strip around the middle. As he hurried toward it, the car started in a puff of blue smoke. It eased into the street and pulled away, but he got close enough to get the license number.

In the morning he called Donovan.

"I saw your splash last night," Donovan said. "Same old Walker. Once you get something, you never let up."

"That sounds like my description of you."

"Maybe so, twenty years ago. Little too old, too slow now. I can't keep up with you young guys."

"I didn't know you read the *Trib* way over in Brooklyn."

"You'd be surprised at what we read," Donovan said. "What's on your mind?"

"Hell, Al, you called me, remember? I'm returning your call of yesterday."

"See how you get in old age? Completely slipped my mind. I wanted you to come by my place, say a week from tonight, for a bit of beef and booze. You've never met my wife. We can sit around and talk old times. You can tell her how great I was before I went over the hill."

"What time?"

"Around seven. Bring somebody if you want to."

Walker thought of the Yoder girl, and what a strange group they would make sitting in Al Donovan's backyard. But he said, "There's nobody to bring, Al. But I'll be glad to come solo, if that's okay. And listen, while I've got you, you could do me a big favor."

"Shoot."

Walker fed him the license number. "Could you find out whose car that is?"

"Is it hot?"

"Not that I know of."

"Sure, Walker, I'll help you out. Same rules as before, right?"

"You scratch my back . . ."

"And you scratch mine. If and when the time ever comes."

Donovan called back about ten minutes later. The car was registered to a Hal Gunther, whose street address lay in a quiet little community halfway between Orange and Union. Walker checked it against his list of little girls, but there was no one named Gunther and no one of that address. He drove there in just over half an hour, not bothering to wear his tie or check in with the office first. The street was narrow and tree-lined, and at midmorning nearly empty of cars. It was strictly residential, some four blocks west of Sanford Avenue. The kind of neighborhood where he had played stickball as a kid. Raced through backyards in bursts of fantasy and sheer joy. Played circus in a neighbor kid's yard, swallowed by time, yet in actual distance not far from here. If it still existed at all.

Walker never went back to his old neighborhood anymore, except in his mind. It was always too painful. There was always some motel, or a new Piggly Wiggly, or worst of all a vacant lot, where people had lived in the old days. But Hal Gunther's neighborhood had escaped the ravages of time. The houses, built in the late 1920s or early 1930s, had held up well. Most were newly painted. What grass there was had been watered and cut, and some of the yards had hedges and gardens. Walker drove past the Gunther house without stopping. The car wasn't there, but Walker could see a big black oil spot on the driveway where it was usually parked. The garage was closed. Probably full of crap. In Walker's youth, people had used their garages for their cars. Today they used them for their crap. Junk they wouldn't ever use again, or think about, or want. It piled up and up until the car couldn't get in the garage anymore and had to be left on the street or in the driveway.

He went around the corner, parked and locked his car, and started back on foot. He walked lazily up the street, to the casual eye a stroller who had nowhere to go and was taking his time about it. But a second glance at the house revealed nothing new. Curtains were pulled across the windows, and it had the look of a million other houses abandoned for the day by working people. He went on down the block and around, thinking. Somewhere there were pieces missing, things he didn't know that went beyond the mother's unknown reasons. Who the hell was Hal Gunther? Somehow Walker hadn't expected a father too.

He was circling the block, taking the long way back to his car and nudging the pieces around in his mind, when he saw the car sitting in a driveway just ahead. It was the same Ford, same coloring, same license

John Dunning

plate—and yes, a shiny oil spot under it, big as a bedpan—parked on a side street about a block from the Gunther house. Most of the houses looked alike. This one differed only in color and a few basics. Like the Gunther place, it was heavily curtained, the garage closed, and the tree out front looked like a dying friend. There was a FOR SALE sign under the tree.

Walker turned in. He would face the elusive lady and play it by ear from there. He could always pretend to be a buyer looking at her house. He rang the bell, but no one answered. He backed away from the steps, and noticed something white through the slit in the mailbox. He opened the top and fished it out. A piece of junk mail, prepared by computer from lists that magazines so unethically sell to anyone who will buy them. The name on the envelope was Mrs. Melinda Baker. The name rang a vague bell somewhere. He had heard it, and recently. He dropped the letter back into the box and hurried around the corner to his car.

He checked the name against his list of missing school kids, and there she was. Robin Baker, age eight, grade three, Robert F. Kennedy Grammar School, about six blocks from there. Robin Baker, daughter of Melinda Baker, who, the record insisted, had taken her daughter and moved to Bakersfield, California.

Robin Baker's last day of school was Tuesday, the day before the circus fire.

In all his nationwide checking, somehow the coroner had failed to find what had been in his backyard all along. Walker drove around to Hal Gunther's place and sat across the street, watching. Now he saw that this house too was for sale. Wind had blown the sign around, making it hard to see from the street. His eyes narrowed. He had all the answers now but the last few. Why had it happened? And who was Mrs.

Baker's neighbor, Hal Gunther, who let her have his car as if it were her own?

Walker didn't go to the office all day. He returned to his apartment for a few hours' rest, then went back to the Baker house. By the time he arrived, it was dark. The car was gone from Mrs. Baker's driveway and was now parked at Gunther's, around the corner. Lights were on in both houses. He parked across from Mrs. Baker's, sank down in his seat and waited.

She came out about an hour later. She was carrying the cloth bag and wore her hair up, tied with a scarf. Her dress was casual. She walked quickly, and to Walker's surprise she turned away from the Gunther house and headed east, toward the bus stop. At the corner she waited under a streetlight. Walker went back for his car.

Following a crosstown bus at night was tricky, but when Melinda Baker got off in an industrial subdivision near Elizabeth, Walker was there, able to park and watch her. She crossed the street and went into a bar.

He got out and followed her inside. She was sitting at the far end, sipping a tall drink. Her bag lay on the floor under her stool. Taking a stool near the door, he watched her in the mirror. She looked to be in her late twenties, slender and good-looking. She wore glasses, bifocals, and was having trouble with them. She took them off frequently and rubbed her eyes. She sat there through two drinks. Then a young stud came in and put the make on her.

They left together.

To Walker, sitting about ten stools away, their talk, and especially their body language, was loud and clear. It was obvious that they hadn't known each other. The stud saw her sitting alone and went right to work. She told him her name. It was so easy it was almost a joke. It had taken less than five minutes for the guy to get to her.

Walker was in no hurry to leave. He thought he knew where they were going: if not to her place, he could at least find her there when he wanted her. He still had some thinking to do about this one. A wrong move could . . . he didn't know what it might do. Melinda Baker displayed all the symptoms of a schizophrenic. Her house was for sale and her daughter was dead. She lived in secret and visited the grave at midnight. She carried a gun and she picked up men in dark bars. Obviously she had given thought to leaving town. In her place, he thought, he might too.

Four

Walker was a great believer in the powers of the subconscious, that part of the brain that worked while the rest slept. He slept late the next morning, went into the office around noon and told Kanin he was working on something that might or might not pan out. Kanin wanted to know what, but Walker wouldn't be pushed. If Kanin knew how close he was to having the Melinda Baker piece ready for the street, he would get that look that all city editors get when they smell a story coming. Then he'd start pushing Walker to get it done. They would ride roughshod over the woman before he could learn what she was about. The tiny details, the little threads of emotion that would make a sensational story something truly fine would be left dangling, hinted at but only half developed.

He drove past the Baker house again. The sign said FOR SALE BY OWNER. There were two phone numbers beneath it, which Walker had copied into his notebook yesterday. An identical sign, with the same two numbers, was posted outside the Gunther house. From a phone booth three blocks away, he tried both numbers. There was no answer at either. He spent his day in the county clerk's office, looking up records of the property transactions. Hal Gunther and Melinda Baker had bought the houses at the same time, from a single source, and had lived there for five years. Mrs. Baker's handwriting was clear and quite ordinary. In the late afternoon Walker ate alone and went home to try the numbers again.

He flipped the TV dial while he looked through his notebook for the numbers. NBC was repeating a special on Radio City. Gregory Peck was host, there were appearances by Ann-Margret and Beverly Sills, and a promise of backstage interviews with the Rockettes. He turned the sound down while he made his calls. Melinda Baker answered almost at once.

"Hello." As Kanin had said, her voice was soft.

"I saw your sign. Is the house still available?"

"Yes."

"How much are you asking for it?"

"Forty-five thousand."

He paused, just long enough. She said, "That's open to negotiation."

"In that case, I'd like to see it."

"Can you come at night? I work during the day."

"Tomorrow night?"

"Sure, fine. Say around eight o'clock?"

"I'll be there."

"Would you mind giving me your name?" she said. "So I'll know it's you. I like to know who I'm letting in."

"My name is Jason Webster."

His first lie. It was an unwritten rule in journalism, Thou Shalt Not Lie. Ethically, a reporter should always identify himself fully to anyone who might find himself quoted in a story. After that, the source is fair game, and anything he says may be published and used against him. A rule of Hoyle, made up by people who never had to play the game.

He made his second call.

A man answered and Walker went through the routine again. He gave the same name, and the man told him to come by tomorrow after work. Five o'clock. Again the asking price was forty-five grand. And again, when Walker paused, the man said he was open to a deal.

Gregory Peck flashed on the Sony screen. Walker wondered if Gregory Peck had ever lied in the performance of his job. Right now Gregory Peck was talking about Roxy, who had opened Radio City almost fifty years ago. The camera panned the splendor of the lobby, while Gregory Peck went on and on about how grand it was. On came the Rockettes. Walker drew up close and peered at the seven-inch screen to watch the girls making up at the dressing room mirrors, laughing and talking to each other just like real people. The incredible world of Diana Yoder, Amish girl.

He looked for her as the camera found the faces of the Rockettes in a series of close-ups. Few were beautiful, but all were nice-looking, white and worked into the regiment by rigid limitations of height and weight. The all-American gals, pure apple pie. But Diana Yoder wasn't among them, at least not for NBC and the nation. The camera finished its probe of the famous line of high-kickers, and each girl said her name. And for nearly an hour Dalton Michael Walker escaped his solitary, slightly bitter world and became a kid again. It reminded him slightly of the old Mickey Mouse Club. *Annette!* Slight curtsy. *Darleen!* Small tilt of head. *Doreen!* Doreen had always been his favorite. His crush on her had lasted two years. In his adolescent fantasies he had imagined her nude. A full twenty years later she surfaced in the buff in a

Gallery Magazine spread. He hadn't even bought the magazine. Somehow it seemed like an invasion of *his* privacy.

He watched for Diana, just as he had watched for Doreen in the old days. When she wasn't there, he was disappointed but hardly surprised.

Gregory Peck told him what it was like being a Rockette, and Ann-Margret and Beverly Sills sat in the empty rotunda and sang some songs. Ann-Margret told Beverly Sills how great she was, and Beverly Sills looked humble and very regular. Beverly Sills laughed a lot. She had always been one of Walker's favorite people.

In the morning Walker took a bus into New York and caught the early show at Radio City. They were reshowing *Fantasia*. He watched it all the way through, trying to rekindle those childlike feelings that had started the night before.

Then the stage show started, and Jesus, it was a spectacle. He never came to Radio City Music Hall without being awed, without realizing what a national tragedy it would be if they closed it. At the same time he knew the inevitability of its closing. It was a lovely dinosaur, a palace in an age when smallness and cheapness were virtues, when people were packed like tuna into mini-theaters and heard more of the marital arguments in the row behind them than they heard of the performance. He estimated the audience at around twelve hundred, and the place was one-fifth full.

But never mind. On came the Rockettes, doing a toy soldier routine that had something to do with the changing seasons. The line formed and did its eye-level high dance. Some inspired bastard backstage, some genius whose mind Walker couldn't begin to cope with, had guided, molded and maybe bullied these girls into line. He didn't know how it had been done, only that it had, and it was dying out to a new kind of entertainment that depended, as Count Basie had said, more on electronics than artists. The goddamn electrician was the most important man in today's big band.

Walker tried to spot Diana Yoder in the line, but couldn't be sure. Afterward, he couldn't help himself. He went around to the Fiftieth Street stage door and told the guard he was a reporter, there to see one of the girls. He flashed his press pass and in a moment someone came to show him in. An elevator took them down to the stage, now draped and beginning the Disney flick again. He walked behind the screen, across the blue floor, where great machines could move sections of the stage up or down. He waited, and eventually some of the girls came along, dressed for the street. Finally Diana Yoder came too.

She was surprised, and maybe a little angry. "Mr. Walker," she said. Her cheeks were red as she came forward.

"I saw your show. I wanted to tell you how great it was."

"Thank you." She stopped about ten feet away and kept watching him suspiciously.

"And to ask you one more time if you'll let me take you somewhere for lunch."

"Mr. Walker . . ."

"Don't say no yet. Afterward I'll take you to Radio City Music Hall, to see the world-famous Rockettes. Eighth wonder of the world. How can you keep turning me down?"

She smiled, giving him a little hope. She came closer and looked at him for what seemed a long time. "I'll tell you," she said at last. "You may take me to lunch, Mr. Walker. Buy me a salad and a glass of tea, and I'll tell you why I won't go out with you."

"Look, what is it with you women?" Walker said over lunch. "Do you work all the time, or do you get Saturdays and Sundays off?"

"We work in shifts. We rotate. Three weeks on, then one week off. When we're on, we work very very hard."

"And when you're off, what then? Do you relax just as hard?"

"We do whatever we want."

"When are you off again?"

"Next week. And I'm ready for it."

They had gone to a small place in Rockefeller Center, a restaurant under the street, in a marble mall above subway level. She seemed to know the waiter, who brought her a chef's salad and a glass of iced tea.

"I missed you last night," Walker said.

She looked confused.

"On NBC."

"Oh, that. I had an awful time getting out of that."

"When you weren't there, I thought I'd better check you out, make sure you're still alive."

"Mr. Walker, when will you people learn that I don't want to be checked out?"

"Just kidding." He held up both hands in a mock truce.

She smiled. "You probably think I take myself awfully seriously."

He shrugged. "Everybody does that."

"It's just that the things that man . . . your editor . . . wanted me to talk about were very painful to me. Still are. And some of them haven't been resolved yet. I still don't know what I'm doing with my life. Can you understand that?"

"Listen, I wrote the book on that."

"Really? Then maybe you do understand. When two forces are tearing at you, pulling in directions that not only are opposites, but are mortal enemies with each other. And you love and hate each almost equally . . . I really don't want to go into it, didn't mean to say even this much. It's just that I want you to understand. When I tell you no, I'm not rejecting you. All I'm telling you is I've got enough problems in my life right now. You seem like a kind and decent man . . ."

"And gracious. Don't forget gracious."

She laughed. "That too."

"And you think going out with me would be just another problem."

"It could be. And I don't need that. Mr. Walker, I don't even need the possibility of that."

"Don't you date anybody?"

Her extended silence let him know that the question was out of line.

Levity returned. He felt her slipping away from him, and suddenly it was important that she not do that. "The nation missed you last night."

"I doubt that."

"Ann-Margret missed you."

"I'm sure."

"Beverly Sills missed you."

She laughed again.

"Even weathered old Gregory Peck missed you. Did you watch it?"

"Sure. I wouldn't have missed it. I saw it the first time too."

"Didn't you think they all looked lonely in that big empty palace?"

"Being lonely doesn't have anything to do with a particular place, Mr. Walker, or how many people are around you."

"Amen to that. Are you lonely?"

Again he had come too close. For a long time she didn't say anything. When she did she was very direct. She looked at him when she talked and said what she felt. "I like you, and the trouble is, I don't want to do that. Why else do people date but to get close to each other? And if you don't want to get close to anyone, what future is there in it but pain and regret?"

"There are other reasons."

"Answer that for me in a way I like and who knows, maybe I'll go out with you."

"You remember Scott Fitzgerald's line about it always being three o'clock in the morning, deep down in the bottom of the soul?"

"Yes, I read it."

"Sometimes people date just to help each other push back the dark."

The sun had dropped low over the Jersey sprawl. Walker sat in his car and waited for five o'clock. He listened to the radio and occasionally looked at the paper she had given him at the stage door. It had *Diana* and her home phone number on it. A Manhattan circuit.

At exactly five o'clock he pulled up in front of the Gunther house. The green-and-white Ford was parked in the driveway, and the living room curtains were drawn back to reveal part of a room, an archway leading back into the house and a piece of refrigerator against a far wall. The man answered his ring. He introduced himself as Hal Gunther. A moment later a woman he called Barbara came out. Walker expected the wife to be the strange Melinda Baker, but this woman wasn't even a good imitation. She was blond, attractive enough in her own way, but clearly didn't try too hard. She was plump, about thirty. Her husband was older by several years, a huge man, bearded and prematurely graying. Streaks of gray were shot through his beard and hair, and his hands bore the hard skin of a working man.

Gunther's face started Walker thinking. It wasn't an old face. Only the regular touches of gray made Gunther look old beyond his years. They went through the house quickly. It was small, two bedrooms, a full bath and an unfinished basement. Walker saw everything, from the color of the telephone to the books on Gunther's shelves. Most of the books were philosophy, which didn't quite go with the hard hands and the slightly stooped shoulders.

He asked to use their bathroom. He turned on the water to cover any noise, then opened the medicine cabinet and looked inside. Nothing unusual. In a corner, set into a wall near the sink, was a linen closet. There were a few things pushed far back, behind the towels: a shoeshine kit, a box of black keys and a small bottle of hair dye, about half full.

He took off the cap. It was gray.

He replaced everything and turned off the water. The Gunthers were waiting in the living room when he came out.

"Well, what'd you think?" Gunther looked nervous, almost like a cat ready to pounce.

Walker sat and faced them. "I was kinda looking for something a little cheaper."

Gunther gave a mirthless little laugh. "God, fella, if you find anything cheaper around here, you'll be in the slum landlord business."

"Still . . ."

"All right, all right." Gunther was impatient, edgy. "How cheap is cheap?"

"Thirty. Thirty-five tops."

"Oh, man, you're wasting our time. We told you on the phone what the price was."

Mrs. Gunther put her hand on her husband's arm.

"Well, it bothers me when people waste my time."

"If it bothers you, then I'll leave," Walker said.

"He didn't mean that," the woman said.

Gunther looked at her, then nodded his head. "She's right, Mr. . . . Webb, is it?"

"Webster."

"Yeah, I don't mean it. We're in a bind right now. We need to sell it pretty quick and get out to the coast, before I lose something pretty important. You know how that is."

"Sure."

"Still, I won't be shafted. Hell, I paid thirty for it."

"Then you won't be losing anything."

"The hell I won't. What do you think inflation is, a working man's picnic? Where do you think I'm gonna get the cash for those inflated houses in L.A. if I let you stick it to me like this?"

"Mister, I haven't even offered thirty yet. This is a pretty small place."

Gunther stood and suddenly, in the deepening shadows of the living room, he looked menacing.

"What are you, some fucking joker?"

"Hal . . ." Mrs. Gunther reached for his arm, but he jerked it away.

"I don't have time for shit like this," Gunther said.

Walker got up too, but slowly, carefully. Gunther was a good four inches taller, and outweighed him by fifty pounds. But it wasn't so much size as the look in Gunther's eyes that bothered him. Gunther's look had something that Walker could only describe as primitive. Savage. Here, he decided, was a man not to fool with.

"I'm sorry, Mr. Gunther. No offense meant."

Neither of the Gunthers said anything. Their eyes followed him to the door and out. At the sidewalk he turned and saw Mrs. Gunther drawing the curtains. Their eyes locked for a second, then Gunther drew her away.

The scene later at Melinda Baker's house was different. He worried for a while that the Gunthers might tell the Baker woman about him, so he started by telling her himself. She seemed disinterested, as if she had no connection with the Gunthers, or with their house. Nervous, extremely jumpy as she talked, she paced and chain-smoked, moving occasionally to the window in the front door, peeling back the curtain an inch or so to peep out into the dark street.

His first impression was that she looked familiar somehow. Her face, finely carved, smooth, almost babyish, reflected first an intense interest, then boredom in the same breath. Her eyes were like buckets of water behind the thick glass of her bifocals. She talked, as she looked, nervously. And Walker had a hunch, when he had been in the house less than five minutes, that she wanted to unload it at any price and simply disappear.

He decided to test her. "Forty-five's a bit steep."

She shrugged. "What do you think's fair?"

He moved through the rooms. The house was of the same general construction as the Gunther place, undoubtedly built by the same contractor at the same time. The birth of mass production.

"I was thinking more on the order of thirty."

"All right."

She had taken him by surprise. "All right what?" he said.

"All right thirty. You can have it for that." She lit a cigarette and walked to the window.

"Just like that?"

"What more is there?"

He pushed her a little harder. "Even at thirty it's no prize."

He was looking down the hall toward the back door. For a moment she didn't respond, and when he turned again two streaks of tears had begun trickling down her cheeks. Her hands were trembling. She looked away quickly, toward the street, and dried her eyes with the back of her hand.

"I owe the bank eighteen on it," she said. "I'll need some cash on top of that, say four, five thousand, to clear up some things. Twenty-three, Mr. Webster. Is that cheap enough for you?"

"It's too cheap, Mrs. Baker. I'll be in touch."

There was something wrong with these people, all three of them. It went far deeper than a little girl's death in a circus fire, but he still didn't know what direction it was going to take next. All he knew for sure was that they had taken the same crisis and reacted to it in different ways. Mrs. Gunther was wound tighter than a drum. Her husband tottered on the brink of violence. And in the agonized eyes of Melinda Baker, Walker had seen the deepest fear he had ever known.

Five

Walker and a guy named Larry Burke sat in an unmarked car up the street and across from the Gunther house. Burke, who was the *Tribune*'s best photog, screwed a long lens into his camera while they waited. It was very early on a Monday morning; the sun hadn't yet broken above the rooftops to the east. The house looked empty and dark. The green-and-white Ford was sitting in the driveway.

In the *Trib* car, Burke sat under the wheel, slouching, two cameras draped around his neck. Walker knew Burke didn't like it. Photographers never like a blind assignment—it took away more option than photogs liked to give up. Photogs liked to run their own show. They wanted you to tell them what the story was, no more, then get the hell out of the way and let them shoot it the way they wanted. That was how the good ones worked. They were often difficult and sour, especially in situations where their talents were subordinated to those of the reporter. Walker had a theory. If you could measure a photog's bile, you could measure his worth. The sour faces usually produced the golden eggs.

Larry Burke was one of the sourest he had seen in a

long while. Burke, too, had won national awards. He had been with the *Tribune* two years, and had a natural antagonism toward pencil men. The argument was always about who had the tougher job. Walker thought the photog's life incredibly soft and cushy. They had no idea what real work was. Like the guy in Texas who had won a Pulitzer for being in exactly the right place at exactly the right time and snapping his goddamn camera at the exact moment when Jack Ruby shot Lee Harvey Oswald. Sure, it was a good picture. It was a great picture, but how could you measure an incredible stroke of luck like that against the hours and days and weeks of mental torture that Walker had endured to win his Prize? But if it made Burke feel better, then fine, let him consider writers his creative and intellectual inferiors.

"We are the only objective historians," Burke had shouted one night in the heat of a barroom argument. Walker had been sitting at the bar, twenty yards away and not involved in the discussion. But something about Burke's arrogance got to him that night, and he whirled on his stool and said, "Bullshit," just loud enough for everyone in the place to hear. The conversation came to a sudden halt, and Walker figured he might as well speak his piece. He stood and went over to Burke's table. "You know that's bullshit, Larry. Are you gonna tell me you never exercise any judgment in your work? That you just take what the camera sees? You gonna tell us you don't decide what to shoot and how to shoot it, and what to leave out of the goddamn picture? Or when you get back in that darkroom, you don't mess with it a little, to bring things out a certain way? You gonna tell us you don't crop the mothers, and then, after all that's done, you don't pick just the right ones, from that stack of maybe fifty pictures, to give to the desk? Bullshit," he said again, and walked out.

They hadn't spoken to each other since, and didn't speak now. The sun was up and the street was bathed in pink. Burke had rolled down his window and was looking through his lens at Gunther's front door when Walker heard the sound of someone coming along the street behind them. It was Melinda Baker, coming fast.

"There's the girl," Walker said. Burke eased himself around in the seat and shot five full frontal face shots before Walker drew in his next breath. With the other camera, Burke took longer shots of the street scene, and Melinda Baker walking under the trees. As she passed them, Burke got her profile with the big lens. He even took a few of her back as she walked away from them.

After perhaps ten minutes inside the Gunther home, Melinda Baker came out with the Gunthers and they all got into the Ford. They were there in the early sunlight for just a few seconds, but in that time Burke shot the roll. The Ford backed out of the driveway and Burke started the car. They went south, then east toward Manhattan, and Burke followed with the skill of an old cop. Walker didn't ask how Burke had learned to tail people. The less you know about some people the better.

They went to the Bristol-Myers plant, parked in a lot nearby and went into the building. Melinda Baker was wearing a dress; the Gunthers were dressed in work clothes. Burke shot and shot until they had disappeared inside and there was nothing left to shoot.

"Now what?" It was the first thing Burke had said to Walker all morning.

"Back to the *Trib,*" Walker said.

Burke just glared at him.

* * *

That night Walker had his first date with Diana
Yoder. They went to a restaurant off Central Park and
later to the New York Philharmonic. Symphony music bored Walker after a while, but being with her
made up for it. After the concert she took him by her
place for some talk and coffee. She didn't offer him
anything alcoholic; he didn't see any booze anywhere
in her place. There were no ashtrays. It was a simple
apartment in the Sixties, a few blocks from the park.
Her bedroom contained a small TV and a wall of
books, mostly history. There was a small single bed,
as in a nun's cell. He found her mind alert and
challenging. There may have been things she didn't
know at least something about, but he didn't find
them on that first date. She talked with ease about
everything from jazz to current affairs. But she wasn't
authoritative or demanding. She challenged him without interrupting or raising her voice, simply by offering slants that perhaps he hadn't considered. There
seemed to be only one passion in her life, the proposi-
tion that women should be equal with men and they
still had a long way to go. She found the hard-line
feminists as arrogant and shallow as that unbearable
housewives group that was working so hard and so
dishonestly to defeat the Equal Rights Amendment.

Briefly she even talked about herself. She had had
some instruction in tap dance, jazz and ballet. She
admitted that she had started late. When he asked
how she had done it, she said, "I worked like crazy,"
and moved along to something else. He never did
learn her age. He learned nothing about her family,
and was a little afraid to ask. When the evening was
over, he knew it without being told. He left with little
fanfare, and didn't try anything, not even a light kiss.
She wasn't a cold person; he could see that. But there

was something about her that completely precluded any such attempts.

Later, alone in his apartment, he couldn't recall one time when their hands had touched.

In the morning, Burke's pictures were waiting on his desk. Burke had printed fewer than ten, but they were fine, as clear and detailed as Walker knew they would be. The first Melinda Baker shot was especially compelling. Burke had caught her in one brief moment with her glasses off. She looked to be about two feet away, staring right into their faces.

Nor was there any mistaking the gaunt, strained faces of Hal and Barbara Gunther. With the long lens, Burke had captured a tension between them that Walker hadn't noticed from the car. They looked angry, as if they had been arguing.

He called Donovan at the FBI and set up a lunch for noon. Walker made the trip over to Brooklyn and they went to a Mexican joint where Donovan had been eating for fifteen years.

Walker showed him the pictures.

"Given the names and addresses of these people, what are the chances of getting a full make on all of them?"

"How far back?"

"As far back as they go."

"Sure, we could do that. Is that what you're asking? I mean, are you doing a feature on the investigative prowess of the FBI? Or are you actually asking me to do your work for you again?"

Walker looked pained. "Al, would I do that?"

"The question is why, old friend? Give me a good reason why I should dig up a couple of private lives for you. The Bureau gets touchy about that these days. Tell me something, Walker. These people in trouble?"

"I think they are."

"Federal trouble?"

Walker shrugged.

Donovan shuffled through the pictures. "So you finally got off the circus fire, huh, Walker?"

Walker shook his head. "Same story."

Donovan stroked his chin. "That's damned interesting." Donovan looked through the pictures again. He stopped at the close-up of Melinda Baker. "This wouldn't be the kid's mother, would it?"

Walker didn't say anything. Donovan passed the pictures back across the table. For a while they didn't speak. Finally Walker said, "It's strictly QT, Al. You've got to promise me that."

Donovan smiled. "Of course."

"That's the kid's mother."

"Well, well, well," Donovan said. He picked up the pictures again, and looked for a long time into the eyes of Melinda Baker.

"No use asking," Walker said. "I don't know any of the answers yet. That's why I need some help now. I need to know as much as I can before I confront them."

"Just remember, I've got to answer to people too," Donovan said. "For you this is a great story. For me it's just another interesting case for somebody else. It's strictly state, pal."

"Call it a favor then," Walker said. "Say it's one I really owe you. Or can I extract payment for all these goddamn lunches I've been buying you?"

Donovan seemed to be pondering it.

"You still coming over Friday night?"

"Wouldn't miss it. I might have somebody to bring, too."

"I'll tell Kim to set another place, just in case."

Several minutes passed.

"Al?"

"Yeah, Walker?"

"How about the pictures? Will you check 'em out?"

"Sure," Donovan said, smiling. His hands closed over the pictures and again he locked eyes with Melinda Baker, for the longest time. "I'll check 'em out."

Six

It was taking a while, but sometimes these things did. Even the FBI, with all its resources and manpower, often came up a day late and a dollar short. Donovan knew from long experience that you never got anywhere in the Bureau by being pushy. Push always had to come from above; then all manner of good things would happen. Cracks would open where there had been only a solid wall before. The bowels of bureaucracy would begin to move, as one of Donovan's younger colleagues liked to say, and the case would get off the pot. With the matter of Walker's pictures, that hadn't happened and wasn't likely to happen. Donovan had sent the pictures on to the main New York office. He didn't give them much thought, except for the few minutes each day when Walker called to check on possible progress. With each passing day, Walker sounded more and more uptight, as if sitting on the big story was taking its toll. It probably was. Donovan had never met a reporter who could stay calm after giving up some of his unwritten story to someone else. Even if that someone were a blood brother, or a trusted best friend, the nervousness persisted until the story got in print, at which point it was promptly wrapped around a fish and forgotten. Long ago Donovan had decided that journalism, despite the strange lure it had for young men starting out in life, was just no place for a civilized human to work. It was like that old saying: there are two things a civilized man should never watch being made, sausage and war. Donovan would add a third: a reporter making his big story.

He liked reporters, and he especially liked Walker, but Donovan wouldn't trade places with him even for the more than twenty years that separated them. Donovan liked his job. It had as much glamour as Walker's, if that was what you wanted. Yes, there was a routine; yes, things sometimes got tedious and boring; and yes, his superiors were probably as insufferable as Walker's. But you never really knew what might happen in the next five minutes. If uncertainty was his cup of tea, the Bureau gave a man that. Not to mention the amenities: a salary that was better than most (certainly better than anything Walker could make); security (you really had to screw up to get fired); a sense of accomplishment (Donovan felt like a vital cog in the American wheel, no matter what had been said to discredit the Bureau in recent years); and yes, goddammit, dignity. People still respected the FBI. They might tell George Gallup or Louis Harris they didn't, but Donovan didn't believe the polls. He knew that a man might tell a pollster one thing, and tell his wife something else.

Still, he understood Walker's impatience, but by Friday even Donovan wondered what was taking so long. He had given the pictures to an old friend named Virgil Craig, who had been with the Bureau even longer than Donovan. Craig was sixty-four, three years older than Donovan, and would be retired next year. Donovan and Craig shared a camaraderie with other Special Agents of their age and longevity. Once a month he tried to make it over to Manhattan for lunch with Virgil Craig and a few of the old heads, some of whom had been out of the Bureau for years. They knew they could count on each other for honest opinion and for material favors, done quickly and without a lot of noise. They were the Manhattan Boys, all serving time in the New York field office at one time or another. New York was the pits to young men making their names in the Bureau. But to the old hands, it was home.

When a working week had passed and Craig still hadn't called him back, Donovan decided to press. But gently.

He called the New York office.

"Virg, Al Donovan here."

"Oh . . . yes."

Donovan caught it at once, a funny edge to Craig's voice. "You okay, Virg?"

"Sure I am."

"Can you talk?"

"Sure. I just feel bad, that's all. Haven't got anything for you yet on those pictures."

"Running into trouble with them?"

Craig paused, then said, "I'm not sure what it is."

"Maybe I ought to get across the river for lunch. We could talk face to face."

"No need for that. We've been busy as hell this week. You know how some weeks are."

"Tell me about it. Look, Virg, I'm not pushing you."

"I know that. It's just . . ."

Donovan waited, but Craig let the sentence drop there.

"I think I'd better come to town," Donovan said. "It's been too long since we had lunch anyway."

"If you want to," Craig said. "But not today."

"You call it."

"How's Monday?"

"Monday's fine. Same time and place."

"Good. Maybe by then I'll have something for you. And I'll see if I can get a few of the Boys together."

"Let's leave the Boys out of this one. Just you and me this time, okay, Virg?"

"Sure, Al, fine, if that's how you want it. I'll see you then."

Still they didn't hang up. Each seemed to be waiting for the other to finish something, something Donovan felt had never quite begun. He said, "Everything all right at home?"

"Wife's a bit under the weather," Craig said.

"Nothing serious?"

"When you get our age you worry, whether it's serious or not."

"Not me, old man," Donovan said. "I never worry about things I can't help."

"Maybe because your wife's thirty years younger than mine," Craig said, faking sarcasm. "If I had a young wife like that, maybe I wouldn't worry either."

"You'd find something to worry about. That's how you are. You'd probably spend all your time worrying about who she's sacking out with while you're slaving away at the office."

"I didn't say a thing, Al."

"On the record, then, for all those things left unsaid. On the record, I don't worry about that either." Donovan let an awkward moment pass. "Listen, Virg, about those pictures. If this is something you'd rather not do . . ."

"Now you are making me feel like hell. I'll see you Monday. And I'll try my damnedest to have something for you by then."

"Good enough," he said, but Craig had already hung up.

Strange, Donovan thought. Damned queer.

He wondered if he should call Walker and try to dig out more facts. He knew that would be a waste of time. Walker had told him what he had told him, and that was all he would get. The Baker woman was the mother of the little girl who had died in the circus fire. The Gunthers were her friends. They were selling their homes. It wasn't exactly a federal case.

He decided to call it a day.

Donovan's home was near Great Neck, about a forty-minute train ride from the Prospect Park center of Brooklyn where he worked with another Special Agent, a secretary and a girl who answered the phones. The trip gave him time to think. Maybe it was just his imagination, but he couldn't shake the feeling that he had dumped something on Virgil Craig's back that was giving his old friend trouble. Just outside Forest Hills he gave his mind a rest, and let his thoughts drift into the past for a few minutes. In the seat across from him, a man was reading the New York *Daily News,* folded over so that Donovan, without straining too hard, could read the headlines on the facing page. A new study had come out. Life expectancy was up again. Seventy-four for women, sixty-eight for men. He could expect to live another seven years, maybe a few more, since he had come this far with no serious problems. Kim, exactly half his age, would probably survive him by thirty-six years. She would live longer after he had died than she had lived already. He would be a brief but, he hoped, important interlude in her crowded life. He wondered how she would remember him in the decades to come. That brought depression, which only compounded the worry of Virgil Craig. Growing old was such hell, and here he was, doing just what he told Virg he never did. Worrying. He hadn't quite lied to Craig. He seldom worried, but when he did he made up for lost time. He tended to drink and brood about growing old, and think too much about the long-gone past and the too short future.

He even worried about the Bureau. He had never wanted the goddamn FBI to mean as much to him as it did. He told himself it was just a job. He'd been telling himself that since his first day in his first post. April 1, 1939: a small resident agency near the Indian town of Nowater, somewhere in central Arizona. He had shared a room with an older agent behind the post office. His partner hadn't been that much older, a few years at most, but already he was disillusioned with the FBI and the building Hoover image. Now Donovan couldn't remember the guy's name. He hadn't lasted long: no one who hated Hoover lasted long in the old days. The things Donovan remembered best about that time were the heated arguments in their room late at night. Even at twenty-two, Donovan was hoeing the hard Bureau line. He remembered yelling at the guy, "For Christ's sake, Barney, if you hate the Director that much, why don't you get the hell out?" That was the guy's name. Barney Southworth. And Barney Southworth had gotten out, a few months later. One morning he had packed his bags and said "Fuck the FBI." Then he had loaded his car and driven away into the desert.

Much later Donovan learned of Barney Southworth's great transgression. Nowater, Arizona, had been used for two things. For young Al Donovan, it was solid training ground. For Barney Southworth, it was Siberia. Southworth had been an up-and-coming agent in the Washington office. A plum assignment. But he had been too impatient, too eager to leapfrog over people and bypass channels. Once he had written to Hoover himself, bypassing his next-in-command, and suddenly Barney Southworth was on the way out. Donovan couldn't even remember Barney's face now.

Forty years will do that. But his own voice came back at him like an old echo. That line about "the Director." Had he really said that, or had all the years—all the tens of thousands of hours spent in a job where thinking like that was not only encouraged but commanded—modified what he had actually said? He must have sounded pretty stuffy to a guy who had been around a bit.

Donovan had been weaned on the book and had never regretted it. In those days the FBI meant something. First there had been the Nazis and the Japs to fight, and later on the Commies. Some people believed foreign spies were everywhere, all through the war and into the 1950s. Kids thought he was some kind of superman. Women, when they found out who he was, got that look in their eyes that telegraphed sex. Radio dramas played up the "counterspy" theme, and Hoover milked that for all it was worth. The Director had made a personal appearance on the first episode of "This Is Your FBI," sometime near the end of the war, warning people about the Nazi spies among them. And maybe some Special Agents *were* after Nazis and Japs, but for Al Donovan the days were filled with tips on cars stolen in Connecticut and driven over state lines. He was in the New York Field Office then, and he chased hot cars, checked out threats against federal officials and occasionally assisted on a bank robbery.

He had never killed a man. Forty years in a job classified hazardous, in most people's minds if not in insurance company briefs, and Albert Harlan Donovan had never had to shoot a man.

Still, the people loved him. It didn't seem to matter how old he got or how times changed. There was always an enemy to fight, just as there was always a Joe McCarthy to exploit a situation and stir people up. It wasn't until much later that the looks had changed from respect to suspicion. The last few years, really, what with all the Watergate business and all the dirt about the Director coming out. The new breed of woman didn't telegraph sex. Maybe it was truly his age, but male ego wouldn't let him think that. Not completely. He still had all his hair (it was white around the edges now, but so what?), and he kept fit with handball three times a week. He had been told that he looked like a man in his forties. Nobody believed him when he told them how old he really was. Kim hadn't believed him when they had first met, two years ago. So it wasn't his age. People just didn't trust him anymore, not as they did when they thought there were Commies behind every bush. In times like these, when he had had too little sleep and carried the burden of intruding on a friend's peace of mind, he actually saw a glimmer of truth in Gallup and Harris.

Donovan's home was truly his castle. Once inside it, the troubles of the Bureau, and of the world in general, faded into the nothings they were. If one true thing could be said about Albert Harlan Donovan, it would be that he had life by the balls. He had done it all, everything he had wanted. He had security and a good pension coming, a lovely house in the suburbs, a frisky young wife four months pregnant, and dammit, he had his self-respect. No matter what the creeps said about Hoover and his dirty tricks, Al Donovan had always done what he believed in, and done it well. The FBI was something he could believe in, and you don't write off a lifetime commitment like that too quickly or too easily.

Donovan had it all. The only thing he didn't have was time.

Kim brought him a drink. Far back in the house, something mighty good was cooking for his guests tonight. She was a fantastic cook, this girl-woman he had married.

And she was perceptive. She saw things, even if she didn't always understand them. If, as some wit had written, knowledge was a person's storehouse of fact and intelligence was that person's key to the storehouse, Kim had built a huge storehouse and was still working on the key. She knew a lot. She absorbed facts and never forgot what she had read or heard. She had been a straight-A student at Syracuse. Straight goddamn A's, all four years. She constantly amazed Donovan with the charming combination of her knowledge and naiveté.

"I felt a kick today." She touched her abdomen, which was just beginning to show.

Donovan looked skeptical. "Isn't it a bit early?"

"All I can tell you was how I felt. How was your day?"

Then Donovan did a strange thing. He looked her in the face and told her about it. Strange, because he never brought things home, never burdened her with the Bureau. He told her about Walker's pictures and the funny feeling they gave him in light of his talk with Virgil Craig. Telling her about it took him back to perhaps ten other times when some case had left him feeling this way. When, for reasons he couldn't touch, things just hadn't felt right. That last time: a so-called suicide at a federal office building late at night in the Brooklyn Shipyard. Very strange. He would have never let that one go as a cut-and-dried suicide, but almost immediately a car from the New York Field Office arrived and the case was taken away from him. Some agent from D.C. took it right out of his goddamn hands. It was almost unheard of, but the other agent had the authority, orders from Roland Simon, Special Agent in Charge. Donovan had been around long enough. He knew when to play it cool, and if ever there were such times, that was one. The hell with it. If it meant that much to the Bureau there had to be a reason, and Al Donovan was too old to start fighting rattlesnakes in the Arizona desert again.

He told Kim about that case too. She didn't understand it. Kim had a single-emotion mind, and she couldn't understand why he had sat still and said nothing if it still bothered him.

"It wasn't my case any more," he told her. "In a sense, anything I said at that point might have been taken as an intrusion."

She shook her head. "That's stupid and short-sighted. Is the FBI always like that?"

"No." He sipped his drink. "Almost never, as a matter of fact. So when they are, you know it's something different, something out of the norm. You might not know what or how or why, but you know it is. And if you've been around for any time at all, you know enough to keep your mouth shut."

"And let it bother you for the rest of your life."

"Well, I don't brood about it."

"What are you doing now?"

"Kim, I'm just telling you. Dear God, it's been months since it even crossed my mind. Don't make me sorry I told you."

"I'm sorry," she said.

"And don't be sorry."

She looked frustrated. "Then how should I be? You never talk about your work, and the one time you do, I can't help you. If I can't be honest, at least let me be sorry."

He stroked her hair. "You do everything right."

"Because I can cook? Because I'm still young enough to make babies?"

"Those things are important."

"But they're not the only things. I told you once I want to share your life. Remember when I got all those FBI books out of the library?"

"I read them. What a crock."

"Which ones? Which ones were a crock?"

"Most of them. It's amazing what the publishing industry puts out as fact. One I read wasn't bad. The blue one." But, he thought, too damn critical of the Director and of established procedure.

"It doesn't matter. The point is, I learned more about the FBI from those books than I'll ever learn from my husband."

"What you've never understood is that most of the time I simply don't want to talk about it. It's got nothing to do with you, and God knows the cases I handle don't present any security problems. It's not that I can't talk or that I don't want to talk with you. It's just that by evening I'm so goddamn tired of it I just want to put it away until tomorrow."

"All right," she said. "Let me fix your drink."

She took his glass and disappeared into the bar. He knew she didn't believe him. There was no way to make her believe him without playing it her way for a while. Talk, talk, talk. Maybe they could have a few minutes of talk at least, after he came home nights. He could tell her about his day and in a while she would see how truly routine it was and there would be peace again. But something about that frightened Donovan. Would there be, instead of peace, a gradual loss of ideal and illusion, and was that perhaps what worried Al Donovan most in the sixty-first year of his life? Would Kim wake up one day and discover how dull his job really was, and how close to the vest he had played it all these years? Hiding out in the Brooklyn office, pounding his home turf. How well he knew it, how safe it was. His record was among the best, and it boiled down to the fact that he knew the territory. No one farted in Flatbush without Al Donovan picking up the scent.

The thought had haunted him, for a full two years, that she had fallen in love not with him but with the FBI. She had had it from the start, that look that he hadn't seen from a woman since the old days. She thought the FBI was okay, really okay, and not just a necessary evil. That figured. She was an only child, daughter of a man who would serve a dozen terms as Republican congressman from the state of New York. Her politics, like his, were right of center, though she was in the middle of some deep shift, and God only knew where that would end. A year ago she couldn't abide people who wanted everything handed to them by the government, and just last week she said she finally understood what welfare was about. Donovan had been afraid to ask. She had started questioning everything: her country, her father, the existence of God, all the rules she had learned in school and now the infallibility of the great FBI. Somehow that scared Donovan more than a hundred men chasing after her lovely tail would have.

The thought occurred to Donovan, as it must have occurred to Walker, that they were a strange group. The dancer, Diana, had made an instant hit with Kim, but to Donovan she was an odd person, moody and deep. He liked her the same way you like your commanding officer in the Army, if you like him at all. With an uneasiness growing out of the vast separation of your life-styles. With the feeling that, no matter what was said, much more was unsaid. With a hunch that a man might live with this woman thirty years and still never know what went on inside her head.

But he loved playing host. Donovan was the only man in the Bureau, to his knowledge, who invited reporters to his home. Most agents had such a fear of the printed word that they constantly tottered on paranoia. The sight of Donovan stoking the fire in his backyard and chatting easily with Walker would have horrified them. Donovan believed that good food bridged any gap, and the food was always good when Kim made it. He grilled the steaks and she provided the fine touches from her oven. Diana Yoder refused alcohol, but had some spiced cider. They talked about Radio City and being a Rockette. At Kim's request, she even did a few high kicks for them on the grass beside the barbecue pit. They all laughed.

They talked about the women's movement, and again Donovan was surprised at how much his wife agreed with the progressive thinking of Diana Yoder. By then a cold wind had come up. They retired to Donovan's den for some brandy and, for the girl, a touch of hot tea. She moved along his rows of books, picking out one occasionally, leafing through it, reading the first page with surprising speed, then putting it back. She stared for a long time at his framed picture of J. Edgar Hoover. It had been taken at a special function in 1969, honoring Special Agents who had served thirty years. Hoover had shaken Donovan's hand for the camera, and later signed the picture and sent it by messenger to Donovan's home.

The girl was intrigued by Hoover. After a while, Donovan told them about his dealings with Hoover. They talked about the revelations of recent years, and Donovan told them what he thought was true and when he thought the press was just having fun. Walker didn't say anything.

In all, it was a highly successful evening. Until ten o'clock.

The phone rang.

Donovan listened without saying more than two words. He hung up the phone and his face was white.

"Al?"

He blinked as he realized that Kim had spoken.

"What's the matter?"

"That was Virgil Craig."

The name meant nothing to Walker. But he noticed that the strange look in Donovan's eyes had spread to his wife.

"I'm sorry," Donovan said, rising. "I'm going to have to go out."

"Oh, dear," Kim said.

"It can't be helped. You've been a lovely guest, Miss Yoder. I'm happy Walker could bring you, and I can't apologize enough for having to run out like this."

She smiled and took his hand as he offered it.

"You and Walker stay a while, keep Kim company."

"Will you be back?" Kim said.

"I wouldn't count on it."

He put on his coat and hurried out. But a moment later he was back, apparently confused. He stood in the doorway in indecision.

"Al?" Now Kim was concerned. "Is there something I can do? Are you feeling all right?"

"Yes, I'm fine. It's not that. I need to talk to Walker."

Walker excused himself and followed Donovan out onto the walk. They stopped just outside the circle of light.

"Those pictures you gave me."

Walker waited.

"I wasn't going to tell you this, but you and I have never played that way before. Just remember, it didn't come from me."

Walker nodded.

"The Gunthers are dead," Donovan said.

"How?"

"From what I know, apparently he went nuts. Killed his wife, then shot himself."

"What about Melinda Baker?"

"Nobody knows where she is."

They looked at each other. Then Donovan said, "You'll have to take your own car. Tell your date she'll have to find her own way home. And for Christ's sake don't get there too soon after me."

Seven

The quiet street where the Gunthers had lived was full of cops. People were at their front doors on both sides of the street to watch the passing parade of lights and black cars. Men in dark suits trampled the grass around the house and into the backyard. Walker got there a full forty minutes after Donovan arrived. He knew the cops would be there for at least another hour, so he took Diana home first. Even death, even a story, wouldn't make him push that lady into a subway late at night.

In his youth he had covered many murders, and they all looked alike from the street. The windows blazed with the lights of the police photographer, and shadows moved beyond the curtains. Measuring. Talking. Shooting flash pictures. Some reporters had arrived, a nightside crew from the Newark paper and a couple of guys Walker knew from the *Tribune*. To them it was just another suicide-murder. In and around New York, it happened all the time. It would rate a couple of lines at best. The photog would turn in a few prints and none of them would make the paper.

Under ordinary circumstances.

Walker moved over toward the *Tribune* team. The reporter was Jerry Wayne, still one of Walker's admirers in the split that had marked his early months at the paper.

"Hi, Jerry."

"Oh . . . hi."

"Better tell your photog not to shortchange this one, Jerry. I've got a hunch it'll see some big action tomorrow."

Wayne's eyes widened. "You working on it?"

"Yeah. I have been for a long time."

"Oh."

"It's okay, don't worry about it. You just keep doing whatever you want to do. We'll work it out together when we get back to the office."

Wayne eased away and began talking with his photographer. The photog looked sourly at Walker. Naturally, he argued about it. But he looked livelier after that, and took more care about what he did.

After a while another car drove up. In it were three men in suits, looking for all the world as though they had just stepped out of an air-conditioned office. Walker knew two of them on sight, from the old days. The man in the back seat, and obviously the one in charge, was Roland Simon, head of the New York field office. Next to him was a guy named Armstrong. Walker didn't remember Armstrong's first name, wasn't sure he ever knew it. A grim man; Walker thought he would have made a fine photog. The third man was much younger, probably still in his late twenties. Walker had never seen him, but two out of three wasn't bad.

The Feds took command almost at once. Roland Simon had some words with the lieutenant from the local police, and the cops fell back and became, with the growing crowd on the sidewalk, mere spectators.

Walker knew then that the investigation, whatever it might become in the next few hours, was just getting started. The press would get nothing until the Feds had sorted through it and decided exactly how they wanted to play it. Walker drifted down the street and around the corner. Halfway up the next block, Melinda Baker's house was dark. The whole block was dark. The trees screened out the streetlights on each corner, and in Melinda Baker's yard deep pockets of darkness melted into total darkness at the sides and behind the house. Walker stopped and unhooked the gate. He went up the steps to the front door and rang the bell, but the house had a feeling of emptiness about it. There wasn't even a creak of a floorboard while he stood there. He knocked, and as he did, two men came around the edges of the porch and stood watching him from either side.

"Who are you?" one of the men said.

"I'm looking for Mrs. Baker."

They came around the porch and up the steps. "We didn't ask you that."

"Dalton Walker. I'm a reporter for the *Tribune*. Who are you?"

They didn't answer. The one with the voice said, "You got some identification?"

"Have you?" Walker said.

"You can show it here or in jail. Suit yourself."

Walker took out his press card. The one without a voice held a flashlight and they looked it over.

"Mrs. Baker isn't home," the voice said, handing the card back to Walker.

"I can see that. What's going on?"

"We have no statement, Mr. Walker. If you want a statement, ask for Special Agent Simon. He's . . ."

"Yeah, right. I know where he is."

"Goodbye, Mr. Walker."

They escorted him to the sidewalk. When he looked

back at the Baker house, from a half a block away, they had disappeared.

Walker didn't see Donovan until perhaps an hour later. He knew enough about FBI procedure to know that Donovan, because he had initiated the probe into the Gunthers' background, would be the agent of record on the case. Donovan would get all the records, all correspondence relating to the Gunther matter, despite the fact that he was assigned to Brooklyn and the killings had happened in New Jersey. That was Bureau policy, and this time Walker was glad of it. At least he could talk to Donovan. But when Donovan did come out, one glance told Walker to keep his distance. Even that might work out well. The deaths had happened on everybody's time but his, and it would be a full eleven hours before he could have his paper on the streets. So the less anyone said now the better.

After a while Roland Simon came to the door. The group of reporters had grown somewhat, from three to six. Walker didn't see a New Yorker among them. Even the *Daily News* had passed up this one. The three newcomers were radio guys. No danger there. Half the time they didn't know what year it was, let alone what questions to ask. The guy from Newark worried him. An older guy: around forty-five, with a dark moustache. Like Walker, he stayed in the background until Roland Simon was ready to talk.

Walker looked at Jerry Wayne's watch. It said quarter to one, and he began to feel better. If the Newark paper was an A.M., most of their deadlines had come and gone. Even if Simon laid the whole number on them, they would have to scramble like hell to get snatches of it into their final. Walker didn't think the guy with the dark moustache was that sharp.

But he wasn't any dummy, either. As the six of

them crowded around Simon, the man from Newark said, "How come this is a federal case?" He went right to the point.

"We're pursuing a lead that goes back to a federal case," Simon said. "No one has called these deaths themselves a federal matter."

"Then what are you guys doing here?"

"I told you."

"Then what case are we talking about?"

"I have no comment on that. I may have one Monday morning."

Walker let out his breath and smiled a little.

"Are you telling me these deaths aren't of any official interest to you, but you're working on something involving them that is?"

Simon gave the man from Newark an icy stare. "I thought that's what I just said."

"Then what . . ."

"I told you," Simon said coldly. "Monday morning. Next question."

Walker stood through it all, while the radio guys asked their dumb questions and Simon filled in the blanks. The dead man was going under the name of Harold Warren Gunther, age forty-nine, occupation laborer. He had worked in the shipping department at Bristol-Myers. His wife, Barbara, was thirty-nine. She had worked at Bristol-Myers too.

"What do you mean he was going under the name?" the man from Newark said. "Was that his name or wasn't it?"

"That's the name he was known by," Simon said.

"Is that the name you know him by?"

"Yes. Next question."

There were no next questions. If they were playing it for a two-graph filler, two graphs was what they would get.

Except in the *Tribune*.

The reporters stepped back and the bodies were brought out. Flashbulbs popped all over the place, as the two stretchers were brought out and deposited in the meat wagon.

The man from Newark came close. "In a pig's eye," he said. "There's more to this one than that."

"You think so?"

"Goddamn right. Don't you?"

"Gee, I don't know," Walker said. "Maybe we'll find out Monday morning."

An hour later, he sat alone in the city room, facing a sheet of blank paper, hoping Donovan would call. Jerry Wayne came in and put a cup of coffee on his desk, then retired into a corner to wait and see what was shaking out of the trees. At Walker's direction, Jerry had typed up a page of notes, giving him all the official quotes along with some firsthand observation. The kid had slipped around behind the house and peeped in through a side window before the bodies were covered. He wrote down what they looked like, where they were positioned and some gorgeous detail. Jerry noted the flecks of blood on the walls, the pistol still clenched in Gunther's hand, and how the gray streaks in the dead man's beard had turned bright red. The kid had a helluvan eye for detail.

Walker had been trying to reach Donovan by telephone since he returned to the paper. First he got Kim, who said Al hadn't come home yet. Donovan had called her, and said he might be another hour or two, but he hadn't indicated where he might be going. On a hunch, Walker called Donovan's private number at the resident agency in Brooklyn. No one answered, but Walker had a strange vision of Donovan sitting alone in that dark office, watching the phone as it rang.

The story was still full of holes and Walker knew it.

He knew too that going with it now would give all the other papers a shot at what might be an even better story, still hidden just under the surface. But he had clearly run out of time. The thing wouldn't hold even through one more edition. Sometime between now and dawn, maybe he could get Donovan or somebody to plug some of the holes; maybe then the thing would start to fit together. Now he had to write.

He began.

The strange death of a little girl in a circus fire three months ago took yet another bizarre turn late Friday night when two close friends of the girl's mother were killed, in what officials are terming a murder-suicide.

The most unusual aspect of the case is that the little girl's body was never identified by the mother. The *Tribune* has learned that the mother was Mrs. Melinda Baker, who lived at 4435 Orange Street, in the township of Stanley.

The Baker woman was being sought by FBI agents Saturday as a link in a "federal case" that Special Agent Roland Simon wouldn't reveal. He indicated that he might have more to say on Monday.

Mrs. Baker was known to be close friends with Hal and Barbara Gunther, whose deaths Friday night brought FBI agents from as far away as Brooklyn. Mrs. Baker and the Gunthers all worked at the Bristol-Myers plant

He made a note to check that in the morning.

and were known to have used the same car on many occasions.

Unknown Saturday was Mrs. Baker's motivation in keeping secret her daughter's identity after the little girl lost her life in the tent fire last July. No one ever claimed the body, and the girl was buried in a pauper's grave at state expense many weeks later.

The *Tribune* learned that the girl was Robin Baker, age 8, who had been in the third grade at Robert F. Kennedy Grammar School. Her final day of school was the day before the fire. The following morning the Baker woman notified school officials that she and the girl were moving to California.

Mrs. Baker and the Gunthers lived in houses of similar construction and age. The Gunthers, who lived around the corner from Mrs. Baker's brown bungalow, were killed at about nine o'clock Friday night.

He shuffled through Jerry Wayne's notes, looking for some description. Wayne got up and came over, trying to see what Walker was writing. Walker turned the page down and said, "Take a walk, Jerry. But come back when people start getting here in the morning. I may need you."

Alone again, he turned back to his job. So far, it was rough but the facts as he knew them were in the right place.

The phone rang, and his story was changed for all time.

"Walker?"

He recognized Donovan's voice.

"Walker," Donovan said again. "Was that you trying to call me a while ago?"

"Sure it was. You at the office?"

"That's right. I thought you might have some things on your mind."

"Sounds like you're the one with problems," Walker said.

Donovan gave a mirthless little laugh. "You might say that."

"Tell me about it."

"You mean for print? Ah, I don't think so, Walker. Not today."

"Come on, Al, don't you whip that Monday morning bullshit on me too."

"That's the way it's got to be. Simon's hoping something will break on it before then."

"And if it does, I'm screwed against the wall."

"Walker . . ." Donovan's voice trailed away. "Walker," he said again a moment later. "Listen to me, Walker."

Walker listened.

"Why don't you try looking under that big investigative nose you get paid so much for having?"

"What's that supposed to mean?"

"Uh-uh, Walker. I'm not leading you around by the hand."

"So we talk in riddles, right?"

"If you want to. Isn't that what you got your big Pulitzer Prize for? Solving riddles?"

"Look, Al . . ."

"You look. Look in your own backyard. That's all I'm saying. I've said too much already. I can't afford to get burned on this."

"Hey, wait a minute!"

"You've got it all now, Walker, all you're getting. Figure it out yourself. See you around."

Walker was holding a dead telephone.

Eight

Walker slammed down the headset and kicked the back of his desk in anger. Then, carefully, methodically, he retraced Donovan's words. Jesus, it had all seemed like such small talk. He went through it again, piece by piece. What the hell had they said? They had fenced through most of it. *Why don't you try looking under that big investigative nose you get paid so much for having?* What the hell did that tell him? What in God's name had he overlooked? He sifted through the elements of the story again, and got nowhere. In none of his notes, in none of his encounters with Melinda Baker or the Gunthers were there any major threads that he could develop now. Maybe Donovan meant something else.

Look in your own backyard. Look under your nose, in the physical sense.

His desk? His telephone? The newsroom.

The newspaper itself.

The *Tribune* was a resource.

The clips.

He got the library key from the spike under Kanin's desk and went up the winding steps that led out of the newsroom. The library, like the rest of the buildings, was closed for the night. Walker let himself in through a back door and turned on the lights. The library had two major resources, the clips and the index. The paper employed twelve clerks who did nothing but cross-index on filing cards every story that appeared in the newspaper every day. These cards were stored in alphabetical order along a far wall, in a row of steel filing cabinets.

Walker checked the obvious listings first. Gunther, Hal; Gunther, Barbara.

Nothing.

Baker, Melinda.

Zero.

He sat at the librarian's desk to think some more. He would have to go into the massive file on the FBI, and check each story, going back God only knew how many years, in the hope of finding just the right one. If there even was a right one. If goddamn Donovan hadn't led him on a wild-goose chase with his cryptic bullshit.

Maybe there was more.

What else had Donovan said? Something about not leading him by the hand. Nothing there. Or was there? Was there something in that, something to do with hands? He thought for a long time, and came up dry.

There wasn't much more. Donovan had said something about his Pulitzer. Possibly, then, the Pulitzer tied in somehow. The only way it could, in time.

He had won it ten years ago this year. Donovan might remember that, because Walker, in the throes of becoming a Great Big Name, had bought a bottle of very expensive wine and they had celebrated together. He got up and crossed the room to the vault, where the clips were kept. He pulled the file on U.S.

Government—Federal Bureau of Investigation for that year, took the clips back to his table and began going through them.

He found it at once. It had been splashed everywhere, in papers from coast to coast. There were pictures of all of them, only they weren't going by the names Gunther or Baker then. Walker unfolded a lead piece and began to read.

Gunther was George Lewis. He hadn't had the beard then, but there was no mistaking those eyes. Barbara was his wife, and her name was Michelle Lewis then. Melinda Baker was Joanne Sayers. They were all products of the revolutionary spirit of the late Sixties: underground types, hardened and rabid. Walker went to the vault and pulled the clips on George and Michelle Lewis, and on Joanne Sayers. All were an inch thick or more.

In the personal files he found stories that hadn't made it into the larger FBI folders. A UPI interview with Joanne Sayers, done eighteen months before she had become a fugitive. Young and pretty, spouting ideals and philosophies and politics. Those were the things they talked about then. Six months later, their first criminal act. They had helped an FBI file clerk named Robert Ordway steal some documents from the Bureau's field office in Philadelphia. There was a lot of flap in the Bureau file about that one, and some of the stories overlapped. The Lewises and Joanne Sayers dropped from sight. They went far underground, joining the revolutionary People's Army in their vow to fight the fascist pigs of America, and to take their fight into the streets if necessary.

They had robbed a bank.

They had shot some people.

One guard had died.

Three years later, the FBI had tracked some of them to ground, in a tiny mountain cabin in upstate New York. There had been what Walker could only describe as one godawful hell of a battle. Usually he remembered big stories like that, but he didn't remember this one. It had happened while he was out of the country, covering Vietnam for *Life* magazine.

Six of the radicals had died in the cabin. The Lewises weren't among them. Nor was Joanne Sayers.

He sat back and took a deep breath. The clock on the wall said quarter to four. Deadline for the Saturday afternoon edition was nine o'clock. He had five hours to absorb all this, draw the links and get the goddamn thing together.

In the newsroom, he read all the clips, making notes from some. By the time he had finished that, a streak of pale light was seeping in through the windows facing east, and the telegraph editor had come in to clip the wires. Jerry Wayne came in and sat in his corner, waiting for word from Walker that he was needed.

Walker worked fast. He threw away the pages he had written and started over, two hours before his first deadline. He slugged the story "death," and typed in the double byline.

By Dalton Walker and Jerry Wayne
Tribune Staff Writers

What the hell? It didn't cost him anything, and for the kid it would be a coup. Even Walker could remember the hunger of the very young.

The man was tall, with streaks of
premature gray in the beard
something about his eyes

He played with that for a while, trying to capture what Gunther had been in one easy, smooth-flowing sentence. He knew before he put down a word that this wasn't going to work as a feature, even with a quick change-of-pace lead that moved right into the hard news. Still, he fiddled with it for fifteen minutes, and finally abandoned it for the traditional approach.

A late-night shooting in a New Jersey suburb opened a Pandora's box of personal tragedy and federal intrigue Friday, and when it was over FBI agents had eliminated two of America's most elusive fugitives from their list of most wanted criminals.

Dead were George and Michelle Lewis, both 34, who had been living at 5023 Nelson Street, in the township of Stanley. The Lewises, wanted on a warrant charging murder and bank robbery, were living under the names Harold and Barbara Gunther, and had been employed in the Bristol-Myers plant near here.

Police said evidence indicated that Mrs. Lewis had been shot once at close range. Her husband was killed with the same gun, which was found in his hand when police arrived.

But FBI agents, who arrived at the scene on the heels of local police, took charge of the case and imposed a mantle of secrecy around it. Roland Simon, Special Agent in Charge of the New York Field Office, said he hoped to have further word for the press on Monday.

It was thought that agents were buying time in an effort to capture Joanne Sayers, a third longtime fugitive, and an intimate friend of the Lewises. Sayers had been living just around the corner, in a house of similar construction and age, and had also

been employed at Bristol-Myers under the name
Melinda Baker.

As Mrs. Baker, Joanne Sayers had been living a
quiet life in Stanley, with a young girl believed to
be her daughter. It was Robin Baker, 8, who
perished last July in an accident, when the main
tent of Circus Ralston caught fire during a performance and burned to the ground.

Speculation then centered on the identity of the
little girl, which investigators at the coroner's office
were unable to establish. But the *Tribune* learned
that Joanne Sayers paid at least one visit to the
unmarked grave where the girl was buried, leaving
flowers there in a midnight vigil.

Though the FBI wouldn't comment on the case,
or on Joanne Sayers' link to the Baker girl, it now
seems certain that her reluctance to identify the
child is the result of her long life as a fugitive.
Sayers . . .

He broke off briefly. He didn't like phrases like
"believed to be" and "it now seems certain" in his
stories. He thought about it and decided to leave it for
now.

The newsroom was filling for the morning grind.
Kanin had come in and was taking off his coat.

Walker began to type again. Kanin saw him and
recognized the look of a news story. He came over.

"You got something going?"

Walker gave him the first two takes.

Kanin read through it quickly. "Has anybody else
got this?"

"As far as I know, everybody else still thinks the
dead people were named Gunther."

"Sweet Jesus." Kanin took the first two pages with
him. He stopped at the news desk and spoke with the

editor there, then sat at city desk and read through it again. In a moment he got up and came back to Walker.

"I don't like the phrase 'FBI eliminated' in the first graph. You make it sound like the FBI killed them."

"Two graphs later I explain that."

"I know, but . . ."

"Okay, you're right. Can you fix it?"

Kanin nodded. "How much of this did Wayne do? Do we need his name . . ."

"He did plenty," Walker said. "Leave Jerry alone, Joe."

Kanin went away and Walker motioned Jerry Wayne over. Might as well make him work for his share of the glory.

"Get the pink dupes from Kanin and make some checks for me," Walker said. "Call the FBI office in New York. There should be some number where they can be reached on Saturday. Ask for Roland Simon and read him what we've got here, see if he'll comment in light of this stuff. If you can't get Simon, call Al Donovan at this number." He scratched both of Donovan's numbers on a pad. "Tell Donovan what we've got and ask him to call Simon. Tell them we go to press in less than an hour."

"Right." Wayne was ecstatic.

"Then call Bristol-Myers and confirm that they had these people in their employ. Get some quotes on what kind of workers they were. Then call the Stanley cops and see if they've got anything new."

Alone again, Walker returned to his work.

The saga began in the late 1960s, and was stoked by the heat of the protest era. The Lewises and the Sayers woman were students together at the University of California's Berkeley campus.

Always active in the school's underground political movements, they were members of Students for a Democratic Society, and later left school to join the revolutionary People's Army.

The People's Army has a history of violence going back at least to 1968, when members planted a bomb in a Boston telephone company rest room. The group later claimed responsibility for the destruction of a Southern Bell transmitting station near Greenville, S.C., and for the bombing of a Public Service Company power plant near Denver, Colo.

The Army attacked anything that smacked of "establishment" values. By 1969 the threat of bombs had forced added security around office buildings and field sites around the country.

The FBI, despite its fabled image, was totally frustrated in its early efforts to capture members of the group. In an era when criminals are more often caught by science than by manpower, the People's Army continued to elude the federal net.

The Lewises and the Sayers woman were billed in FBI posters as true criminals now. They allegedly robbed a bank in Los Angeles in late 1969, along with two other Army members now dead. About $25,000 was taken in that noonday holdup, and four people were shot when a guard tried to stop them. The guard, Albert Hook, 57, was killed.

For a time, the Army members seemed to disappear. One FBI official theorized that a string of "safe houses" had been established, where they could hide without fear of detection.

Not one member of the group was arrested between the bank robbery in November 1969 and the looting of FBI files in Pennsylvania almost two years later. At first that seemed to be the work of one man, Robert Ordway, a file clerk in the Philadelphia field office.

Ordway, who had worked for the Bureau for seven years and had top secret clearances, took some files and the journal of an agent, apparently with the intention of leaking the documents to the press. The files, and especially the diary of the agent, who had recently died, were described by FBI spokesmen as "very sensitive."

But when Ordway was arrested two days later, only part of the file was recovered. The FBI refused to say whether the dead agent's diary had been among the recovered items, and no hint was ever revealed as to what it might contain.

Ordway, then 32, suffered appendicitis while being held in a prison hospital ward. Complications developed in the operation that followed, and he died February 1, 1972, without ever going to trial.

That smells, Walker thought. And for once, he wasn't thinking about his prose. The Ordway deal smelled from the first line.

Kanin came over, flushed with the glow of handling a big one. "How much more?"

"Another take, maybe two."

"Hurry it up. We're getting tight."

"I know what the deadlines are."

From across the room, Jerry Wayne called, "Hey, Walker, I got Roland Simon on the line, madder than hell."

"Switch him over." As he strapped on his headset, he said to Kanin, "I may have some adds to chase in."

"Make it fast," Kanin said.

Roland Simon came on the line.

"Goddammit, Walker . . ."

"Careful, Mr. Simon, I'm quoting you. It's been a long time."

"Not nearly long enough," Simon said.

"Look, I'm on deadline. Are you going to talk to me or not?"

"I'm asking you, man to man, to hold that story till we catch the Sayers girl."

"No way, Simon. Not a chance."

"Walker . . ."

"You're wasting your breath and my time, and time's one thing I've got no more of right now. Are you going to confirm some facts for me or not?"

"I'm not confirming anything."

"Then we've got nothing to talk about. Lucky I don't need you, Simon. The clips here at the *Tribune* have everything I need."

"Listen, I'll say this one time and goddammit you'd better listen. There's nothing I can do to keep you from publishing that story. But if you do, things are going to get unpleasant as hell." He tried to temper the threat. "For all of us."

"That's a gorgeous quote, Simon. You always were good for a line or two to liven things up."

"Your profession may not have any restrictions on it, but you sure profess to have some ethics. Now you tell me, Walker, what are the ethics of jeopardizing an investigation before the suspect is arrested?"

"That won't work either, Simon. The press has no interest either way in your investigation. The *Tribune* has no stake in whether you catch the Sayers woman or not. We just report what's happening. But I'll have to argue ethics with you some other time. I will say this, Simon. If you think the Sayers woman doesn't already know what happened in Stanley tonight, you're crazy. She hasn't eluded you all these years by being stupid."

Simon was silent for a moment. When he spoke again, his voice was calm, flat. "Here's my statement, Walker. You ready?"

"Shoot."

"The FBI attempted to capture Joanne Sayers, suspected bank robber and murder suspect, by drawing a curtain of secrecy around the Lewis killings for forty-eight hours. It was hoped that . . . scratch that. All news media agreed to cooperate with the forty-eight-hour embargo, and to allow the FBI to release the facts at a Monday news briefing. Only the *Tribune* refused to go along."

Walker looked up at the clock. "Is that it?"

"One more line," Simon said. "You can quote me on this, and Walker, I'll expect to see this just as I give it to you. In my opinion, the *Tribune,* and particularly its reporter, Dalton Walker, bears the responsibility for whatever happens to the Sayers girl, in the event we do not take her quietly."

"Good shot, Simon. Let me ask you a few things."

But Simon had hung up.

Kanin came over, foaming at the mouth. Walker put a sheet of paper in the typewriter and banged out what Simon had told him. "This should go in as an add. Fairly high up."

Kanin frowned when he read it.

"Come on, Joe, show some guts. The goddamn guy's bluffing," Walker said.

"It's a pretty good bluff. This'll have to go up to the old man."

"Oh, for Christ's sake, here . . ." Walker put another sheet in his machine and typed out a few more sentences.

Simon's statement failed to acknowledge that the *Tribune* initially tipped off the FBI on the fugitives' whereabouts. A *Tribune* reporter had been working on the circus tent fire for more than two months, and it was this reporter who passed along photographs of the suspects to the FBI early last week.

Donovan wouldn't like that. Walker paused for a moment, then went on.

Also contradicting the agent's statement was the behavior of Simon and other agents at the death scene. The FBI didn't ask for the cooperation of the press. The agents didn't share anything with the press, and it was only when Simon learned that the *Tribune* had the story anyway that he claimed otherwise.

Kanin read it over Walker's shoulder. "You're a mean prick, Walker," he said, smiling.

"It gets us off the hook."

"Yeah, it does that." Kanin looked up at the clock. They were right on deadline. "How much more?"

"As much as I can get in. Five, ten graphs."

"Make it fast. What doesn't make Saturday we'll run back Sunday."

Again Walker wrote.

For a time after Ordway's death, the secret documents dropped from sight. Then, in September 1972, more than seven months after Ordway's death, the *New York Times* published excerpts from the files, revealing how former FBI director J. Edgar Hoover had used his influence to stop probes of organized crime figures. Some of the backstage struggles between Hoover and Robert F. Kennedy, former attorney general, were brought out in detail.

Both Hoover and Kennedy were dead by then, and the revelations, though sensational, came about almost in a vacuum. All the alleged abuses had happened in the past, and while the *Times* reports triggered outcries in Washington for FBI reform, no new information came out of the closed hearings between members of Congress and the new Bureau hierarchy.

In January 1973, the Washington *Post* published a story, compiled from the files and from interviews with two People's Army members. Excerpts from the dead agent's diary were published, and a picture showing the closed journal was used with the story. Again, the report detailed alleged FBI dirty tricks, but the reporter wasn't allowed to see the last part of the diary, which the People's Army "general" said would be released later.

That later never came. Less than a month after the *Post* story, FBI agents found a central Army hideout, a remote cabin in upstate New York. There . . .

His telephone rang.

"Walker? Roland Simon here."

"Yes, Mr. Simon?"

"I want to retract what I said earlier. Publish what you want. The FBI will have no comment."

"The FBI has already had a comment."

"Well, I'm taking that comment back. It was made in the heat of the moment."

"I thought they taught you guys not to make comments in the heat of the moment."

"Walker, do you always have to be difficult?"

Kanin was standing over his shoulder, reading the last take and motioning with his hands that they were out of time.

"Sorry, Simon, I've got to go."

"Walker . . ."

But now it was his turn to hang up.

"Listen," he said to Kanin, "I've got a graph or two to finish, then one more add from Simon."

"We'll have to cut it off there."

Walker wrote.

> . . . agents fought a fierce battle with Army mem-
> bers inside.
> Five men and one woman were killed in the
> gunfire. Joanne Sayers wasn't in the house. Neither
> were George or Barbara Lewis.

"That's it!" Kanin shouted. "We're out of time."
A copy boy plucked the last take out of Walker's
hands. Walker rolled a new sheet into the typewriter,
slugged it "insert two death" and wrote:

> Simon later called and retracted his statement.
> "Publish what you want," he said. "The FBI will
> have no comment."
> He said his earlier statement was made "in the
> heat of the moment," and should be disregarded.

Walker ripped the page out of his typewriter and
hurried over to Kanin. "Let's chase this in, right
below the Simon insert."
Kanin read it and marked it for the backshop. "You
really are a prick, Walker. I guess that's what makes
you so good, your ability to make people look like
assholes. Helluva piece."
Walker was reading Kanin's dupes. "Not too well
written."
"Who gives a damn? It's in and that's what counts.
You've got six hours before the Sunday city, so you
can sit here and fiddle with it all you want. Write me a
masterpiece for Sunday, Walker."
"Things like this: 'Joanne Sayers wasn't in the
house. Neither were George or Barbara Lewis.'"
"What's wrong with that?"
"It's obvious that they weren't in *that* house. They
were just killed last night."

"Don't you think it's important to remind the reader?"

"There are better ways of doing it."

"Then be my guest. Write me something stunning for Sunday."

"Joe?"

Kanin looked up at him.

"Go to hell," Walker said.

Walker did fiddle with it, taking all six hours to work up an entirely new piece for Sunday. He wrote a story half again as long, using some of Jerry Wayne's notes to give the kid's signer some legitimacy. And the Sunday piece read well, but the more he looked at his rush job, the better it looked to him. The writing wasn't anything special, but Kanin was right: he had gotten the facts in, and had them straight. It had been a long time since he had to write under pressure like that. He felt good. He felt like part of the paper, and it had been a while since Dalton Walker had felt like part of anything. He remembered something an editor had once told him. A really good reporter can write hard news almost as well under deadline as he can with all the time in the world.

Maybe there was some hope for him yet. More likely, he was just riding the crest of a big one, and would come down hard in the morning. He gathered in Jerry Wayne, who was rereading the piece for the tenth time, took him to a bar up the street and got him soused on three bottles of beer.

The day was going fast by the time he got home. His story was everywhere, screaming at people from every news box on every corner. The telephone was ringing as he came in. That figured.

But no, it was Diana Yoder of the Rockettes. "Congratulations. Is that what they call a good story?"

"It'll do for now. How'd you see it already? I didn't know the *Tribune* got over to New York."

"They've got it on TV. They're attributing everything to your paper, so I figured that must be your story. Happy?"

"Delirious. How can I make up for running out on you last night?"

"No apologies necessary. I can see for myself how important it was."

The illusion of importance. Even she could see it. Only Walker knew that the story had no real importance. The screaming headline, the coal-black type: none of it mattered, except to four people, two of whom were dead.

He was starting down already. "Let's go somewhere," he said.

"I'll come to your place," she said. "I'll bring some food we can eat there."

"I don't know. My place is pretty grim."

"I think I'll survive. Tell me how I find it."

He told her, and afterward he settled back and savored the day. She had saved it for him, lifted him just by being there. He savored her coming, and the prospect of an evening in. At last he knew that he could move on to something else. The death of an unnamed little girl would haunt him no more. Melinda Baker, Joanne Sayers, whatever the hell her name was, was the FBI's problem. He had it in print, and now he could forget about it.

Nine

A heavy rain had started by the time Diana arrived. She wore a simple overcoat, hooded and belted at the waist. Rubber boots, no umbrella. She took off her coat in the hall and shook out her hair, then hung the coat in the bathroom, over the bathtub. She had brought a bag of groceries, her offering of celebration. Walker took it as something more, a sign that he had passed muster with her. She had accepted his friendship, nothing more, and he had to be careful with her, and with himself, so he wouldn't upset that.

She ran on a delicate balance of thought and instinct, just as he did. She followed her hunches, but could reverse herself in a minute if events proved her wrong. Walker was determined not to do that, not to disappoint whatever expectations she had of him. He found himself playing a role that didn't quite feel right, and as a result, was tense all the time, like a silly teenager. He found himself thinking about her religious background, wondering where she stood on that now, and how, and if, he could possibly fit in. He wanted her, but he was afraid. She was the only woman in years who had frightened him.

And the crazy thing about that was, she was so

natural. She didn't talk religion, didn't seem to disapprove of anything he did. She had found the bourbon where he had hidden it in the kitchen cupboard, and had fixed him a drink. She didn't have any with him, waiting instead for her tea to boil, but he noticed that she had really laced in the booze. She made a hell of a good drink, as if she had been tending bar downtown for years.

When her tea was ready, she brought in the steaming cup and sat facing him, holding it between her hands. For a while they sat in silence. He thanked her for the drink.

"You know," she said, "I'm not even sure what I should call you. Somehow Dalton doesn't seem to fit. Do you go by anything else?"

"Only very occasionally, my very best friends call me Mike. My middle name."

She looked at him, her head tilted slightly. "Hmmm."

"Mostly, though, people call me Walker," he said simply. "I'm comfortable with that. People have been calling me that for so long now that I hardly ever answer to anything else."

"Yes," she said after a while. "You do look like a Walker. Somehow that fits just fine."

Again they had run out of words.

"Look," she said suddenly. "I like you, Walker, but you're driving me crazy. You're letting yourself be inhibited by all kinds of things I can't even guess at. You're putting me on a pedestal, don't you see that?"

He nodded slowly and sipped his drink.

"You hide your whiskey because you're afraid I won't like it. You watch your language to an embarrassing extent. How many times have you chopped off something just as the talk is getting interesting? Why do you do that?"

"You're right, I'm probably afraid you won't like it."

"If I don't like it I'll tell you so. Then we'll either stay friends or we won't. But I can't imagine anything you'd say that would offend me that much."

"I guess I'm still feeling my way along. I didn't want to turn you off even before I get to know you."

"And you're afraid the world you inhabit will turn me off."

"Something like that."

She shook her head. "You are all wrong, Walker. It's the pretense that turns me off, not the words. It's true, I come from a background of Puritanical values, but I've been in the city a long time. Ten years now. Do you think anybody could live in this city for ten years without hearing all the words there are to hear? Dozens, hundreds of times? What do you think this is, Victorian-era New York, when men protected women like that? Could I even pick up a novel today without seeing all the things my father once said were so unspeakably evil? Damn it, Walker, don't put me in a shell like that."

"I'm sorry."

She shrugged again, and laughed at herself. Her cheeks reddened. "Suppose we fall in love and get married." She laughed again. "What then, Walker? Are you going to go through life hiding your whiskey and watching your language? Or are you going to change that character you spent thirty-five years building, just for me? Would you be able to do that? Would you want to?"

"You've made your point," he said. "I apologize for treating you like a kid."

"Fine. Now that we've got that settled, I'll fix you some dinner."

* * *

"It's a simple Amish dinner," she said, setting the dishes on the table. "Nothing special."

They ate quietly. Over coffee, she said, "I'll tell you about myself. Maybe that'll help. I have three brothers. My parents are both living. I haven't spoken to my mother or father in ten years. I see my youngest brother, Michael, once or twice a year, and he brings me news from home.

"My parents are very traditional, very much of the Old World. If I went back now, even though we haven't seen each other for ten years, they'd shun me. It's got nothing to do with love, it's what they believe, what they were raised to believe, from their parents and grandparents, on back as far as anybody can remember. Outside people don't understand it, but it's their way. It doesn't mean they don't love me, but they wouldn't speak to me until I'd confessed my sins and been admitted back into the Church. Then all would be forgiven. I'd be expected to take up the traditional woman's role and become a farmer's wife. That's what they are, farmers. I'd be expected to marry a good Amish boy and settle down in Lancaster County, Pennsylvania."

He didn't comment, and she was silent for a long time. When she spoke again, she had shifted slightly into a new train of thought.

"I'm not a Puritan, Walker. I wasn't born to be one, not a good one, anyway. There are some things they ingrain into you, and you never really work them out of your system. Good things. Belief in God. Brotherly love. Sharing work and enjoying what fellowship you have with your brothers and sisters. Some of the things that happen there are fantastic. The things people do for each other. Back there, you're truly your brother's keeper. Not like here. There's a sense of belonging, if you do belong, that you won't find

95

anywhere else. But if you don't belong, your life there can be hell. Sometime I'll tell you all about it. About them and me."

She took a deep breath. "Look, I don't drink myself, but I don't mind those who do. I don't like drunks, though, so if you're one of those, I guess we won't get along. Otherwise, everything's fine. So far, I think we're doing all right, don't you?"

"I think we're doing fine, Diana."

"I like your company," she said.

And suddenly Diana blushed, filled with the self-consciousness of an introvert caught talking too much. "Mercy, I haven't made a speech like that since Lincoln freed the slaves." She gave a dry little laugh.

Walker drained his drink, leaned over and squeezed her shoulder.

She covered his hand with hers.

They sat for hours, listening to the rain and talking in spurts. They drank black coffee and talked about prisons. Walker told her about his personal prisons, his years of sporadic self-exile from the business he loved and hated. She found strong similarities between that and her own background.

"Sometimes you have no choice," she said. She had moved over next to him and now sat nestled under his arm. "I started learning that very early in my school years. Second or third grade. In the early Fifties, the Amish farmers were starting to catch a lot of heat for not schooling their kids. Did you know that the Amish don't send their kids past the eighth grade? They feel threatened by the school system. They're afraid the kids will see too many earthly pleasures and will want to break away from the Church. That's what happened to me.

"I'd always been a restless child. I'd never been really comfortable with the life they mapped out for me, but it wasn't until I got into school that I started to see some alternatives. Michael tells me things are different now. The Amish have built their own schools, so their kids won't have to truck with outsiders. But when I was growing up, there were no Amish schools. There was a big confrontation between the farmers and the school board. We lost, the kids were made to go through eighth grade at least. In second or third grade, I met a girl named Billie Morris, and Billie wanted like crazy to be a dancer. She had books on dance, on ballet and modern dance, filled with the most gorgeous pictures you ever saw. Her parents had money; by our standards they were rich. They bought her everything she wanted. I couldn't get over it, how *much* she had of everything. The books thrilled me. She used to lend them to me and I'd take them home and hide them in the barn. I'd read them at night by lanternlight. Until my father found them and burned them.

"You might say that was the beginning of my rebellion. You can imagine how I dreaded telling Billie Morris. For a week I avoided her. Finally I couldn't put it off any longer. And you know what? She didn't care at all. She said they were old books and she was getting tired of them anyway. She'd make her dad buy her some more. Over the next few months, the rift grew between the family and me. I became the black sheep. My older brother Daniel, who's always followed the teachings of the Church to the letter, thought I was a terrible heretic. He stopped speaking to me long before I broke with the Church. Michael tells me he's married and has his own farm now. Children. Two boys and a girl. And I'm sure he makes them tow the mark."

"Making that final break must have been hard."

"Not as hard as you'd think. It had been coming on by degrees for years. I'd been getting regular thrashings and one day, about two months before my seventeenth birthday, I decided I'd had enough. I packed my bag and walked out, in the middle of a workday, when Father and the boys were still in the fields. I told my mother I was going to New York, and I'd write.

"No, the hard part was staying away. No one who hasn't been raised in the Amish faith could understand what a huge, wonderful, terrifying place the outside world is, when you come into it all of a sudden like that. You have no skills. You don't know how to behave around people. How do you survive? The only thing you know is your housework and your Church, and now there's no house to work in. There's no family to put food on your table and give you a bed at night. You have no money and little more than the clothes on your back. Where would you go?"

"I don't know."

"I did what every Amish girl who's ever run away from home has done. You either give up and go home or you find refuge where you can, in God, which is the only thing you know. In my case, the Mennonite Church, which is fairly close to the Amish, but somewhat looser in its rules. The Mennonites, for example, can have electricity in their homes. They don't have to do without all the modern wonders, like Old World Amish. They don't have to ride in buggies, or use horses for plowing. Their bathrooms are inside the house. Things you take for granted, the Amish child has never known for himself. So you might say I came up like a diver who's been under water too long. Slowly, by degrees. I found a Mennonite family who took me in. I worked for them a year, until even their standards became too much to bear, then I broke away from them too. In the city I took simple jobs. I studied dancing, went to night school, got my high school diploma. And I found a Protestant Church that was close enough to the old teachings to give me the comfort I wanted, but loose enough to give me some breathing room.

"I got secretarial jobs, worked nights as a waitress. One day there came the chance I'd been waiting for, a dancing job in a roadhouse revue. Up in Connecticut. It meant casting off the last of those old chains, rejecting my home and Church and everything they stood for. It was something I'd always wanted, but I was afraid. I was certain it would lead to disaster."

But it hadn't led to disaster. Yes, her nervousness had cost her that first job in Connecticut, but there were other jobs, other parts. She played in a theater-in-the-round production of *Little Mary Sunshine,* and after that went on the road, to Colorado, where the wave of dinner-theaters offered jobs and new vistas. Her courage had seen her through lean times. And one night a girl from Radio City had seen her dancing in a Village play, and had met her backstage. They became friends, and the girl talked her into auditioning at Radio City.

"Here I am," she said, with a sweeping motion meant to simplify the complicated. "Now you know the story of my life."

Diana said she had never wanted to be a star, so the anonymity of the Rockettes suited her fine. She had never wanted anything but to dance. To dance and get paid for it was the ideal. She had read an article describing the sensations of free-fall parachuting, and she thought dancing was like that. Her brother Michael understood her. The others didn't. Her parents didn't know that she worked at Radio City. The last time he was in New York, Michael had come to see her perform. He had been thrilled by the wonder of it, and afterward he had gone home to his pregnant wife Trudy, and the patch of land he was leasing from brother Daniel until he could save enough money to buy his own. And he had written to her, and they had thought about each other. But Michael had never told anybody.

It was two o'clock in the morning. They had talked for eight hours, and had come to know each other well. Diana worked for the Democratic Party, licking stamps in election years. She did volunteer work with the handicapped, and she liked baseball. She went to Yankee Stadium when she could, always alone.

"Would you ever go home?" Walker said.

She thought for a long time. "Sometimes I want to go back so much, it really hurts me. It brings tears to my eyes. I'd give anything to be able to go home for a visit and be on good terms with everyone. Just like other people. How I'd love that."

"Would you ever go back for good?"

"Once I actually had my bags packed. I was ready to go, but somehow I just couldn't get on that bus. Somehow I couldn't make that final step. Because I was afraid of just that. It would be final. I got away once. I couldn't do it again. I don't think I'd ever have the strength to walk away a second time."

"You would," Walker said.

"You think so?"

"People like you always find the strength, if it's the right thing to do. God, listen to me. As if I'm any great authority on what that is."

"You make me feel good."

"It's always easier the second time around. My profundity of the week, in case you're interested."

"You make me feel that I could do anything."

He leaned over and kissed her. At first she didn't move. Then her hand came up and touched his cheek.

"There's another reason I left home," she said some

moments later. "The Amish, as you might imagine, have rules about . . . fooling around. As I grew older, I found it hard to obey those rules."

They looked at each other.

"That's why you're here now," he said.

"One of the reasons. Not as strong as the others, but there's no use denying it."

Again he touched her shoulder. "Would you like to stay here tonight?"

"I thought I had."

Walker dreamed of a line of Rockettes, all naked, doing high kicks on NBC. He stirred and came awake. Once awake, he tried not to move because Diana had her head resting on his bare chest. He felt drained yet full, a fullness he hadn't known with a woman in years.

He had always been able to find sex, and in his youth that had been enough. Bar-hopping. Whore-hopping. Just the brutal, physical act of getting off with someone. Give him an hour in any strange town and he could find someone to sleep with. Someone lonely, like himself, and maybe she would be as good-looking as the ones with all the ideas about perma-nence and a lasting thing. Looks didn't have anything to do with it. The foolish fantasies of youth, come back now to haunt him. In his early twenties, he had seldom been without female company, sometimes a different woman each night. He had developed a thick skin and a brash manner. If one woman turned him down, the one just a seat or a table away was ready and waiting.

He must have been thirty years old before all that started wearing thin. Now he went a week or two, sometimes longer, without a date. Even when he did date, he didn't always make a pass at the girl. He wondered if he was losing his juice. Then he fell in love, with a Jewish girl named Lois Berman, and she loved him back. Fairly late in his sex life, Lois Berman had given him the gift of giving, and he had never been satisfied with store-bought sex again.

Diana knew about that too. She was no thirty-year-old virgin as she came to his bed. It was clear from their first contact that, to her, he came first. And he had. She knew what she was doing, and there was simply no way he could make it for her. It had been too long.

Later. In another hour, things would be different.

He slipped out of bed without waking her. Going into the kitchen, he sat at the table and thought about being happy. He had never been a happy man. But at this moment, he was as happy as he had been in years.

Maybe, just maybe, it was good enough.

He had been there about ten minutes when he thought he heard her stir, but then realized the noise had been distant, farther away, and muffled. It sounded almost like someone knocking at his door. He slipped into his pants and went into the living room. Half a room away, Diana stirred and called his name.

"I think somebody's in the hall." He draped a shirt across his shoulders.

She sat up. In the dark he could see the pale hint of her breasts. "What time is it?" she said.

He looked at the clock. "Quarter to five."

There was no question. Someone was outside.

"Who is it?"

The knock came louder.

"Who is it?" he said again.

Still no answer. He looked at Diana and his male ego got the best of him. The girl would think he was afraid of his own shadow.

Walker opened the door, and the woman came

toward him, forcing her way into the room. Melinda Baker. Joanne Sayers. She looked like a drowned rat. Her hair streamed down her face and the makeup around her eyes had run down her cheeks. She had lost the bifocals, but not the gun. She held that steadily in her hand, pointed straight at his throat.

Ten

Donovan spent Monday morning in his office, doing busywork and waiting for the telephone to ring. It did, several times, but that one call he expected never came. The silence was enough to drive a man nuts. They had zipped up the Lewis-Sayers case and put a lid on it thirty-six hours ago. Roland Simon had told him to sit still and wait for further word. Since then, nothing. The fact that Walker had blown the lid off the case should have produced a few waves, but so far, not a damned thing. The phone call he had been expecting since Saturday night, when Walker's story had hit the streets, had still not come. Donovan had stayed home all day Sunday, the phone within arm's reach. He had no further word on the Sayers girl, either from the Bureau or from Walker. The way things were going, he half expected Walker to find her first.

Donovan was nervous. It was another of those strange ones. He hadn't liked the smell of it from the first and it didn't get better with time. So he had called Walker and had given him just enough to find the rest. He thought his conscience was clear, but his first reaction, when he sent Kim over to Jersey for the

Saturday *Tribune,* was one of horror. No matter how well you know a reporter, you can never quite visualize his story in print. It was never even close to the way you would have done it. The words were the same (Walker had been hard on the Bureau in a few places, but that was Simon's fault), but somehow the images were different. Put it under a roaring headline, strip it down the right side of Page One, and damn, it sounded as though the world was ending.

Donovan always had very mixed emotions whenever some tip of his resulted in a big story. Power and guilt were the usual feelings. He felt like a traitor, and at the same time he enjoyed seeing what he had done materialize into an important event. He salved the guilt by telling himself that Simon was wrong, it would have come out anyway, there was simply no way you could hold a thing like that back. And because Simon had mishandled it, both Simon and the Bureau would look like hell in the press. The thing that bothered Donovan most was Simon's parting shot: that the *Tribune* must bear responsibility if the Sayers girl wasn't captured without a fight. If Walker had to bear that cross, the full weight of it must finally be passed on to the shoulders of Al Donovan.

He was constantly amazed at how little government agencies like the FBI knew about dealing with reporters. Donovan's attitude was simple. You kept sensitive material out of their hands as long as possible, but why try to fight them when they had it anyway? That's when you stepped in and helped them. You only fought the fights you could win. He had learned that from Hoover, long ago. Young agents coming along today didn't seem to understand that, or believe it. They came with ready-made chips on their shoulders, always ready to stonewall everything. Trying to tell them how to get decent press was like reciting Longfellow to a tree. You might think it penetrated, but when you went back the next day, the tree hadn't changed.

At midmorning, he put his desk in order, locked up his work papers and went into New York for his lunch date with Virgil Craig. He was glad he and Craig had agreed to meet at the restaurant: he didn't want to be seen in the field office today. Craig was early as always: sitting alone in a corner looking like an old doctor, or perhaps a broker. Donovan slipped in opposite him and they murmured a few words of greeting. Donovan noticed, as he had on the telephone, that Craig seemed distant, almost remote. They ordered lunch, then Donovan said, "Well, Virg, I guess you can forget about those pictures."

"Turned into quite a fracas, didn't it?"

"That it did."

"I figured you'd want to be there."

"I appreciate the call. I'd appreciate something else, too. I'd like to know what's eating you."

Craig didn't answer.

"I'm serious," Donovan said. "Ever since I gave you those pictures, you've been cool as hell."

"Have I?"

"Now see, that's just what I mean. What kind of bullshit answer is that? We go back too far for that kind of grind."

"You know me," Craig said. "Always the careful one. Always trying to follow the book, right, Al? I almost didn't call you Friday night."

"I'm glad you did."

"I still wonder if I made a mistake. I told you on the phone, make up something if you have to. Just don't tell them I tipped you."

Donovan sighed and looked at the table.

"I've always played it too safe," Craig said.

"Funny. I was thinking the same thing about myself just the other day."

"You never played safe a day in your life. You don't know what playing it safe is. Me, I look for a cool spot if things get too warm. We're different kinds of animals, Al, and you might as well admit it. It still surprises me that we've stayed friends all these years."

"What kind of talk is that? You don't see me sticking my neck out."

"You would, though, if you had to."

"Sure I would. That's why my career's been so much brighter than yours."

Craig shook his head. "The fact that we've ended up at about the same level's got nothing to do with it. It's for different reasons and you know it. You never could stand office politics, and I couldn't stand the heat at the top." He stirred some sugar into his tea. "The thought hit me the other day, and it was a pretty rude shock. I've spent thirty years in the wrong business. It's true. I never should have been in the FBI, Al. I should have been what you're always saying I look like. A country doctor. A lawyer, maybe."

"You are a lawyer." Donovan smiled.

"Maybe I should have practiced. Now all I want is to retire quietly. No fuss, no bother. Just retire and do whatever retired people do."

You poor bastard, Donovan thought. He said, "Okay, so what's it all mean? You're beating all around something. Can you just give me a simple answer?"

"Sometimes there are no simple answers. Sometimes, no matter how hard we look, two and two just don't add up."

"Then give it to me raw and I'll add it up."

Craig thought for a long time. "Here it is, then, as much as I know. And Al, after this it's your baby. Do with it or don't do whatever you want. Just don't tell me about it and don't say we talked." Craig sipped his tea. For a while, Donovan thought he wasn't going to talk at all. Then he said, "For a couple of days after you gave me those pictures, it was pretty normal procedure. Then funny things started happening."

"Funny how?"

"There was a lot of flutter from above."

"Stands to reason. They had made them. Somebody knew we had some pretty important criminals on our hands."

"A *lot* of flutter, Al. From *way* above. This started coming down Wednesday, and went all through Thursday. There were notes between here and D.C., and I was cut completely out of it, which you know isn't normal procedure at all. Normally these things would work back through me to you, as originating agent. Right? So Simon called me in twice. Asked a lot of questions about the pictures. Where I'd got them. When. How."

"You told him?"

"Sure I told him. What would you have done?"

"I'm not blaming you, Virg, I'm just asking. Go ahead."

"I told him I'd received them from you on Monday. He wanted to know where you had got them. I said I didn't know. He said he'd get back to me and never did. He never got back to me at all."

"That it?"

"That's some of it."

"What's the rest of it?" Donovan was beginning to believe that Virgil Craig was right. He should have been a lawyer.

"Well, think about it. When were the Lewises killed?"

"Friday night."

"And when did all this static start floating around the office? More than forty-eight hours before. Does that sound right to you?"

"Nothing sounds right to me. How does it sound to you?"

Again, the long silence. "What do you usually do when you've got identity on people like George and Michelle Lewis? When you've got them and you know where they are, what do you do? Do you wait forty-eight hours, give them a chance to get lost again? In any office I ever worked in, you go out and pick them up."

"Maybe they didn't have them made yet."

"Then why all the fuss?" Craig frowned. "Al, you'd have had to be there Thursday morning to believe it. They burned up the wire between here and D.C. Simon was on the phone all day. Later I heard that some people were coming into Kennedy around midnight."

"What people?"

"I didn't ask and they didn't say. It was after closing time. I was still in the office, getting my stuff together to go home. All the secretaries had left, and Simon was in conference with that young kid, Kevin Lord. They'd been at it over two hours then, between phone calls to Washington. The door opened and Lord came out. He got some papers out of the box and went back into Simon's office. Just before the door closed, I heard him say, 'You want me to go to Kennedy tonight?' And Simon said, 'Hell no, you stay out of it.'"

"That might have meant anything. Might not have related to this at all."

"Like you said, Al, you add it up. Frankly, I don't know or care. I'm just telling you what happened."

"Okay. Then what happened?"

"Then I went home and got myself a drink."

"Is that it?"

Craig nodded. But there was something else. Donovan could feel it.

"Virg?"

Again the long silence. Finally Virgil Craig said, "Did you see the *Daily News* Sunday?"

"Sure. I read all the papers."

"The last edition?"

"Jeez, I don't remember what edition. Is it important?"

"Here." Craig reached into his coat pocket and took out a small clipping. The headline said MAN IN CRITICAL CONDITION AFTER ROBBERY ATTEMPT. Donovan read through the story and gave it back.

"The guy isn't named," Craig said.

"Happens a lot in journalism," Donovan said. "They can't make the guy, or if it's a likely fatal they'll hold up the name till next of kin's been notified."

"That's not the case here. This man's one of us."

Donovan blinked.

"He's from the Bureau," Craig said.

"How do you know that?"

"Simon put a ring of people around his room at Riverside Hospital. I was on it for a while. We were to let no one in, especially reporters. But I guess Simon covered his tracks pretty well, because no one came."

"Virg . . ."

"Wait, let me get it all out. Now that I've started, let me finish and then you can have it. The guy's name is Blanton Smith. That's not the name he's admitted under. He's in the hospital as Joseph Collins. But he's Blanton Smith, and he's with the Bureau out of Washington."

Donovan didn't say anything.

"He was shot up real bad, Al. Took three in the chest, high up. They didn't have much hope for him when I was there early Saturday."

"And this was supposed to be a robbery attempt?"

Craig touched the news clipping. His face was deadpan.

"Where'd they pick him up?"

"Just off Tenth Avenue, not far from the Lincoln Tunnel. That's what the report said, anyway."

"Who found him?"

Craig shrugged his shoulders.

"Anything else?"

The waiter brought their lunches. Craig seemed lost in thought for a while, picking over his food. "When I got up there, around two o'clock Saturday morning, he had just come out of surgery. The ether was just starting to wear off, and he was crazy, you know, delirious. He started to moan and talk. I couldn't understand any of it, except for one word. 'Bitch.' He said that over and over. 'The bitch.'"

"What time'd they bring him in?"

"To the hospital, you mean? Around eight-thirty. Must have been found a few minutes before that."

Donovan turned it over in his mind. "It's strange, all right, and the timing's right. Just about the time the Lewises were killed. It might fit in or it might not."

"Whether it does or not, it's off my chest."

The waiter came. Virgil Craig indulged himself. He ordered dessert. "You like football, Al?"

"What? Oh, sure."

"How do you like the Steelers this year?"

They parted outside the restaurant. From a phone booth, Donovan called his office. There were several messages; none from Walker.

He called Riverside Hospital and asked for a condition report on Blanton Smith. The woman said they had no one of that name registered.

"How about Joseph Collins?"

"Are you a relative?"

"No, just a friend."

There was a long delay. When the nurse returned,

she said, "Sir, Mr. Collins passed away about three hours ago."

He tried calling Walker at the *Tribune* and got a gruff man named Kanin. "Walker hasn't been in all day," Kanin said. "But that's nothing new."

He called the office, told them he was out for the day, and took the train home.

Kim greeted him at the door, on her way to a shopping spree. She was surprised to see him home so early. He took a drink into his den and sat under the picture of J. Edgar Hoover, drumming his fingers.

Some ugly thoughts were forming in his head.

He reached for the telephone and got the number of Blanton Smith in Washington. He shouldn't make the call from here. He knew that. There should be no record that Al Donovan had tried calling the dead man's home.

The hell with it. He placed the call.

A woman answered. She sounded very cheery, as if all was right with the world. He asked for Mr. Smith.

"Mr. Smith is out of town. Who's calling, please?"

"Is this Mrs. Smith?"

"Yes."

"When do you expect him home, Mrs. Smith?"

"I'm not sure. He had to go to New York for a few days. May I ask who this is?"

"I'm a friend of his. My name wouldn't mean anything. You understand that, don't you, Mrs. Smith?"

"Yes. Of course I understand."

Yes. A good agent's wife would understand. Still, he had to be sure.

"Is this the Smith who works for the FBI?"

"Yes it is. Is there anything I can do?"

"No. Thank you."

He hung up.

There was nothing Mrs. Smith could do, nothing

anybody could do. Blanton Smith was dead and his widow didn't even know it. Donovan wondered how they would tell her. He wondered what the explanation would be, what kind of story they might concoct.

He tried Walker again. Kanin told him Walker hadn't come in or called in, all day long. Donovan tried Walker's apartment. There was no answer.

He went into the bedroom and found Kim's address book. Now, for some awful reason, he found himself in a mental block. That girl, Walker's girl. He couldn't remember her name. Younger, he thought it was. She and Kim had hit it off. Maybe Kim had taken the number.

Yoder. Diana.

He tried her apartment. No answer.

He waited awhile, and had himself another drink. At last driven by an increasing sense of curiosity, he called Radio City. The person there didn't want to cooperate. He identified himself as an FBI agent and was put through to someone else, who told him that Diana Yoder had called in early that morning, and had quit her job. No notice. No explanation. Nothing.

"Son of a bitch," Donovan said, placing the phone gently in its cradle. "I wonder where *they* went."

Eleven

In the morning Donovan tried Blanton Smith's house again. A man answered.

"Mrs. Smith isn't available."

"That's okay, it's Mr. Smith I wanted to talk to."

"Mr. Smith is dead."

So. They had broken the news, sometime during the night.

Donovan pretended shock. "Dear God, how?"

"An accident. Who is this?"

He hung up.

It was almost a rerun of last night. Walker wasn't at the *Tribune,* and he hadn't called in. The Yoder girl wasn't home, and they weren't at Walker's apartment. The only new wrinkle was that Blanton Smith's death had finally come out in the open. As an accident. Probably a closed-casket case, who would be buried in Arlington by tomorrow.

Throughout the morning, Donovan tried to reach Walker. He isolated himself from the small office staff and kept to his room, staying on the phone throughout the morning and declining two offers to break for coffee. At eleven o'clock a call came through from the New York office.

114

"Donovan? Roland Simon here."

"Hi," Donovan said. He never knew how to address Simon. The young turks in the field office called him Mr. Simon, but Donovan—a full fifteen years older than Simon—felt slightly degraded by that. The use of Simon's first name suggested an intimacy he didn't feel, and the last name without the "Mr." seemed a bit too arrogant. Usually he used no forms at all. He slouched down in his desk.

"I thought you handled the press well," Donovan lied.

"It's not the way I'd have wanted to handle it," Simon said.

"Under the circumstances, it went as well as you could expect."

"I was wondering if you could get over to the city this afternoon."

Donovan, anticipating the question, had already looked at his calendar.

"I'm supposed to be in court. I may have to testify this afternoon."

"You won't," Simon said. "I know about the case, and it'll be continued until tomorrow."

"Oh."

"Well then?"

"Well then, sure." He knew he wasn't being asked. He was being politely ordered, and the next order wouldn't be so polite.

"Fine," Simon said. Some of the ice had disappeared from the edges of his voice. "See you here. Three o'clock."

The phone clicked off. Donovan put the receiver down slowly and looked up at the clock. It was noon. He called Walker. Walker wasn't in. Somehow, he didn't think Walker would be.

* * *

He skipped lunch and went to Walker's apartment. The old lady who managed the building looked at his credentials for a long time, then reluctantly led him up the three flights to Walker's door. She stood at the threshold and watched while he walked through. The place smelled slightly stuffy, as if it had been locked up and no one had been there for a while. He moved into the kitchenette and found the remains of an old meal still in the sink. The dishes hadn't been washed, and he guessed they had been used late Saturday or sometime Sunday.

The bed was mussed, and there was a smear of mud on one of the sheets. The covers had been tossed carelessly on the floor and left there. He crossed the dark room and looked in Walker's closet. Some of Walker's clothes were still there. The dresser told the same story: the drawers were partly full, indicating that perhaps some clothes had been taken. But he couldn't tell for sure.

He went over to New York an hour before his meeting with Roland Simon, and went through the Yoder girl's place. This time the manager let him roam at will. He went through her apartment carefully, as much out of personal curiosity as professional interest. The girl was a strange one. She intrigued him. Her bedroom was simple. A picture of Christ hung over her bed. Across from that, a Ruysdael reproduction, a grassy Dutch meadow with a heavy cloud bank. The apartment was incredibly neat; not a speck of dust anywhere. The hardwood floors were for the most part uncovered, though each room had an oval rug in its center. He went through the notebook by her bedside, where the telephone was, and found the notation *Walker*. Under it, Walker's telephone numbers at work and home. He went into the bathroom. In her medicine cabinet, he found a container of birth control pills with six missing, beginning on Monday and ending Saturday.

It told him little that he couldn't have figured out anyway. That the girl and Walker were becoming pretty thick pretty fast. Perhaps they had run off to get married. Now there was a thought. An angle, as they said in Walker's business. But it didn't quite mesh with the Walker he knew. Still, what did mesh? At his best, Walker was unpredictable, given to sudden impulse. When all the chips were down, Donovan could picture Walker doing something dumb like that.

He arrived at the field office a few minutes early, and was kept waiting for almost half an hour. When at last he was shown into Roland Simon's office, he found the remains of a continuing discussion scattered around him. The desk contained a number of closed files, and one that was open. The open file was on what had become fixed in everyone's mind as the Sayers case.

The air was blue. Simon was a chain-smoker who looked at you with puffy eyes and coughed a lot. Seated on his right was a spotless young agent, Kevin Lord. Donovan didn't know him, except by sight and through grapevine reports that he had become one of Simon's pets. He wore a dark gray suit and had his hair styled. He was about thirty. Across from Kevin Lord was Joe Armstrong. Donovan had seen Armstrong off and on for more than twenty years. Armstrong was Lord's opposite in almost every way. Heavier, older, with craggy features and a flat nose. If Kevin Lord's face had been carved in marble, Armstrong's had been pounded in clay. His clothes clashed, but in a quiet way. The FBI didn't like conspicuous dressers. Over the years Armstrong had found a way to accommodate Bureau guidelines and his own atrocious taste. His eyes reflected keen intelligence, but disinterest. Donovan guessed that Armstrong was bored by life.

Armstrong made an imposing figure when you walked in on him. Somehow he managed to inhibit you without even moving, or without looking your way. Simon sat back in his swivel chair and seemed to be searching for a way to begin. Finally he said, "Al, we've got a problem."

It was the first time Simon had ever used his given name. Kevin Lord leaned toward him and Armstrong just gazed at him with bottomless eyes. Donovan wondered if they were going to sweat him, catch him in a crossfire between them. But it was Simon who continued talking. "We've got a delicate situation on our hands, and only part of it has come out in the press. We hope we'll be able to keep it that way."

"He's telling you no more leaks to your reporter friend," Armstrong said.

Donovan bristled. So it was a sweat job after all. "Shove it, Joe," he said. "If there's a leak around here, it's not me."

"Then the son of a bitch must be a mind reader," Armstrong said.

"Walker was working on this story long before we were. It's natural that he'd have some background."

"Just as natural as you thinking of it as a story. To me it's a case. Maybe you should have been a newspaperman, Donovan."

"I'm trying to tell you how he thinks, in case you're interested." Donovan looked at them and decided to play it straight. "You want to know where Walker got his information, then ask him."

"We would," Simon said. "Only we can't find him."

"Besides," Armstrong said, "we all know that'd be a waste of time, don't we? This Walker cat wouldn't tell us anything."

"Then I'll tell you," Donovan said. "He called me

late Friday night, early Saturday morning. I don't know what time it was. I told him no go, whatever he got on this he was going to have to get himself. And he found it, gentlemen, right there in the *Tribune* vaults. Any fool can see that his story was written from clips."

"Yeah," Armstrong said. "Any fool can see that."

Lord picked up the attack, but in a smoother, more civilized voice. "The thing is, we think Walker was still a few steps from being able to write that story when he left the scene."

"What makes you think that?" Donovan said. "Did he tell you that?"

"Use your head," Armstrong said. "Why'd he give us the pictures?"

"Because," Lord said, "he didn't have the ID's made yet. He needed our help on that."

"We had those pictures a week," Donovan said. "A lot can happen between Monday and Friday. Maybe he had them made by Friday night."

"And maybe the Pope don't wear a high hat," Armstrong said.

Simon flexed his fingers. "Well, we didn't call you in here to argue."

"You could have fooled me," Donovan said.

"We're all on the same side," Simon said. "We all want the same thing. Once we get the Sayers girl, the papers can do anything they want. I don't give a damn."

"Look," Donovan said impatiently. "Walker's no dummy. Sometime between the morning he gave me those pictures and the morning after the Lewises were killed, he pieced it together. You're asking me how. I don't know how. All I know is that somewhere he got a name, and it wasn't from me. I know what I think, and I told you that. Once he had the name, the rest was duck soup."

"Fish soup sounds more like it," Armstrong said. "That smells stronger."

"All right, can it, Joe," Simon said. "This isn't getting us anywhere. What we're saying, Al, in our charming way"—he smiled crookedly at Armstrong—"is we know how you work with the press. And that's fine, we understand it. It's unusual, but fine, it's your way and up to now we've had no complaints. It's done us some good turns in the past to have friends in the news business."

"Friends who are really friends," Armstrong said. "Not jerks like this Walker character."

"Walker's a goddamned good reporter," Donovan said. "You don't want a friend, Joe, you want a lackey."

"Gentlemen, you're straying again," Simon said. To Armstrong, he said, "May I finish, please?"

Armstrong shrugged.

"All right, part of our problem is that we don't know exactly what we've got here." He paused to light a smoke. "You all read Walker's story."

They nodded, all but Armstrong, who merely looked bored.

"You know about the Ordway matter," Simon said. "You know that some important, critical Bureau documents are still missing from that case. That's why Joe was sent up here, to help us recover those papers."

"At any cost," Armstrong said. He looked at Donovan. "What was that phrase your friend used? 'Very sensitive'?"

"He was quoting the Bureau's spokesman, I believe. That was our definition."

"Our definition, as run through their mill," Armstrong said. "And rewritten from old newspaper clippings. When we made that statement, we thought we'd have those documents back in a few days."

"A lot has happened since then," Kevin Lord said.

"A hell of a lot," Armstrong said. "The whole political climate of this country has changed, thanks in no small part to jerks like this Walker guy. They put their junk in the newspaper without even starting to understand the consequences. And suddenly everything's different. People want blood, and it's our blood they want. So we want those records back."

Donovan knew better than to ask what the records contained. But Simon, anticipating the unasked question, said, "None of us knows what's in those Ordway papers."

Donovan looked at Armstrong, whose face remained a mask.

"But we know what we need to know," Simon said. "The Ordway papers contain items of national security, and they're top priority. More important than the girl's capture." He looked at Donovan. "More important than anything you've ever done for the FBI, Al."

Okay, he thought. I'm impressed. Now what?

"I'm assigning you and Kevin to work with Joe on their recovery. You'll form a loose team, under Joe's direction, and will work out of your office in Brooklyn."

"I don't understand that," Donovan said. "That seems like the long way around."

"Let me put it another way. We think Walker at this point knows more about the case than we do."

"You've seen what Walker knows. It's all there in his story."

"We don't think so. We had a meeting yesterday, and some startling patterns came out of this story. We know that he's met Joanne Sayers, at least once while she was hiding out as Melinda Baker. We know the pictures originated with Walker. We know he'd been working on the case more than two months, so in a sense he's had that much head start on us. And we know he won't stop until he's got that Ordway file in his hands, and splashed it across the front page of his paper. Even you, Al, will have to admit that."

Yes. Even he had to admit that.

"We've got to shortstop that," Simon said.

"At any cost," Armstrong said.

Donovan couldn't resist slipping them a needle. "Those things aren't so startling. You should have had a tail on Walker from the moment his paper hit the street."

Simon cleared his throat. There was a long awkward moment. "That was a busy morning for all of us, Al. And hindsight is a great thing." There was another long pause. "So. I want you to work out of your office, just as you've always done. Walker will contact you, sooner or later."

"Maybe. Maybe not."

"If he does, I want you to play it straight with him. Work with him, offer to help. Anything to find out what he knows. Joe and Kevin will also use your office as a home base. You'll meet there at the end of the day, go over what you've got, and Joe will report to me. Any questions?"

He had none.

"I don't have to tell you, this takes priority over everything. Go anywhere, do whatever you have to. If you need help, pick up the phone. The entire office is at your disposal. I'm not kidding, men, I want those goddamned records back."

The three of them went out together. At Armstrong's direction they went to a coffee shop and sat in a corner booth over three steaming cups. They talked for fifteen minutes, quite long enough for Armstrong to establish command.

"Lord, I want you to go over to Jersey. Interview people at Bristol-Myers. Then talk to people all along the block where the Sayers woman lived."

"We've already done that," Lord said. "I have the reports."

"I don't want the goddamned reports," Armstrong said. "I want *you* to do it. Do it again. Do it a hundred times if I tell you to. We're gonna break this bastard, if we have to ask the same people the same questions a thousand times. You got that?"

To Donovan, as they were paying the bill, he said, "You come with me."

They each paid for one coffee. On the sidewalk, Armstrong waited until Kevin Lord had disappeared around a corner.

"You and I will take off for Brooklyn," he said. "And listen, Donovan."

Donovan listened.

"I want you to remember two things. I'm running this show."

Donovan faced him coldly. "What's the other thing?"

"The Sayers girl. No matter what . . ." Armstrong paused, to give the words their proper weight. "No . . . matter . . . what . . . I want that little baby handed to me. You got that?"

Donovan got it.

An hour later they walked into the Brooklyn office. There was a stack of messages on Donovan's desk. Busywork.

"Get rid of that," Armstrong said. "Get it assigned to somebody else."

Donovan went through the messages while Armstrong looked over his shoulder. At the bottom was a note that made them both sit up. A Mr. Walker had called, just after noon. No message. He said he would call back, sometime tonight.

Armstrong was smiling. "You see, Donovan? Just what I thought. Working with you pays off, real fast."

"If he's going to call tonight, he probably means at my home."

"Good. You got a spare bedroom?"

Donovan nodded.

"Then I accept your invitation, for the duration. Let's get going. He might call early."

When they arrived, Kim told them they had just missed Walker's call. "That's okay," Armstrong said. "He'll call back." They planned to use two phones. Donovan would take the call in his den and Armstrong would listen in on the kitchen extension. They waited, watching the phone, but the call didn't come. At seven-thirty, Kim served dinner.

Donovan discovered that Armstrong had a certain rugged charm, which he could turn on and off at will. He raved about Kim's cooking, and about their home; he called Donovan by his given name as they passed plates across the table. He ate heartily, the ultimate compliment to a cook's labors. Donovan could see that the charm had had its effect on his wife. "I like your friend," she said as they met briefly in the kitchen. "He seems very nice."

"Things aren't always what they seem," he said coldly.

Her eyes followed him out of the room, and he knew he shouldn't have said it, shouldn't have involved her in it in any way. Armstrong was his problem; let it stay that way. Now all he wanted was that Walker should call and convince them all that he and the Yoder girl had run off for a long weekend. That he knew nothing more than what had been in his story and wasn't pursuing it any further. Then maybe Armstrong would get out of his house and take his case somewhere else. That hope faded and went out when the phone rang. Kim moved toward it, but Donovan motioned her to stay still. He went into the den and lifted the receiver. In the kitchen, Armstrong lifted his so quietly that Donovan didn't hear as much as a click.

"Mr. Al Donovan?"

"Yes."

"Hold please for long distance."

He was in a telephone booth somewhere. Donovan heard the coins dropping in the slot as the operator directed. The coins seemed to come endlessly. At last the operator said, "Go ahead, please."

"Al?"

"Yeah, Walker. Where the hell are you at?"

"Never mind that. Listen, I got no more change, so whatever we say will have to be kept to three minutes. So you listen and I'll talk. First I need your word on something. This has got to be between you and me. Your word on that."

Donovan writhed.

"Al?"

"Yeah, Walker?"

"Is something wrong?"

"No, of course not. It's just . . . how can I give my word until I know what you're talking about?"

"Listen," Walker snapped. "It's about the Sayers thing. Now do you want to help me on this or not? I haven't got much time."

"Sure I do."

"Then tell me it'll be kept private, between you and me, until I say otherwise."

Armstrong pushed his way into the den, gesturing with his hands and eyes. Gesturing yes.

"Sure," Donovan said. "Just between us."

Armstrong hurried back to the kitchen phone.

"Okay, then. The Sayers girl is with me."

Donovan felt his pulse quicken.

"Al? You still there?"

"I don't know," Donovan said, trying to laugh. "That's an awful big load you dropped on me."

"It's no load, Al."

"Listen, Walker, if you're trying to help her get away, that can get mighty goddamn sticky . . ."

"I'm trying to help her give herself up. Listen, if you want to get technical about it, I've been her prisoner since Saturday. Does that make you feel any better?"

"I don't know." It was a bad scene in either case. "Ah, Walker . . . where are you?"

"Doesn't matter. We won't be here long enough to matter anyway. The kid wants to give herself up, but she's scared. She's sure she'll be killed the way the Lewises were."

"Lewis killed himself, Walker."

"She doesn't believe that. Now listen. I've told her about you, and she wants you to take custody of her. Nobody else. We'll tell you when and where, later."

An operator cut in. "Your three minutes are up."

"All right, Al, I've got to run."

"Wait a minute!"

"No more time. Call you in a few days."

The line went dead.

Armstrong came in, grinning. "Pay dirt," he said. "Who'd have thought we'd hit it this quick? See, pilgrim? Sometimes my hunches do pay off." He had a small notebook in his hand with some figures on it. "There's no way we can find out where that call came from. Next time he calls, we'll have a trace ready. Right now we'll have to make do with a little crude arithmetic. You got a map of the United States?"

"In my car."

"Get it."

Armstrong dialed the operator, then asked for the chief operator. He identified himself as an FBI agent, and was still talking when Donovan came in with the map. They spread the map out on a table and Armstrong drew an almost perfect circle, with its center near Donovan's home. The circle's outer edge cut across northern Maine, through mid-Ohio, across the Kentucky-West Virginia line, through southern Virginia and parts of North Carolina.

"That's the area we're working with, given the amount of change your buddy fed the phone," he said. "He's done himself some traveling."

Donovan didn't say anything. He was thinking about Diana Yoder, also gone from her home and job. He thought about the rumpled bed at Walker's place, and a vial of birth control pills with six pills missing. The girl would have gone to Walker's to spend the night. Had Joanne Sayers walked in on them? If the Yoder girl was with them, could she be a link in the search for Walker's destination?

She was a farm girl, with roots somewhere in the Midwest, he thought. He looked at Armstrong, but he didn't say anything. That was an element he was keeping to himself.

Armstrong's mind seemed to be running in the same direction. Links. Roots. He called Roland Simon's private number. "We may have a break," he said. "The Sayers woman is with Walker. On the road somewhere. He just called here, fifteen, twenty minutes ago. Now listen, I want every possible tie she has to points north, south and west of here. Yes, him too. I know it's a tall order. Just hurry it up, will you please?"

He hung up and faced Donovan. He seemed lost in thought.

"It's a waste of time," he said softly. "We've got to try everything, but this won't cut it."

"How do you figure that?"

"The kid's not stupid. She's not going anyplace where she's got ties."

"I'm not so sure about that," Donovan said. "She depended on Lewis for quite a few years. With him dead, she may be confused. She might try anything."

"Maybe." Armstrong stared at the phone. "Uh-uh," he said. "She's going to get the Ordway papers, from wherever they're stashed. You can bet me on that one, Donovan. She's going after those files. They're her insurance now."

"They're probably traveling in Walker's car. Should be easy to spot, once we have it narrowed down a bit."

Armstrong shook his head. "You still don't savvy, do you, Donovan? I don't want them picked up."

Donovan just looked at him.

"I don't want any bungling county sheriff getting his hands on that girl," Armstrong said. "I don't want any other police agency in on this at all. We'll get them ourselves. Just us."

Twelve

They were in Ohio. They had been driving without rest since morning. Walker and Diana shared the driving, while Joanne Sayers sat in the back seat and watched them. Walker couldn't see the gun, but it was there somewhere, curled under the blanket on her lap like a tiny snake. Joanne Sayers didn't seem to get tired. She seldom spoke, even to give directions. Both Walker and Diana knew where they were going now. They had a weathered road map, which one read while the other drove. But there was no need. The great tollway out of Philadelphia ran straight to Chicago. The Pennsylvania Turnpike became the Ohio Turnpike, distinguished only by the changing faces of the pirates who manned the tollbooths and collected their booty. Three bucks and change, to drive another two hundred miles. What a world.

They had gone to Philadelphia first, after spending most of Sunday locked in Walker's closet. Joanne Sayers had been on the run, and confused from lack of sleep. In the two days before the Lewises were killed, she had felt something brewing. Like the warnings of Cassandra. Perhaps she had sensed them out there, taking her picture, passing it along. She only knew things were coming to a head somehow, and that nagging hunch had kept her awake, alert. It wasn't until she had read Walker's story a dozen times that the plan had occurred to her. Diana was a complication, but a minor one. She would have to go along for the ride.

Joanne Sayers had locked them in the closet together, and had slept through the day on Walker's bed. Then they were on the road. They hadn't talked much in those early hours. Joanne Sayers had given the orders, and Walker did what he was told. In the time they were locked in the closet, Joanne Sayers had tried to do something with her hair. But the rain had wrecked it. It had matted against her face while she slept, and brushing had only made it worse. Walker drove all the way that first day. Occasionally his eyes met hers in the mirror. She was alert; she had slept well. As they neared Philadelphia, she directed him off the freeway and down into a commercial-residential subdivision. They drove for a long time, skirting the city and apparently lost in the suburban sprawl. But she knew exactly where she was going. They came around toward the south, and she directed him to turn in again toward the city. They were on a busy street of businesses and gas stations and drugstores. She told him to turn again. By then it was dark. They had pulled into a narrow alley behind a row of stores. The buildings were connected by a common front, and each had an upper-floor apartment.

"Get out," she said.

They walked along until they came to a back door. By then it was so dark they could barely see her. She motioned them aside and knocked on the door. When no one came, she knocked louder. At last a light came on in the window directly above them.

"Now," she said. "You two will do exactly as I say. Exactly."

A moment later the old building began to creak as someone moved toward them from inside. "You will not speak," she said. "You will not talk either to me or to each other. I will introduce you as friends, and that's all anybody needs to know. I'll direct you to a room and you'll stay there until my business here is finished. It may take all night."

Walker grunted as the door opened, revealing a shaggy-looking man in a sweatshirt and jeans. The man had long hair and a beard. He seemed startled to see Joanne Sayers, and even more startled to see someone with her. The words between them were short and to the point. It was obvious that she had come to cash in some old debts. The man clearly was frightened. He led them through a back room. Joanne Sayers brought up the rear. They went into a bookstore, then took a winding set of stairs into the upper apartment. The upper floor consisted of three rooms and a kitchen. The rooms ran the length of the building, and were laid out one after another. Joanne Sayers directed them into the farthest room. There was a double bed with no sheets, and a table and two chairs and a lamp. There was one window, in the far wall, which looked down into the alley where the car was parked.

Joanne Sayers turned on the lamp. She had closed the door and the three of them were alone in the bedroom.

"I hope you'll be comfortable here." She said it without sarcasm, as though she meant it. She moved around and looked at the window. It squeaked loudly when she opened it. "Just like an alarm clock." She looked down into the alley. "That's a long drop, people. With four legs, chances are you'll break at least one of them. But just to make sure, I'll sleep in the car."

She left, and returned a few minutes later with blankets and a sheet. "Make yourself comfortable. It's not the Hilton, but it beats the hell out of a closet."

They didn't see her again that night. Walker didn't go near the window. Diana didn't even suggest it. She made the bed and they crawled in together, fully clothed. She hadn't said much the whole day and didn't say anything now. He lay beside her in the dark, wondering what she could possibly be thinking.

Walker awoke several times during the night, once to the sound of arguing voices. He heard the man scream, "Are you crazy? Have you completely gone nuts?" And in that icy clear voice, Joanne Sayers said, "You keep your goddamn voice down, Billy. Now I'm not gonna tell you that again." There was a long silence, and Joanne Sayers said, "There are people trying to sleep back there." Their rage settled into a subdued intensity, but the argument went on for a long time. Much later the light went out, the thin yellow line disappeared from the bottom of the door, and the arguing stopped and the house was quiet.

She came for them before first light. She sat on a chair in the dark, about ten feet from the bed. "Billy's cooking us up some breakfast," she said. In the pale light Walker couldn't see the gun, but he knew it was there somewhere. She crossed to the window and looked out. "I'm glad you didn't try to jump. Really glad."

Walker sat on the edge of the bed. "Like you said, it's a long way down."

For almost a full minute her back was to them. It would have been easy to jump her. She turned and put on the lamp, and some of the desperation had melted out of her eyes. She even smiled a little. "I didn't sleep in the car. I figured what the hell, if you jump, you jump. There comes a time when you don't care as much."

He moved suddenly and the gun came out.

"I'm not at that point yet," she said. "So don't make me shoot you. I wouldn't like that."

"What do you want from us?" Diana said.

"From you, nothing. You just happened to be in the wrong place at the wrong time. So you come with us."

"I'm due in at work today."

"That's tough, lady." Joanne Sayers sat in the chair and looked at them. "Will you be missed?"

"You'd better believe it."

"Must be nice. Me, I could drop dead and fall off the end of the world. Nobody'd miss me."

"People already miss you," Walker said. "They're looking all over for you."

"That's funny, mister. You're a real scream at six o'clock in the morning." She paused, then said, "You know, I had a hunch something was wrong, the minute you came at me with that Jason Webster act. Oh, you were good, but I have this sixth sense that won't let me rest. Only sometimes it doesn't start working till too late. Like that night, after you'd gone, it struck me that something wasn't quite right about you. I couldn't quite put my finger on it. Chemistry maybe. Do you believe in ESP, Mr. Walker?"

"I don't know."

"Well, I've got it. Not real strong like some people, but it's there and I know it. Maybe half a dozen times in my life I've known things without being told. The day Martin Luther King died, I kept seeing visions of a black man lying in blood. I tell people that and they think I'm making it up. Do you think I'm making that up, Mr. Walker?"

"I don't know you well enough. Some people would make up something like that, just for effect."

"Not me. I don't do things like that. I've been told I should work on it, develop it, but I wouldn't want to do that either. But I know it's there. Like when Robin died. My little girl, remember, Mr. Walker? I knew then that it would lead to something like this."

"It had to figure, didn't it?" Walker said. "Did you really think you could keep that covered up forever?"

"Why not? It was just an accident. What did she ever have to do with any of this? All this got started years before she was born. She was just a sweet little kid."

"With no name. Didn't you think somebody would be curious about that?"

"We didn't think at all." She took a deep breath. "Sure, I thought of that. But we'd given up thinking individually so goddamn long ago. As a group we just reacted, like animals. That's what you do when they've been after you that long. Just react. And when they get close, you've really got just two choices. You either run or you dig in and try to ride it out. What would you do, Mr. Walker? We'd been there for a good long while and nobody had ever come close to us. We were as secure as we'd ever been, and we were all so fucking tired of running. We had done that, years ago. There was no organization any more, nobody to help us hide until we could start again somewhere else. Sure, I wanted to go anyway. The hell with the houses. I just wanted to leave 'em there and get the hell out. I had bad vibes from that first damned day. But George wouldn't hear of it. He always had to run things, George. Your classic male chauvinist pig, and look what it got him. My judgment always was better than his."

"Look." Walker sat forward on the bed. "Why don't you turn yourself in? You haven't got a chance."

"I see. Is that your best advice for today, Mr.

Walker? Well, we'll see." She pursed her lips and looked at Diana. "What do you do, dear?"

"I'm a dancer."

"No kidding. Where do you dance?"

"Radio City."

"No kidding."

They just looked at each other. After a while, Joanne Sayers said, "I always wanted to see the Rockettes, ever since I was a little girl. I never did get to see them. I was going to take my little girl over next month, for her birthday, to see the Empire State Building and the Rockettes. Maybe we'd have seen you there. Jesus, that must be a buzz."

"It's a kick," Diana said, smiling.

Joanne Sayers smiled back. She looked at Walker. "Your girlfriend's got herself a sense of humor. I like her." She stood and moved to the door. "Breakfast is about ready, if my nose tells me anything. So I'll give you the script for the day. Right now we'll go out and eat. Then you, Mr. Walker, will sign a paper giving Billy title to your car."

"Why should I do that?"

"So we can sell it. Never mind, you'll do okay. I'll see that you get a much better car in trade. That'll be my gift to you, Mr. Walker, for being such a sport. Then you, Miss . . . what's your name?"

Diana told her.

"You will call Radio City, whoever you call there, and quit your job."

"You've got to be kidding."

"It's better this way. Nobody to wonder, nobody to come looking for you. And it'll just be for a few days. When they find out why you had to do it, they'll fall all over themselves forgiving you. Take my word for it, people are like that. Once they hear how you were taken prisoner by the big bad public enemy, they'll fall all over themselves giving you your job back.

Right now you'll do it the way I tell you. No extra words, no fooling around with the phone. I'll tell you what to say and you'll say that. Then you'll hang up." She looked at Walker.

"You going to make me quit too?" he said.

"I don't know. Your job seems more flexible."

"I'm an eccentric. The only time they'll worry about me is if I do call in."

She laughed. "That's lovely. You're both lovely. Such lovely people."

"We're going to Chicago," she said later. They were sitting around the breakfast table, finishing the coffee that Billy had made for them. "We're going to drive there in Mr. Walker's new car, which Billy is going to buy for him. There's only one hitch in all of this. Billy must not be implicated in this in any way. I want your word on that. Both of you."

They didn't say anything.

"In exchange, you, Mr. Walker, will get a new car and a big story. And you, Miss Yoder, will get out of it older and wiser, and without harm."

Billy looked at them, and there was fear in his eyes. "Believe me, I got nothing to do with it. I'm just doing what she says, just like you. Jesus, I could get screwed to the wall for this."

"They can see that," Joanne Sayers said. "Can't you see that, Mr. Walker?"

"Sure, I can see that."

"Then give us your word."

"Sure," Walker said.

"What about you?"

"I'm not anxious to get anybody in trouble," Diana said.

"I didn't ask you that."

"All right. You have my word."

Billy looked from face to face. "How do we know . . ."

"Oh, Billy, you don't know. Sometimes you take a chance. What other choice do you have? You either trust them or kill them, right? I don't want to kill them, do you?"

Billy fidgeted.

"Everybody knows how reporters are," Joanne Sayers said. "He won't turn you in. It's that silly code they live by, something like protecting a source. Isn't that what you call it, Mr. Walker?"

"Something like that."

Billy looked into Walker's eyes. "I don't like it."

Joanne Sayers ignored him. She opened her cloth bag, resting the gun carelessly on her lap, and took out several large bundles of cash. She gave the money to Billy, and told Walker to hand over his car keys. "Now, let's make this short and sweet. Real simple. Billy's going downtown and buy us a car, using my money and your car as a trade-in. He's going to get it registered to Joan Brox. That's me. I have a bank account in Chicago under that name. When we get there, I'll sign it over to you."

Billy took the key and stuffed the money into his pocket.

"Get us something nice," she said. "A station wagon, something with lots of room. You like a station wagon, Mr. Walker? And you'd better get snow tires. The Midwest isn't any picnic this time of year."

Billy left. For a while none of them spoke.

"Four thousand dollars," Joanne Sayers said. "Four grand plus your car. Billy knows cars. He should be able to get us something nice."

"You sure throw your money around," Walker said. "I thought you needed money."

"Things have changed since that night, Mr. Walker. Where I'm going now, I won't need money at all."

They were on the road again, driving a pale blue Plymouth wagon with twelve hundred showing on the odometer. They had stayed another night in Billy's back room, and now Joanne Sayers seemed more relaxed, more willing to talk. She asked about their jobs, and prodded them for details. And in time, she talked about herself. "Can you possibly imagine what it's like, being bottled up that long? You get to where you're scared of your own shadow. Every man who looks at you twice becomes something sinister. For a while you forget that sometimes men look at women for other reasons, that everybody on the streets isn't a cop waiting to bust you. In a real sense, George Lewis was my jailer, Mr. Walker. Can you understand that?"

"Sure."

"I doubt it. What do you know about jails? George called all the shots. I was under his thumb for such a long time, and that can be a special kind of hell, Mr. Walker. Having your life depend on someone whose mental process is so different from yours. The one thing George had was a track record, and I respected that. We had been hiding for years, and for the last five years without a goddamn soul to help us. George had proven himself smarter than the whole FBI. The Feds had gotten to the others, but never to George. He was too smart for them."

"Then why were you afraid?"

"Because it only takes one mistake when you live like that. And because he had some blind spots. One of them was his chauvinism. I told you, George Lewis had to run everything. He'd never take Michelle's or my word for anything, even if he knew in his heart that we were right. To listen to him talk, you'd think here is a very liberal man. College-educated, with all his instincts and philosophies in the right place. But beneath all that, he was insecure. He needed a woman to boss. Barbara—Michelle—fit that role perfectly. He tried to make me fit it too, but I wouldn't. Jesus Christ, George could talk some grand philosophy, he just couldn't live up to it. If I had a suggestion to make, I'd have to work at it for days, plant little seeds of it so he'd think it was his idea to begin with. You ever know anybody like that, Mr. Walker?"

He nodded. "Some of my best friends are knee-jerk pointy-headed idiots."

"What about you? Can I call you Diana?"

She nodded too. She said, "Sure, I've known people like that, but never very well. My family made no bones over where a woman's place was."

"Sounds lovely. No wonder you escaped."

Diana didn't say anything. After a long silence, Joanne Sayers said, "Listen to me, both of you. What I'm going to say is very important. That fear we were talking about before, it's still there. Right now I'm scared out of my mind. I'm screaming inside. You wouldn't know what that's like. What have you ever had to be afraid of? All I'm saying is, I don't want to ride all the way to Chicago with a gun in your back. This can be ugly or it can be fairly civilized. Either way, we're going to do it. It's my first positive move in ten years, the first time I don't have to depend on George Lewis to think for me. I know exactly what I'm going to do, and I'll kill anybody who tries to stop me."

Walker met her eyes in the glass. "I wonder if you would."

"Don't wonder!" The gun came up and pressed against his neck. "Don't wonder," she said again, but softer. "Don't make that mistake even for a minute. For the first time I see what I've got to do as clearly as I've ever seen anything. I know there's a price to pay, okay, I'm willing to face that. I know the price is high. I'm willing to face that too, but I'm not willing to die to square it. I want to live, even if it is behind a wall. You two are elements of my plan. Nothing more than that. I like you both. I don't want to hurt either one of you. But I will if you make me. You can count on that."

They must have gone another ten miles before she spoke again. "I killed a man Friday night."

Walker looked back at her.

"I'm just telling you that so you'll know I mean business. I'm not afraid to shoot if I have to."

There was another long silence. Her words had cast a pall over the car. The quiet was like an increasing weight on all of them. Joanne Sayers broke first.

"Look, I'm not going to kill you. For God's sake, I was talking about an entirely different situation back there."

"Who was he?" Walker said. "The man you killed."

"Who knows? Some agent, you can be damned sure of that. FBI probably, but he might have been from any of the intelligence agencies. They're all the same to me. When the man came after me, I didn't ask for his credentials. All I knew was it was him or me, Mr. Walker. You can believe that or not. I don't care."

But she did care. She wanted them to believe her; she seemed to need it. "It was him or me," she said again. "He made the same mistake George made. He underestimated me, and I shot him before he knew what hit him. Then I shot him twice more, to make goddamned sure he wouldn't get up. Because if he had, Mr. Walker, he'd have killed me, as sure as we're sitting in this station wagon."

They had been talking sporadically for a long time, and had crossed into Lancaster County. Diana watched the rolling countryside pass with a growing nostalgia. They were on Route 30 west, at Joanne Sayers' direction. "We'll keep to the smaller roads for a while, see how it goes," she had said. "Maybe later we'll get on the freeway and make some time, if it feels right." She seemed content, looking out at the farms, at the rows of trees and buildings in the distance. Diana squirmed and tried to keep her eyes on the road. But her attention wandered across the tilled earth, and Walker knew she was out there somewhere, washing clothes in a bucket behind her house. Watching her father kill chickens. Working through the day to feed the men. No TV, no radio, no newspapers. Books only as a necessary evil. The simple pleasures. Moonlight and laughter and a walk along a riverbed, and even that only occasionally. Mostly work.

Voices from another lifetime.

They passed an Amish family, riding along the highway in a buggy. The man and his sons wore black, wide-brimmed hats, black pants and jackets, pale shirts. The woman wore a long dress and a bonnet. Their horse was a chestnut mare, the buggy simple but well-built. Its wheels were wooden, with no rubber even on the rims.

Diana turned in her seat as the car passed them. Her eyes followed them until they disappeared behind a truck coming along. Her head turned slightly and she looked into Joanne Sayers' eyes. "Crazy goddamn people," Joanne Sayers said. "Sometimes I think all people are a little cracked, but I'll never understand why even crazy people would want to live like that."

"If you don't understand it," Diana said, "why talk about it?"

She turned in her seat and faced the road. Joanne Sayers made a sucking noise with her mouth. "My, aren't we touchy all of a sudden?"

"Diana comes from around here," Walker said.

Diana turned her freeze his way, letting him know he had violated a trust. He tried to apologize with his eyes.

"You're Amish?" Joanne Sayers said in disbelief.

Diana didn't say anything. She huddled against the door and watched the road.

"I don't believe it," Joanne Sayers said. When it became apparent that it didn't matter what she believed, she said, "Where's your home?"

"I don't want to talk about it."

"Come on, I'm interested. I didn't mean what I said back there. That was just something you say when you get bored, and when you really don't understand something. Sometimes I'm like that. I say things all the time without thinking first."

When Diana still didn't speak, she said, "How was I supposed to know I'd offended you?"

"You weren't."

"I'm sorry."

They let it lie for a while. Suddenly Diana said, "I live . . . used to live . . . on a farm. Twenty or thirty miles from here. That was a long time ago."

"How long?"

Diana told her.

"Is your family still here?"

"Yes."

"Thirty miles which way?"

"North."

"North, that's toward the turnpike, right?"

Walker nodded in the mirror.

"Would you like to go up and see them?"

"No."

"It wouldn't bother me any. They wouldn't have to see the gun. You could have a visit and we'd be gone, just like that."

"I don't think so," Diana said.

"Seems a shame to be this close . . ."

She turned in her seat and looked at Joanne Sayers. "I don't want to."

"All right. Would you even like to drive by?"

"No. Not even that."

But the spell of the land had come over her. A few minutes later she admitted that she might like to drive by, as long as they didn't have to stop. She directed Walker onto the next state highway north. Twelve miles up, another state road cut through going east and west. They took that for a few miles, until she directed him north again. They were on a narrow blacktop road, fenced on both sides. Plowed fields, looking barren and abandoned for the winter, stretched away on either side of them. In the distance he saw a barn and a cluster of houses.

"That's my dad's place."

She was dry-eyed, but her hand was shaking. She pointed ahead, where a buckboard was entering the highway. "Watch out for that. Cars look out for horses along these back roads."

They came up slowly as the buckboard turned toward them. In it was a lone man, perhaps forty years old. They saw him clearly as they approached. Dressed in the Amish garb, he also wore a full beard, which tapered to a point. He had no moustache.

"Some of these horses are skittish around cars." Her voice was flat, as if the words were simply mouthed without any thought.

"I'm watching," Walker said.

The man in the buckboard passed slowly. He looked straight ahead as they went by. Again, Diana turned and watched him until he was out of sight.

"You know him?" Joanne Sayers said.

"Yes."

She seemed very close to tears then, but she didn't

cry. She didn't say anything as they drove past the houses.

Then, as if no time had passed, she said, "That was my older brother Daniel back there in the buckboard."

They picked up the interstate after a while. Walker got his toll ticket and soon Lancaster County slipped behind them. Diana sat quietly, lost in thought. Joanne Sayers told him to turn on the radio. A few minutes later, she told him to turn it off. They were well beyond Harrisburg when Walker asked if she would mind telling them her plans.

"This may surprise you, Walker," she said. "I want to give myself up. I'm tired of running."

"Why didn't you do that last Friday? It would have been much simpler then."

"Not as simple as you think. I told you, I want to stay alive. That's all I've been thinking about these last few days. My best chance of staying alive is to bring it all out in the open. Everything I know about these people you love so much. Once it's out, I'm no longer a threat to them, am I? The only reason they'd kill me then would be revenge. And they don't operate that way. That's one thing I can say for them."

She lit a cigarette and cracked her window. "You're to be my instrument, Mr. Walker. I'm going to give you a story you can't refuse to print. Once it's in print, the pressure's off me and on them. Let them squirm for a while. Then and only then will I give myself up. If they catch me before we do that, somebody's going to die. Never mind. Forget I said that. Do you have any friends in law enforcement?"

He told her about Donovan. For a while she didn't say anything. Then she began to ask questions. She was annoyed that Donovan had been an FBI lifer. Her questions focused on their personal relationship, and the one thing she kept coming back to was trust. Did he trust Donovan? How had that trust proven itself over the years? And that was how they happened to be in Ohio, just across the state line, when she let him call Donovan at home.

Thirteen

They stopped for dinner somewhere off the highway. It was a family restaurant, noisy and crowded and well lighted. Joanne Sayers put the gun in her cloth bag and the three of them went in together. An uneasy truce had developed between Walker and Joanne Sayers. It was as if suddenly she understood him, and knew she had nothing to fear. He was a reporter on a story; he would follow it, but wouldn't try to change it with any heroics. She sat apart from them, in a corner of the booth opposite them, the bag in her lap. "Eat hearty," she said, smiling. "This party's on me, remember? And on this trip you never know when you might eat again."

She seemed to enjoy the lights and the crowd. She tried to press dessert on them, but Diana refused. Then they were all standing at the register together waiting for Joanne to pay the check, and the hostess was taking a long time with the family ahead of them. Suddenly Joanne Sayers grew very nervous. She pushed ahead and put her check on the counter, covered it with three tens and said, "Keep the change." Then she hurried them out to the car, where they sat for a moment, under the restaurant's neon light. Joanne Sayers was breathing heavily.

"What's wrong?" Walker said.

"I don't know. Just wait a minute."

They waited for several minutes. She watched each incoming car, scanning the faces of the people as they walked in.

"I don't know what it is," she said. "Cat just walked up my spine."

"You're just jumpy."

"You got that right, Mr. Walker." She gave a nervous laugh. "All of a sudden I'm jumpy as all get-out, and I don't know why. Maybe it's the night, I don't know. It hit me right there at the cash register, while I was waiting to pay the bill. I just felt like the place was full of cops. I got to thinking about that call you made, and suddenly I felt like the place was full of cops."

"You watched me make it. That was hundreds of miles from here."

"I know it. But I didn't stay alive all these years by not trusting my instincts. Right now my instinct is working overtime. Something . . . not right." She leaned forward and Walker could feel her breath on his neck. "I think we'd better hole up for the night, see how it looks tomorrow," she said.

They found a motel half an hour later. It had two bedrooms, and the only windows were tiny crank-outs, too small for a body to pass through. They settled in, Walker and Diana in the back room. After a while, Joanne Sayers asked them to come out to her room, and they sat and talked and watched the news on a flaky TV set. She tried to ask Diana about her home, and got nowhere with that. "We'll be in Chicago tomorrow," she said, to no one in particular. "Chicago." She looked at Walker. "Then you can have your story and we can put an end to all this."

They didn't say anything.

"Jesus," Joanne Sayers said, "I'd give anything for a shower."

"Go ahead," Walker said. "We won't go anywhere."

"Really?"

"What does that instinct of yours say?"

For almost a minute they battled with their eyes. Then she took her cloth bag into the bathroom and put it on the closed toilet seat. She didn't close the door. She watched them the whole time, while she stripped off her clothes, even from the shower. She was under the water ten minutes or more, soaking up the luxury of it. She washed her hair with motel soap. When she stepped out, Walker noticed how hard and tan her body was. Diana watched her too. Joanne Sayers had a lovely body, long and lean.

"In Jersey I was in a nudist camp," she said. "After a while you forget all that crap they beat into you when you're young. Stuff like being ashamed of your body. It took me a long time to get over that. When I was a kid in high school, I had a phys-ed teacher who was bad news. When I was thirteen, I was very sensitive about having hair on my body." She touched it with her fingers, then gave it a final pat with the towel. "I've heard that's a pretty common thing with girls that age. This woman embarrassed me every chance she got. Just little things, but to me they seemed like acts of incredible sadism. She really got on my case. And the goddamn system takes up people like that, protects them and punishes you. Somehow they become right and you're wrong, always. Did either of you read Orwell? *1984?*"

"I did," Diana said.

"It's like that scene at the end, when they take the guy and put the cage of rats over his head. At that point you'll do anything, betray anyone, if they'll just go away and leave you alone. Oh, this bitch eventually stepped over the line. They usually do, people like that. She leaned on the wrong man's little girl, and she was fired, but I was too damned relieved to feel anything close to satisfaction. She put a fear into me that lasted for years. Would you believe me if I told you I was twenty-one before I let a man touch me?"

"Why shouldn't we believe you?" Walker said.

She wriggled into her clothes. When she came into the room, some of the fear had gone from her eyes. "If you ever wanted to walk away from here, that was your chance. You must want that story real bad, Mr. Walker."

"Let's say I'm curious."

"Fine. Let's say that." She motioned toward the bathroom. "Your turn."

Diana closed the door, and was gone a long time. Joanne Sayers sat on the bed across from Walker, the half-open cloth bag within easy reach. He could see the gun, nestled there in its bed of money. Fifties and hundreds.

She was brushing out her hair, grimacing as she looked in the mirror. "This'll be stiff as hell, but maybe I'll live now. Your girlfriend got any hairpins?"

Walker said he didn't know. After a while, he said, "Tell me about your little girl, Joanne?"

She looked at him, sad and angry all at once. "What for? So you'll have another piece of your goddamn story?"

"Just so I'll know."

"I didn't like it much, the way you wrote that."

"I thought I played that part of it your way."

"What would you know about my way? It's time somebody started stacking the facts on my side."

"Come on, you know better than that."

"Oh, yes, you reporters. Must be objective, what a

laugh. Mr. Walker, whenever people play it straight with me, I'm the one who comes out wrong. Maybe I am wrong. I helped George and Michelle rob a bank and it's been all wrong ever since. It's like one act colors your life a certain way, and nothing you do from then on has any real value. What am I, some animal without any feelings? I'm not supposed to have a child and love her the way other people do, right? And what did that kid have to do with any of that? To her, George and Michelle were Aunty and Uncle. Then she dies in a freak accident, and you come along, and damn it, you just won't let it rest. Just mentioning her in the same article with all that stuff about me—well, it had a dirt on it that I couldn't get rid of."

"Then why come looking me up?"

"Because, in spite of all that, it had a kind of honesty to it. Jesus, it hurts me to admit that. Even more than the honesty, it had a compassion behind it. Maybe I thought you'd help me put it right."

"Maybe I will."

The brush hung suspended over her head. "What do you want to know?"

"We're just talking. Just rapping back and forth. You can tell me whatever you want to. Don't tell me what you don't want to."

"I suppose you want to know about her father?"

"If you feel like it."

"It could have been any of half a dozen men. How'll that look in your newspaper?"

"We'll never know."

"All right." She went on with her brushing. "I know who the father was. I wouldn't be able to prove it, and you're not gonna believe it, but I know the exact moment she was conceived. It could have been a lot of guys, but it wasn't. It was this one, and now his name doesn't matter because he's long gone and he'll never come back. And I wouldn't give him the time of day if he did. Feelings do change, Mr. Walker. Nothing's eternal, no matter what the love songs say. So her father isn't important. His role was almost accidental. I'd call it casual, though it sure didn't seem like that then. He was just there."

"You must have had second thoughts about keeping her."

"Mr. Walker, I had second thoughts about *having* her. George made an appointment with an abortionist, but I wouldn't be bullied on something like that. I told him it was my decision, not his, and I'd do it if and when I was good and goddamned ready. That was one part of my life he couldn't run. She was my little girl, and I just told George to fuck off if he tried to take too much. What we had was between us, nobody else. And then she wasn't a baby any more. She was a real little girl. A kid, with a personality and her own way of doing things. And that brought out my terror all over again. What if I got busted then? What would happen to my kid? It bothered me all the time, damn near ruined my health worrying about that kid. I had dreams of being killed, shot down in front of her, real bad stuff like that. Whoever would have thought that she'd die first? Some freak accident. Who would have thought that?"

Diana came out in a swirl of steam, patting her head dry. She didn't say a word, just went back into the rear bedroom, leaving them alone. But Joanne Sayers had said her piece for the night. She tied her hair back in a frizzy ponytail and put out the light.

"Mr. Walker?"

"Yeah, Joanne?"

"You could stay out here tonight. If you want to."

"That wouldn't be too smart, Joanne. But thanks."

"Sure." She laughed. "Anytime."

Fourteen

The car slipped through the quiet Philadelphia streets. The glare of the early morning sun bothered Armstrong. He was a night person. He hated harsh sunlight, but on this Wednesday morning he was full of hope. They had had a phenomenal break, the kind you dream about but never get. The bills from the Sayers-Lewis bank robbery had turned up, one big chunk, three thousand dollars' worth. That had been one of their hole cards for years, the fact that the bills had been new and that the serial numbers were all consecutive. But the money had trickled in, a few bills at a time, and from various parts of the country. George Lewis had been too smart for a trap like that. Then, late yesterday, a sharp-eyed clerk in a Philadelphia bank had spotted the wad, big enough to choke a horse. Armstrong left Donovan and another agent to baby-sit the phones, and he and Kevin Lord took off for Philly.

It had been a simple matter after that, tracing the money from the bank to the car lot, where the nervous manager had taken it in trade the day before. The man chain-smoked and chewed Certs nonstop. He had been uneasy with that much cash lying around; he couldn't wait to get it on deposit. He bubbled with useless chatter and information before Armstrong got the purchaser's name as Mrs. Joan Brox. The car had been bought for Mrs. Brox by a Bill Neal, who owned a bookstore on the south side. Bill Neal had used Walker's car as a trade.

The sign in Bill Neal's window said OPEN 10 A.M., CLOSE 5 P.M. It was after ten, but there was no sign of life inside. "You go around back," Armstrong said. "Just in case this turkey gives us some trouble." Lord pulled to the curb and they got out. Armstrong walked to the front door and peered in. He rapped on the glass but no one came. The pounding became harder, more insistent, until he actually rattled the glass in the storefront. At last the door above the circular staircase opened and a man came down.

Bill Neal was one of those yippie types that Armstrong detested so much. One of those bearded nonconformists who were really the biggest conformists in the world. They all conformed to their idea of what the rest of the world loathed. They hadn't had an original thought in twenty-five years, since the beginning of that beatnik crap in San Francisco of the early 1950s. They all looked alike, smelled alike, wore the same beads and faded jeans; same long hair, same beards. They smoked the same cheap dope. It was their way of saying screw the world, because they couldn't handle it. Bill Neal was just like all his brothers. Sit him down in a classroom, tell him to work out something logical, and he's lost in five minutes. He drifts through life like all the others, bumming from parents, stealing, playing poker with food stamps. Sucking the blood from people who worked for a living. Bill Neal's bookstore, what a laugh. Armstrong would bet Bill Neal hadn't sold a book in two months, if that was even the cat's real name.

Bill Neal, or whatever his name was, came forward slowly. They had seen each other from a distance, and if Bill Neal could have his way the distance would get nothing but wider. Just as Armstrong had known Bill Neal, so had Bill Neal recognized Armstrong. An enemy by blood, a creature of another world. Fuzz. A pig. Oh, yes, Bill Neal had had his run-ins with the pigs, Armstrong had no doubt of that. Right now his heart would be pounding away in fear and loathing, wondering what they would make him on, perhaps knowing, and wondering if there was any escape. No, Bill Neal. There is no escape, you have made one mistake too many, and the grim reaper is here to collect.

Bill Neal stopped about five feet short of the glass. "What do you want?"

Armstrong held up his watch. "It's after ten. Sign says open ten ayem. You run a business here or not?"

"I'm closed today," Bill Neal said. "I'm sick."

Not as sick as you're gonna be, Armstrong thought.

Bill Neal turned away and started back toward the steps. Armstrong pounded on the glass. "Open up, buddy. We've got some things to talk about."

This time Neal came closer, and peered through the glass. "Who are you? What do you want?"

"Open the door and I'll tell you," Armstrong said sweetly.

"If you're a cop, let me see your badge."

Armstrong fished out his wallet and held it close to the door. Still, Bill Neal hesitated, as if by stalling a few more seconds, something might happen to save him. Armstrong waited patiently, and patience was not one of his virtues. He could almost see the wheels turning in Bill Neal's head. When they had all turned, he would open the door, because there was nothing left for him to do.

He opened the door.

Inside, the place smelled like stale grass. There had been a helluva pot party there last night, a tidbit that Armstrong might want to use later. He would bet that upstairs, hidden away somewhere—but not so carefully that he couldn't find it—was a dope stash. Maybe grass, maybe something harder, something he could really use to sweat Neal. Never mind that he didn't have a warrant, never mind that he couldn't make Bill Neal on any drug bust without one. What he needed was a lever, to pry Neal loose from information on the Sayers girl. A dope stash would do as well as the next thing.

"What do you want?" Neal said. "I haven't done anything."

"You've done plenty." Armstrong walked along the rows of books, as a browser might. They were all cheap discards, throwaways, books you buy in a garage sale for a dime apiece. "Nice front you've got here," Armstrong said.

"Man, what the hell are you talking about?"

"You're no more book dealer than I am. What's your real business?"

Bill Neal didn't say anything.

"What's your name?" Armstrong said.

"Bill Neal."

"What's your real name?"

"That is my real name."

"You got a birth certificate?"

"Hey, man, what is this? You can't just walk in here like this and start asking me questions. I got a right to a lawyer."

"What do you need a lawyer for, Bill? If you haven't done anything, what do you need a lawyer for?"

"I don't like being hassled. You . . ."

"Me what? Me pigs? Us pigs? That what you were gonna say, Bill?"

"No, I wasn't gonna say that. Say, what is this?"

"Just a friendly little talk between you and me. That's all it has to be, Bill. You interested in keeping it like that?"

A light of hope had come into Bill Neal's eyes. "Sure I am. I got nothing to hide. What do you want?"

"You're willing to cooperate?"

"Sure. I got nothing to hide."

"Do you know Joanne Sayers?"

"Who?"

"Let's cut the shit, Bill. I thought you were gonna help me."

"I am, man, I am if I can. Ask me something I know about."

"You trying to tell me you don't know Joanne Sayers?"

"Never heard of the lady."

Armstrong waited a moment. It stretched into several minutes. He browsed among the bookshelves, looking at the titles, letting Bill Neal's tension mount. Letting it get tight, like a drum covering, before he punctured it with his next question.

"You didn't let Joanne Sayers stay here two nights ago?"

"No, man, nobody stays here."

"You didn't go down to Arnie Blake's car lot and buy her a blue Plymouth wagon, serial number 45327-J?"

"Jesus, you got one helluvan imagination."

"Bill, you're in big, big trouble."

The hope had disappeared from Bill Neal's eyes. In its place had come the despair of the cornered.

"Let me tell you what you're in for. Joanne Sayers, as you well know, is a fugitive. She's been wanted almost ten years now by the federal government. The man with her was a reporter. We have reason to believe she kidnapped him and forced him to accompany her. She stole his car, forced him to sign it over to her, and you, Bill-boy, sold it for her. You hid her out. You helped her keep this man prisoner here against his will. You bought her a blue Plymouth wagon and then you helped her get away. You're an accessory to bank robbery, kidnapping and murder, Bill, and you're going to prison for a long, long time."

He looked in Bill Neal's eyes. Sometimes it worked, sometimes not. In this case, it had driven Neal deeper into his shell.

"I don't know about any of that," Neal said.

"Okay," Armstrong said. "Let's go upstairs."

"What for?" Now Bill Neal's face registered open alarm.

"I've been called a pig so many times, I'd like to see how real pigs live. You lead, Bill."

The upstairs, as he knew it would be, was a shambles. Old food lay molding in the sink, and dishes were piled up from days ago. Papers were everywhere, and the dirt on the windowsill was a quarter of an inch thick. He didn't see any dope; Bill Neal wasn't that dumb. But there were some rolling papers on the coffee table, such as it was, and next to that was an open package of condoms.

Armstrong walked through the place. He went into the back room, where the bed was still mussed from Monday night. "This is where the reporter slept, right, Bill? And maybe the Sayers girl too. She wouldn't want him too far out of sight, would she?" He came back slowly. "Oh, she's a smart one, that Sayers girl. She's got a grand plan in all of this. I can see her mind working on it now. Do you know what she's doing, Bill?"

"I told you . . ."

That was as far as he got. Armstrong had come alongside and balled up his fist. He drove it into Bill Neal's gut, without any warning, and Neal wasn't ready for it. He doubled up on the floor, writhing, gasping for breath.

"Jesus Christ," he gasped. "You mother . . ."

Armstrong kicked him hard in the ribs. He felt the bones give. Then he walked to the window and looked down at Kevin Lord in the alley behind the building. "It's a nice day out, Bill. Too bad you couldn't cooperate. Hell, you might even be out there now, enjoying the sun. What's about to happen to you wouldn't be happening at all." He came back into the room. Bill Neal had rolled over on his back and was watching Armstrong in absolute terror.

One thing about a yippie's hair: it was made for grabbing. Armstrong grabbed a big handful and jerked Bill Neal's head up off the floor. With his free hand he flattened Neal's nose against his face. Blood poured out of both nostrils.

Armstrong stood up, careful not to get any of the pig's blood on him. He reached into his coat and took out a pair of rubber gloves. That always scared them. Bill Neal couldn't have been more frightened. He was living his ultimate nightmare. Armstrong took out his gun, put it through a series of terrifying clicks, grabbed the pig's head again and held it against his pig-brain.

"Now Bill." He breathed heavily into the pig's face. "You got one chance and one only. If you want to sing the same song, it'll be the last tune you ever play. One time, Bill. Did Joanne Sayers stay here?"

"Yes."

"Did she have the reporter with her?"

"Yes. And . . ."

"Never mind the ands and buts. You just answer my questions. When I want some elaboration, I'll ask for it. Did she use the name Joan Brox?"

"Yes."

"Where's she headed?"

"She didn't say."

Armstrong clicked the gun.

"Later . . ." Bill Neal was almost beside himself with fear. "Later . . . overheard her . . . telling the guy."

"Walker?"

"Yeah . . . that's his name."

"Telling him what?"

"Chicago."

"She's going to Chicago."

"Yeah. Yeah."

"To do what?"

"Don't know."

Again came the click of the gun.

"I don't know!" Neal sobbed. "I swear!"

"Does she have a bank account there?"

"Yeah . . . yeah. Said she did."

"Under what name?"

"Brox."

"What bank?"

"Don't know."

"Okay." Armstrong released his grip and let Bill Neal's head sink to the floor. "That's easy enough to check. By God, you'd better be telling me the truth." He got up and went to the window, motioning for Kevin Lord to come in through the front door. A moment later, Lord mounted the steps and came into the room.

"What happened to him?"

Bill Neal was bleeding into a dirty rag.

"Son of a bitch tried to jump me. He was okay until I mentioned the Sayers girl, then suddenly he went nuts."

"He tell you anything?"

"Let's say I got a lead. Book this prick, will you? Call it harboring a fugitive. The Sayers girl stayed here at least one night, with this guy's full knowledge of who she was. While you're at it, do a full check on his background. I think you may find a lot of other stuff on him. Christ, do I hate pigs like this."

"What about you?"

"Never mind about me. I'm gonna follow my nose a bit. You get back to New York and ride herd on Donovan. I don't trust that bastard any more than I'd trust this one."

An hour later, Armstrong checked into Philadelphia International Airport for a midday flight to Chicago. He identified himself and got clearance for his gun. He checked the other gun, a precision rifle with a telescopic sight, through luggage.

He didn't know how much time he had, but Chicago was one hour behind Philly, and that had to be a plus. During his wait, he phoned ahead to the Chicago field office, and cleared his arrival with the SAC. They would have a car waiting for him. They would run down the banks for him, both in town and in the suburbs. That was the kind of job the FBI did better than any other agency on earth. The SAC said he would have the information on Joan Brox by the time Armstrong arrived.

As the plane circled out of Philadelphia, Armstrong almost felt good. He felt better about the Sayers matter than he had in years. That uneasy tension he had learned to live with, the waiting forever for the shoe to drop, was over now. The gods were with him at long last. For the next hour, he savored the job he had done on Bill Neal. Those pigs were all alike. All you had to do was look the part, play a little rough, and they opened up like a sack of beans stabbed with a knife. Just promise them a quick death, and mean it. Their imaginations did the rest.

Fifteen

"Now comes the tricky part," Joanne Sayers said.

"Why tricky?" Walker said. "You've got the key. It's not as if you were robbing the damned bank."

"Tricky because I'm nervous. If anything's going wrong, it'll be here. My nerves are shot. I'm afraid I'll kill somebody if there's even so much as a sneeze in that bank."

They were sitting in the blue station wagon, parked around the corner from the Chicago Bank and Trust. Joanne Sayers had directed Walker carefully, so he wouldn't drive directly past the bank. Diana sat in her place on the driver's side of the front seat. She hadn't said much since yesterday.

All through the day their relationship had deteriorated. For a while, yesterday, they had managed an air of civility and near friendliness. But today, as they approached Chicago, Joanne Sayers withdrew into herself once more. She took fewer chances with them, and kept the gun in her lap. Her eye contact with Walker was continuous. She gave clipped, terse orders that took them off the highway and through suburban developments. It was the Philadelphia scene all over, a game of hide-and-seek, with the sought always on the move. They came into town on the Skyway, but she told him to get off and drive toward the lake. They hit Lake Shore Drive, and suddenly they were downtown. They passed Soldier Field, went through the Loop and on beyond Tribune Tower.

"Another *Tribune,* Mr. Walker. The big time."

"I know. I worked there once."

"You've worked everywhere once."

They didn't say anything for a minute. Then Joanne Sayers said, "I've got a super idea. Why don't you offer your story to all the papers at once? Sort of a highest bidder thing."

"It doesn't work that way. Not as long as I work for the one."

"My, such ethics."

"All right, put it this way, then. Newspapers don't like to pay for stuff. They wouldn't pay five grand, say, to solve the Kennedy assassination."

"I don't believe that. You're being modest again."

They had left the downtown, and had reached the edge of Lincoln Park. "Keep going," she said. "It's way out near Wrigley Field."

Twenty minutes later, they sat parked at the curb. Joanne Sayers didn't move for a long time. Her eyes darted across the street and down it, scanning each face. Her breathing was heavy. A clock hanging over the street said two-thirty.

"Okay," she said. "Let's go."

They got out and started up the street. Walker and Diana went ahead. Joanne Sayers was about five feet behind them, still looking, her eyes like black snakes. She watched the windows too, looking for faces there, for any sudden flash of light, for any movement that didn't blend with the crowd. They reached the corner. Half a block ahead, Walker could see the sign: CHICAGO BANK, and under it, in smaller letters, AND TRUST.

She stopped.

"Wait a minute." She seemed to be struggling for words. "Something's not right. I can feel it."

"You're paranoid," Walker said.

"Shut up."

"Joanne, it's just like in the restaurant last night."

"Maybe. Maybe not. But in this game I only get one mistake."

"Come on," Walker said. "Let's go get the stuff and get this over with."

"No!" She backed away and clutched the bag against her. "Back to the car, quick!"

In the car, Walker turned and leaned over the back seat. Again the gun had come out and was resting on her lap.

"This is the last step," he said. "But it's one you've got to make, sooner or later. You've really got no choice."

"There's always a choice."

"Look, I'll go get the stuff for you."

"Shut up, goddammit, I'm trying to think."

They waited for about five minutes. Walker saw that her hands had begun to tremble.

"Good idea," she said nervously. "Or it would be, if you'd just tell me how you'd pass for Joan Brox. They make you sign before you can get into those deposit boxes, Mr. Walker. For a big-time reporter, you don't know much. No, I've got a better idea. Diana will get the stuff."

"Me?"

"I don't see anyone else named Diana here."

"I don't want to."

"Listen, sister, I'm not asking you. Nobody's going to hurt you. It's me they want. Come on, it's time you paid your way for all this fun you're having." She reached into the cloth bag and brought out some bank forms. "Here's my signature. Joan Brox. See how simple I made it? Big, sweeping J. Clear letters. Big, sweeping B. Nobody's going to question you. They don't have any handwriting experts right there on the spot. They'll eyeball the two, and if yours looks like mine, you're in. Simple."

"I don't want to," Diana said.

"Here." Joanne Sayers ripped some paper out of a pad and passed the bank forms up front. "Practice for a few minutes, until you can write like that."

"I told you, I'm not going to do it."

Joanne Sayers sat forward. A mean light had come into her eyes. "How'd you like to see your boyfriend's brains blown out?"

Diana began to write.

"That's better," Joanne Sayers said. She looked over the back seat. "See? You've got it already. See how simple it is? I wouldn't know the difference, would you, Mr. Walker?"

Walker didn't say anything.

"All right," Joanne Sayers said. "Take off."

They watched until Diana had turned the corner and started up the street toward the bank.

"All right," Joanne said. "Gimme a pencil."

She wrote something on a scrap of paper.

"Now get out," she said. "Leave your keys in the ignition."

She got out behind him, and left the paper on the driver's seat.

"Now what?"

"Now we walk." She nodded toward a tall office building on the corner.

They went inside, and caught the elevator for the top floor. From the end of the hall, she could look down into both streets. She had a clear view of the bank, and down the other street she could see the car.

"Perfect. Now we wait. Relax," she said, as much to

herself as to Walker. "If everything's okay, it shouldn't take long."

They waited and watched. Below them, people scurried like ants.

"I'm sorry I had to say that, back in the car," she said.

He just looked at her.

"Sometimes you have to say things like that, to get people moving. You know I wouldn't do that. I wouldn't shoot you, Mr. Walker."

She took a deep breath. "Unless I had to."

The bank was crowded. For the first time Diana understood, if only a little, what Joanne Sayers was feeling. She was tense, and every face was an enemy. Guards seemed to be especially threatening, even when none of them looked at her. She crossed the crowded lobby, waited behind an old man and at last signed the foreign words. *Joan Brox.* A man showed her into the vault.

It was a simple procedure, something thousands of people did every day. But she wasn't one of them. She had never owned anything valuable enough to be kept in a safe-deposit box. So the man had to show her the routine. Then, alone in the curtained room, she opened the inner box and lifted out the two thick manila folders inside it. Under the folders was the leatherbound book, gold-embossed with a star emblem on its face. She couldn't resist opening it and looking at the first page. There was a name there: Malcolm Dawes. The handwriting under the name identified him as a Special Agent of the FBI. The date in the upper corner was December 1968.

For some reason, it gave her a shiver. Whatever paranoia had infected Joanne Sayers had also worked its way under her skin. She gathered up the files and slipped the diary into one of the folders. Then she put the box back into its slot and walked out of the bank.

She didn't look around, but her imagination was running wild. In her mind she saw a street crawling with federal agents, crisscrossing behind her, peering out of dim doorways at her back. If she turned around suddenly, she could almost catch them, but not quite. It was that kind of nightmare.

She walked to the corner and went around it without looking back.

In fact, there was only one man behind her who mattered. The street was teeming with people, and to an untrained eye they all looked alike. It was late on a Wednesday afternoon, payday for several nearby factories, and the lines at the tellers' cages were long and slow-moving. People went in and out of the bank in a steady stream. Armstrong came out about thirty yards behind the girl. She had surprised him. He had expected the Sayers woman; he had half expected Walker to come to the bank. Guys like Walker would do anything for their stories, and Armstrong was prepared for that. But this was a new face, someone he hadn't ever seen. That brought up disturbing new possibilities. Joanne Sayers was as slippery as an eel. Had she kidnapped someone else? Was she forcing a new hostage to make the pickup for her? Something like that would be a disaster. Even the possibility shortened his already tight timeframe. The more people involved, the greater the risks. He had to get the files, and fast.

The SAC had been superb. By the time Armstrong had arrived in Chicago, everything had been worked out, every base covered. Chicago had been alerted by Washington: Armstrong was on a priority matter; they were to lend support and ask no questions. If it had been simply a matter of picking up the Sayers woman, it would have been easy. They could have ringed the bank with agents, ringed the whole goddamn neighborhood with agents. But Armstrong knew better. The files were the important things, and Joanne Sayers knew that too. The files had to be retrieved and destroyed, and Armstrong had to know in his mind that there were no copies. That meant no agents, no big stakeout, no one but him and the girl. The Bureau had to stay clear of it, beyond lending assistance in mechanical areas that required sheer manpower.

Walker's involvement made Armstrong more nervous than he wanted to admit. Anticipating that Walker might pick up the files, Armstrong had had a car parked in each block for five square blocks around the bank. One master key fit them all: one hell of a challenge in two hours' time, but again the Bureau had come through. He had four additional manned cars standing by, in case he walked out of the covered area and had to be picked up fast. In his pocket he carried a tiny radio, and hoped he wouldn't need it. With luck, he could wind it up this afternoon, be out of here on the first flight to D.C., and let Chicago worry about the mess he would leave behind.

He had correctly anticipated the general makeup of the bank's customers. He wore what most of them wore: casual work clothes, no tie, shirt open at the neck. He didn't wear a sports coat, but luckily the weather was cold enough to allow him an overcoat without suspicion. Just under his left arm, the gun nestled.

A strong wind blew in off the lake. The girl disappeared around the corner and Armstrong fought back a desire to run after her. He continued on at the same regular pace, stopped at the corner, cupped his hands and lit a smoke. Only then, and almost casually at that, did he look down the street. To anyone watching, he was a man adrift, money burning a hole in his pocket, looking around for something kinky to spend it on. He seemed lost in indecision for a few seconds, then moved on down the street after the girl.

Maybe Joanne Sayers was watching him, standing in the throngs just a few feet away. Waiting for him to move, to commit himself. Or maybe, just as likely, she was holed up across town somewhere, waiting for this girl to make her drop and beat it. He was approaching his moment of truth and he knew it. Soon he would have to commit to a course of action and take his chances. His eyes moved on past the girl, scanned the street and picked up the blue Plymouth with temporary tags. There was no one in the car.

He was still one jump ahead of her. He looked back over his shoulder, as anyone might before jaywalking in midblock. The four corners contained a drugstore, a gas station, a department store and a high-rise office complex. He started across slowly, toward the plain black car parked at the curb.

He reached it and slipped under the wheel, just as the girl pulled open the door of the Plymouth. There, in the shadows of his own car, he watched her keenly. She looked puzzled for a moment, then got in and seemed to be reading something. She slipped over and started the car. He started his.

The Plymouth came past him and turned right at the corner, away from the bank. He eased out into traffic and blended in behind her. At the corner she turned right again, then again, and still again, coming back into the same block. She eased the blue Plymouth back into its original parking place, and Armstrong's heart pounded faster. The Sayers girl had tricked him. They had set him up.

From the window high above the street, Joanne Sayers watched intensely. "There he is," she said. "Same black car."

"How can you tell that?"

"It's the same car. They followed her around the block. Watch him."

But the black car didn't stop behind Diana. It went past, down the block and disappeared far beneath them.

Diana, still clutching the two thick folders, stepped out of the Plymouth and started up the street toward the office building. In her free hand, she carried the scrap of paper with Joanne Sayers' instructions. She stopped at the corner and waited for the light to change.

A block away, Armstrong had made his commitment. He jerked the black car to a stop and leaped out, leaving it in a tow-away zone. He hurried back along the sidewalk toward the office building. For a terrifying moment he didn't see the girl at all. Then she moved between some people in the intersection. She was crossing the street, coming straight at him. He blended in with some shoppers and she passed not five feet away. He stepped in behind her. The game was over. If Joanne Sayers could see him from wherever she was staked out, it was all over anyway.

The girl went into the office building, and Armstrong followed her in. The place was packed. She stopped at the bank of elevators, and for the next minute Armstrong stood so close he could have touched her. He watched the red floor indicators giving them information on all four elevators. The third one was coming first. By the time it had arrived, the people were packed in around the door, ready to load. They pressed in, the girl among them, Armstrong to the far rear. The girl looked at the buttons but didn't press any of them. Most of them had been pushed anyway.

The elevator eased upward. It was the slowest

elevator Armstrong had ever seen. It slowed at each floor, then squeezed itself to a standstill, waited a few seconds and slowly opened its doors, reluctantly letting the passengers escape. Floor by floor. An eternity. Gradually the ranks thinned, until there were only five of them in the cage.

Two floors from the top, they picked up a contingent of white-shirts going up to the cafeteria. They laughed and talked loudly: four men in their twenties accompanied by two women who looked and talked like secretaries. The girl inched her way back until Armstrong could feel her body against his. He eased his hand up and unbuttoned his coat.

What happened next was like some slow-motion nightmare. The door eased open and there she was. Joanne Sayers stood not ten feet away, nervous as a cat, ready to jump. Her eyes found his perhaps a second sooner than he saw her. In that second, her bag dropped to the floor and the gun was in her hand. Someone laughed, a laugh of disbelief. It cut off abruptly as Armstrong reached for his own gun and tried to push people out of the way with his free hand. Joanne Sayers fired. A woman screamed. The bullet tore through the wood paneling at Armstrong's elbow. It was a lousy shot, a shot made too quickly, from too many pent-up nerves, and he would see that she never got another. But again, she had that split-second edge. Her second shot tore through his neck, spinning him around even as his own gun was coming up. Shock, cold and sudden, raced through him. He never felt his fingers open, but he heard his gun clatter on the floor. He twisted around and she shot him again as the door closed. Once for good measure in the gut.

The people had parted like the Red Sea, and were littered across the elevator floor at his feet. The elevator shimmied and started down. Armstrong sank back against the wall and reached out for support.

There was nothing to grab. He began to slip down to the floor.

Out of shock came panic. One of the secretaries began screaming and one of the men pushed the emergency stop button. The elevator stopped between floors. An alarm went off.

Armstrong sat there, watching his blood ooze out.

Sixteen

Someone had kicked Joanne's bag in the scuffle, and money was scattered down the length of the hallway. She whirled as the door closed, ready to fire again, but faced only an empty corridor. Everyone in the elevator had jumped back, all but Diana, who leaped out as the shooting started and sat on the floor about ten feet away. Walker stood flat against a wall, waiting. An alarm went off, and almost at that exact second the express elevator came. Joanne Sayers grabbed her bag, leaving the loose money on the floor, and pushed them ahead of her into the cage.

The elevator stopped only once going down, at the halfway point. Two men got on, so engrossed in some corporate argument that they paid no attention to the ringing bell. Less than thirty seconds later the elevator reached the ground. The lobby was still full of people, and word was passing among them that there had been a shooting and that one of the elevators was trapped between floors. Joanne Sayers pushed them through it, through the revolving door and into the street. Outside, the world went on as if nothing had happened. Half a block away, the bank looked strangely different, all its menace gone. People hurried past, unaware that a shooting had happened. The distant wail of an ambulance was already dying out. It was for somebody else.

Walker looked back just once. Joanne Sayers was about twenty yards behind them, the bag draped over one wrist while the other hand, still clutching the gun, was buried in the pocket of her dress. And Walker, though he really didn't like himself for it, was thinking story. He couldn't help it; that's how his mind worked. The shooting of an FBI man was a story. But it was one he would never write, because he had been swept out of it, because he had lost his objective voice and was now a part of it, because of half a dozen reasons that might not make much sense to anyone else. Let them have it, it was nothing more than a cop story on its face. The real story was still to come, still to worm its way out of those files that Diana clutched against her breast.

They reached the Plymouth and Joanne motioned them inside. Again, Walker drove. He had to give Joanne her due. She handled herself in a crisis like one cool number. Inside the car, she took charge as if nothing had happened. She told Walker to drive straight ahead, straight past the door of the office building. By then a crowd was beginning to gather on the sidewalk by the front door. She didn't look back. As with everything else unpleasant that happened to her, she found a way to deal with it and move on. The bank robbery, the years of loneliness, the long strings of faceless men, the death of a little girl she had loved very much: these things were part of an irretrievable past. Add to that the terrors of the elevator. It was done, gone. Maybe later she would have a reaction, when she was alone and wouldn't show her weakness to anyone. Now Walker didn't even hear a slight quiver in her voice.

"Well," she said. "That was too bad."

That was all they said for a while. Walker understood without talking that they were finished with Chicago. He drove south and east, the way they had come, and she didn't correct him. Maybe she was confused. Maybe she didn't know yet where they were going or what they would do when they got there. Somewhere outside Gary, he said, "You're taking a hell of a chance, you know, sticking with this car."

"You think I haven't thought of that?"

Again, they lapsed into that awkward silence. She asked Diana for the files, but kindly, her voice just above a whisper. Walker kept his eyes on the road. It was the twilight hour, the worst time of day to drive. The freeway stretched on forever, luring them on.

"I've got a hunch," Joanne Sayers said suddenly. She had brightened visibly. "I don't think it matters what car we're in. Mr. Walker, I think maybe we've won."

"I don't follow that."

"I know you don't. But you'll understand better when you've had a chance to read these files. Then you'll know it all."

Walker shook his head. "I don't see what the files have got to do with what car we're in. Your reasoning doesn't make sense."

"Look, think about what just happened back there. Use your head, Walker. There was one man. Just one. Doesn't that strike you as odd, just a little bit?"

"It struck me," Diana said. It was the first thing she had said since the shooting.

"Tell him, then," Joanne Sayers said. "Our star reporter can't put it together by himself."

"That's all," Diana said. "I thought, where are all the others, and there weren't any. I kept waiting for them to kill us. To open up on us right there on the street. I'll never forget that feeling as long as I live. I just knew the place must be crawling with police."

"See, Mr. Walker, for all your highly touted investigative skills, your girlfriend's out-thought you. That's the heart of it. There was only one man. That's what this whole thing is about. That man and me. Why do you suppose that is, Mr. Walker?"

He didn't say anything.

"They don't want the other cops to be involved. They're taking no chance that these files might get into some police chief's hands. Or even into the hands of others like themselves, who aren't involved in it. Does that make sense, people? They want to write an end to it with one bloody period. The end of me."

"Joanne . . ."

"I know, I know; you think I'm paranoid. You've already told me. Let's see how you feel after you've read the files. For now, let's play my hunch and stick with this car. It'll be safer than all the bullshit hassle involved in getting another one. Think about it, Mr. Walker. I'm betting my life that I'm right. They won't put out any bulletins on us. They'll go like they're walking on eggs from here on out."

She lit a cigarette and cracked open the window. "They don't want to catch me. They want to kill me."

They stopped late that night, somewhere in Indiana away from the highway, and found a small motel off the beaten path. The motel consisted of a ring of log cabins, each with two bedrooms and a kitchen. Joanne Sayers put them together in the back room.

"We'll be up awhile yet," she told them through the open door. "In the morning you can decide what you want to do." A moment later she came into the bedroom and dropped the files between them. "Read. Both of you. I want you to read every word of these tonight, and in the morning you can decide for yourself how you want to do it. Keep the door open until you're done. I want to watch you while you read them."

It took a long time to go through it all. Walker passed each page to Diana as he read it, and found her waiting for each one. She read with amazing speed, and he had a feeling she never forgot what she had read. Halfway through, the fear began. "I don't think she should read any more of this," he said.

"Both of you," Joanne said through the open door. "That's why you're here. I want everybody in the world to read that stuff, Mr. Walker. There's safety in numbers."

Two hours later, he closed the diary. They had read that together, with Diana waiting for him to turn each page.

"Now you know," Joanne said. "Now they have to kill you too. I'm sorry if I seem to draw comfort from that thought, but I do."

She got up, leaving her gun on the bed, and began to gather up the files. Walker could have reached over and picked it up.

She turned and looked at him, amusement spreading across her face. "Now do you believe me?"

"Yeah, Joanne. I believe you now."

Seventeen

Boiled down to basics, it read this way. The men were assassins, specialists in death. They did it for their country, took that ultimate step in the name of patriotism, and that was supposed to make it all right. They were an elite corps, known as Mechanics in the trade of death. They were sprinkled throughout every intelligence agency, and some could be found in the largest metropolitan police forces. Some knew others. No one seemed to know them all.

They were especially effective because they had the full resources and manpower of the departments, agencies and bureaus that employed them. Fifty men might be employed in the pursuit, but one man did the job. The top men in those agencies—the chiefs, directors, agents in charge—seemed to have no real knowledge of the Mechanics, or the nature of their work. Impossible? Maybe, but pinning them down was going to be a hell of a job. Going back up the chain of command became difficult, and after a while impossible. They were expert in muddying the water, and finally, when all else failed, they stonewalled. Some of the highest walls were apparently built by those who simply didn't know.

John Dunning

There were some key contact men, who moved freely between the agencies and departments. Beyond that, responsibility blended into an eternal gray. Another you and me story, Walker thought; ultimate responsibility was shared by all. We let this happen. It's our fault.

Shit.

Malcolm Dawes had been a career man. He was a young turk, graduating from the FBI Academy in 1952 with new skills and a conviction that the Red menace must be met at any cost. Dawes hadn't drawn the line at murder, but if his diary could be believed, he had never pulled the trigger himself. He was a disciple of punitive philosophy. People who sold out their country didn't deserve to live. So he hadn't been too shocked when the loose network of killers became known to him, slowly, by degrees. It was a rough old world. People who played for those stakes had to be prepared to pay the price.

Dawes had been thirty-two years old in 1961, when a leak developed in a Central Intelligence Agency operation in Europe. Dawes had been assigned to the FBI office in London. Most people he met didn't even know the FBI had offices overseas. Most people didn't know anything about the world he lived in. It was partly a case of watchdogs watching the watchdogs, of one agency working against another, of operations cloaked in shrouds of jealousy and chauvinism. Malcolm Dawes worked well with everyone. Old Hoover would turn over in his grave if he could know how close Dawes had been with some CIA men in West Germany during those years. There the cooperation was surprisingly fluid, the people in tune with each other to a degree that other working agents wouldn't have thought possible. Skids were greased. That was a term they all loved to use then. Skids were greased, and Dawes had some excellent sources and contacts

178

that helped the CIA in more cases than he could remember.

Nobody seemed to be in charge. Nobody gave orders, at least not that final order. It was just something that became known, and the Mechanics moved on their own. Leaks were plugged. In his business, a little knowledge was truly a dangerous thing.

Especially when the knowledge came from faulty briefs. Malcolm Dawes had prepared one such, on a man known as Hollister. A double agent, whose body was found in a muddy French river one Sunday afternoon. Hollister had played a dangerous game and lost.

An innocent man. Imagine the effect on Malcolm Dawes, a man of conscience for all his hardening experience, when the murder of Hollister didn't plug the leak. Dawes tried to chalk it up to bad luck. Handling dozens of cases over the years, you were bound to make an occasional mistake. Sometimes people had to die, for no other reason than that they played the game and were mistaken for someone else. It sounded good, only Dawes' conscience wouldn't let it go. He thought about it at odd moments during his workday. He saw the eyes of Hollister, a man he had met only once, staring back out of his medicine cabinet mirror.

The mistake he made was getting close to Hollister's widow. He started by sending her some money. Mrs. Hollister came to see him, and hadn't been fooled a bit by his contention that the money had come down through Bureau channels. She was a smart woman, smart and pretty. They talked over coffee about her husband and the dirty job he was involved in. And in the end, Hollister had been a patriot, not much different in attitude and philosophy than Dawes himself. Hollister had been killed for being in the wrong place at the wrong time, and for bearing a strong resemblance to someone else.

Dawes met the Hollister children. He had dinner at the dead agent's house. In Mrs. Hollister he found a lonely woman, not unlike his wife, Marie. He saw an easy mark, a conquest without struggle, and he might have justified it with the simple truth: that here was a woman who wanted and needed him. But he couldn't do it, and it had nothing to do with Marie. It wouldn't have been the first time that he had run out on Marie.

For Dawes there had been a turning point. Like the hawk turned dove by the sickening diet of war and death, Dawes underwent a rapid change of political philosophy. The change deepened and grew like a monster in a scientist's lab. In this case, the lab was himself, the monster his own heart. And suddenly Malcolm Dawes became a man with a very big problem. Soon he began to detest his work. Then he began to hate the FBI. Finally he hated the country that had put him there.

That autumn he learned about the cancer. He had been coughing all summer without letup, and then he knew why. He left Europe, and quickly, in the privacy of his own den, he began writing his journal.

Maybe you couldn't even call it that. It was handwritten in one of those leatherbound books that stationers sell as diaries. For Malcolm Dawes it had become a confessional, a tool of summing up. Walker thought he was a pretty fair writer, faced with a final awful deadline. He had gotten to the heart of what he wanted to say very quickly, with straight, simple words. The words were devastating: a scathing indictment without the extra baggage of adjectives and adverbs. In the end, that was what made it so powerful. The facts spoke so well for themselves. There were two pages of names. Powerful figures in the Justice

Department, FBI, CIA, Army and other military intelligence networks, who had had personal dealings with the Mechanics. Then the names of the killers themselves, a partial, smaller list supported by the files, and by the ring of truth shot throughout Dawes' last testament.

Perhaps it was enough. No newspaper would name names on Dawes' say-so alone, but Walker knew that a powerful story could still be written from the diary without going into specific charges against individuals. He could cite the cases. He might even get away with naming the high-ups who supposedly had knowledge of how the Mechanics worked. Naturally they would all deny it, but his facts would be nailed down so strongly that they would have to be careful about what they said denying it. Nobody would know how much more he had, how much the official records might contradict what they now told the press. An outcry would follow, demand for the original diary and records. Finally, when the newspaper had done its job, the documents could be handed to a congressional investigative committee. Let them get the bastards up in front of lights and cameras, and sweat the facts out of them.

Walker stayed up all night, rereading, making notes. The folders contained the original files stolen from the FBI, which in turn had contained some cross-files from other agencies. The pages in the diary made repeated reference to the files, and to cases of what became known in Walker's mind as spontaneous assassination. It was a good phrase. He would use it somewhere, high up in his first piece. Somewhere the spontaneity had to have originated, but they had protected themselves well. On the face of it, it had just grown, like the cancer in Malcolm Dawes' body, from a single cell now lost in the maze. Suspicion. Then distrust. Surveillance. No orders, anywhere, but in every case the victim was so well set up that he almost invited murder. Bodyguards suddenly disappeared, or were shuffled away on a fool's errand, leaving the man exposed just long enough. The Mechanics always seemed to know who and when and how, and nobody ever told them.

All the obvious ones were here. Allende in Chile. Ngo Dinh Diem in Vietnam. The attempts on Castro. But Walker was amazed at how many cases were domestic nobodies, guys in the federal government that he had never heard of. People with access to sensitive material. Those who had stumbled over something in the files. Men with consciences who, from a warped viewpoint, suddenly became a security risk. That was the trouble with operations like this. They started to protect America and ended by protecting only themselves. And murder was the result in either case. After a while "national security" became a broad blanket indeed. It would cover almost anything.

The man in Brooklyn whose death was ruled suicide. A man working in the federal center west of Denver. Another in Miami, just a year before Dawes' own death. Walker struggled with the material, letting it boil around inside him before he began to write. "America, it's a hell of a place you've come to," he said aloud. Diana, half asleep on the bed across the room, looked at him curiously.

By early morning he had the bulk of it finished. He had filled a yellow pad with notes and was ready to phone it in. He had put a Chicago dateline on it: no harm there; they knew he had been in Chicago anyway.

His first paragraph did the job, got to them where it hurt. He listed the well-known cases and hinted of more to come. He got the words "spontaneous assassination" in, which pleased him. He looked at his watch.

He couldn't remember now if Indiana was on Central or Eastern time. His watch said five-thirty, which might be six-thirty back in Jersey. Time to call. He called from the phone beside his table.

Kanin answered on the first ring.

"City desk."

"Hi, Joe, it's Walker."

There was a long silence.

"Don't smother me with your enthusiasm."

"What am I supposed to do, give everybody half a day off just because you've decided to phone in? All right, Walker, I'll ask the obvious, if you insist. Where the hell have you been?"

"I've been in Chicago. Right now I'm in a motel somewhere . . . near there. Joanne Sayers is with me. Do I have your attention?"

"Go on."

"First I want to ask you something. Did you get a wire story out of Chicago about some cop getting shot up in an office building?"

"I'll have to ask the news desk. Hold on."

He was gone perhaps two minutes. When he came back, he said, "FBI agent named Armstrong?"

"Yes."

"Wait a minute. Are you telling me you witnessed that?"

"Yeah, but . . ."

"Well, why didn't you phone in last night, for Christ's sake?"

"Because I'm phoning in now. Do you think you could shut up and listen a minute?"

Kanin barely breathed into the telephone.

"So tell me about it," Walker said. "Read me the piece."

Kanin read it. An FBI man named Armstrong had

been shot in an elevator of the Barnes Office Building on Chicago's north side. Witnesses said the man was shot by a woman in her early thirties, who escaped.

"I assume it was Sayers," Kanin said.

"The cop didn't identify her?"

"Not according to this. It really isn't much of a story, Walker. Three graphs, just the facts. It was probably a big deal in Chicago. It would have been here too, if we'd known the woman was Sayers."

"So now you know. Look, it just happened last night. Do you want this or not?"

"Oh, by all means."

"Then plug me into somebody and I'll dictate. It'll be a long piece. You'll need somebody to call Chicago and check out the cop's condition, get any possible statements out of there. Is he still alive?"

"He was as of last night. Wait a minute, I'll switch you over. I'll give you Jerry Wayne. He already knows some of this. And Walker, don't hang up when you're done dictating. I want to talk to you again."

He went through it smoothly, dictating commas, periods and paragraphs. Wayne took it quickly, and had no comment until he was finished. "It's a helluva story, Walker. Kanin's already got the first six takes. They're haggling it over up front."

"That figures. They'll have fun with this one."

"Kanin took one peek at that first take and got right on the phone to Byrnes. I think Byrnes is on his way over now."

"Good."

"I think they're talking to the lawyers too. You've got some pretty tough stuff in here. Wait a minute, Kanin wants to talk again."

"Well, where the hell is he?"

"Still up front. He said to keep you on the line."

"Sorry, kid. Being kept on the line makes me nervous."

"Then better give me your number so he can call you back."

"Tell him I'll call him back. Fifteen minutes."

"He won't like that."

"So what else is new?"

Walker hung up.

He could almost see the pandemonium at the *Tribune*. Absolute chaos. So now he would learn what the bottom line was on Byrnes, what the differences were between the show he ran and the show he talked. He didn't envy Byrnes, having to make a quick decision like that. It would have been so much easier getting a story like this by wire. They would simply banner it across Page One and be done with it. Passing along that final responsibility to the AP made it so much easier to take. Nobody's ass was on the line; it was all somebody else's doing. Somebody far away, in a wire service office in New York or Washington. If the story was wrong, the AP would correct itself. The *Tribune* would run it, saying, listen, people, it was the AP that screwed up. Things were different when it came from your own man, even if he had won a Pulitzer. Walker knew that. He understood that management mentality, had been keenly aware of it throughout the writing. At the last minute, he decided the hell with it, and put it all in. All the names, every connection Dawes had been able to establish clearly. Let it be the *Tribune*'s problem; he would get rid of it in one gush. And who could tell, they might print it. Stranger things had happened. Jonah had lived in the belly of a whale for three days and three nights.

He had thought of all their possible arguments, and of his own. He had played it out a dozen times in his head. Was he willing to risk his name and reputation on what he had written? No doubt about it. But it wasn't a fair comparison and he knew it. His name probably meant a lot less to him than their newspaper did to them.

Joanne Sayers knocked lightly and opened the door. She saw the notes on the table beside him.

"You did it."

"I did it."

She sighed. "Good."

"Not good yet."

"Why not?"

"We don't know yet if they'll print it."

Walker called back a few minutes later. This time Jerry Wayne answered, and immediately switched him to Hiram Byrnes' private line. Kanin was still back there, and they got on a three-way hookup.

"Walker? Hy Byrnes here. That's quite a surprise you had for us this morning."

Bad start, Mr. Byrnes. Walker took a deep breath.

"A couple of our lawyers are reading it over now. You understand that, don't you? We've got to be right on a piece like this."

"We are right. But I understand your concern."

"It's a helluva reader, Walker. Simply one helluva piece. I don't think there's any doubt that we'll go with some of it today, across the top of One. What bothers us are the names."

"I spelled them all right."

"When they bury him, he'll make a joke about it," Kanin said.

"If we had the documents here in our hands, we'd feel a lot better," Byrnes said. "How long do you think it would take you to get back here?"

"That depends."

"On what?"

Deadline

"On whether we come right back."

"How are you traveling? By car?"

"That's right."

"If we wired you plane tickets, for you and the Sayers girl, you should be able to get in here this afternoon. I wonder if it would hold till tomorrow."

Walker didn't say anything.

"You understand my position, Walker. Goddammit, I'd love to be able to go with the whole thing at once, but I've got to at least have those papers and that diary in house first. We'd want the lawyers to look through them. And we'd probably have to contact the people named . . ."

"I know the procedure."

"Then what do you say?"

"I'll have to call you back."

"What for?" Kanin snapped.

"Because the documents aren't in my possession. They belong to the Sayers girl."

"The FBI would probably argue with that," Kanin said.

"The FBI argues with everything," Walker said. "Anyway, I'll have to ask her permission."

Now Byrnes had a strange edge to his voice. "Walker?"

"Yeah?"

"You're not aiding her in any way?"

"Why would I do that?"

"Because if you are, we could get in one helluva bad light."

"You? What about me? I know the laws on aiding a fugitive. If it makes you feel any better, I've been her prisoner since Sunday."

"You never really say that in your copy."

"I like to stay out of my own copy if I can."

"I don't see how that's possible, on one like this," Kanin said.

187

Walker felt his warning sensors go off.

"Kanin, leave my stuff alone, will you?"

"Oh, I wouldn't touch your goddamn precious prose. I know better than anyone how sacred every word is."

"All right, you two," Hiram Byrnes said. "Walker, Joe's right. It's going to be tough as hell trying to report this as though you weren't even there. We'll need all the details from you on this abduction bit. Maybe we'll run it as a sidebar, and let the main story stand by itself. If we can ever get it straightened out. How does that sound?"

Lovely, he thought.

"Walker? You still there?"

"Sure."

"Let me switch you back over to Wayne. Give him notes on what happened, everything that happened since last Saturday. Don't worry. We'll handle it right."

That's what the Watergate burglars said, Walker thought. He said, "All right. Give me back to Wayne."

Byrnes clicked the phone. "Get back to me when you're through." The operator came on and Byrnes said, "Transfer to 222."

Walker hung up. He looked at Joanne.

"Must have got cut off."

"What'd he say?" She looked nervous, expectant.

"It's not what he said. It's what he is. They're not gonna use it, Joanne. Not the part that counts. No way."

It was light outside, and Diana fixed breakfast, and they sat around the table to talk about it. The gun had disappeared. Walker didn't see it again. Joanne Sayers had made them part of her. If she bled, they bled; if she died, so did they. They all seemed to know that without ever saying it, and now the only conversation necessary was on what to do next. The idea of flying back to New Jersey bothered Joanne. "What guarantee do we have that they'll print it even after we give them the documents?"

"None," Walker said.

"Not even somebody's word?"

"They can't give us their word, Joanne."

"Jesus!" she fumed. "How can they *not* print a story like this? Walker, I can't believe this."

"All right, look at it from their viewpoint. If you want to understand what you're up against, you've got to do that. Even if they've got the papers, there are no guarantees. If the FBI can discredit this Dawes, if they can cast enough doubt over his mental state, we might have a big problem. Joanne, they're a bunch of scared little minds. They live their whole lives for the big story, then one comes along and they don't know what to do with it. They see it as going on the line, and that bothers them. It doesn't bother me much. They know that, and *that* bothers them. I'm an oddball. I might take chances that they wouldn't take. And they're trying to make decisions, weighing all these things, a thousand miles away. You remember the Pentagon Papers case?"

"Sure."

"Remember when Ellsberg first leaked that stuff out? There was a big flap at the *New York Times* about whether they should publish or not. I couldn't believe it. Here was the best newspaper in the country, with the biggest story of the decade, and they were hassling about it. I remember thinking then, wow, that's the big time. And I wondered then what would have happened if Ellsberg had leaked that stuff to any other newspaper. The *Washington Post?* Maybe. But the others? Forget it. There's no way a newspaper in Dallas or Rapid City, South Dakota, is going to put itself at the fulcrum point of a story like that. It's like a dinosaur eating its young. They might want it, but then they turn around and destroy it before it's even had a chance to breathe. I don't know a newspaperman in the country who won't argue like hell about this. They'd come right up out of their chairs if they could hear me talking. They'd get red in the face and raise hell. Sure, they'd publish the Pentagon Papers, you bet, as long as they can look back and see all that glory from here. As long as they didn't have to make the decisions all the way along the line. The hell with them. Ellsberg was right. He gave the stuff to the right paper."

"Then why don't we?"

"I've given that some thought. Yes, ma'am, I truly have."

They were on the road again, drifting like a sailship on a windless day. The tide took them easterly, toward the sun, across the fertile fields of Indiana. They kept to the back roads now, speaking little, listening to newscasts when they could. There was nothing on the radio about Armstrong or Joanne Sayers.

"That'll change by tonight," Walker told her. "I don't know what the *Trib* will use, but you can bet when I don't call in again that they'll get some hacked-up version on the streets. Both AP and UPI will carry it on their A-wires. You won't have much time after that to make up your mind."

"I can't think like this," Joanne said. "Maybe you can think under pressure like this, but I can't. We need a place where we can stop and rest, without worrying about every car that passes. Will you help me?"

"I'll help you if I can. I'm not too anxious to go to jail with you."

"I want to get it in print. That's the kind of help I need."

"I'll keep trying. That's my job."

"We need a quiet place. A place to think." Joanne looked at the back of Diana's head. "I think I know a place."

Eighteen

This time, Diana let herself be led home without comment. Seeing her father's farm that first time had brought her to a turning point. The man at her side, the girl with the gun, all the events of the past week were absent from her thoughts. Some point of basic personal conflict had come to the surface at last. Now she had to make the choice she had never made. Her escape from the farm long years ago hadn't involved free choice at all. She had been a terrified adolescent, and she had been running from those childhood ghosts ever since.

So once again they drove along that narrow black-top road in Lancaster County, Pennsylvania, looking out across the even-plowed fields toward the cluster of houses in the trees. It was midafternoon Friday, almost six days since Joanne Sayers had come to Walker's and taken them hostage. They had driven late at night, and had started early in the morning. Now, they parked and sat for a long time at the side of the road, none of them certain of what to do next.

"What a lovely place," Joanne said.

"My parents always worked hard to keep it up."

"I can see that." She rolled down the window and

looked across the field. Far away they heard a voice, someone calling. They could see some movement in the yard behind the house, under the trees and around the barn.

"It's dinnertime," Diana said. "We always ate two meals a day. My father thinks that's healthier than three. So we ate at dawn and again around three o'clock in the afternoon. Then nothing else till morning. My father especially believed in going to bed on an empty stomach."

"Your father sounds like a wise man," Joanne said.

"Wise and blind at the same time. He's a tough taskmaster, and death on discipline. He doesn't seem to understand feelings. If he does, he won't tolerate letting them interfere with what he considers duty. God comes first. Then family."

"And country third?"

"Maybe country not at all, I don't know. I never really heard him say that much about it. My father's no patriot. He'd never go to war for his country, if that's what patriotism is. If the Communists took over, that'd just be God's will. He wouldn't ever kill a human being, even to save another. He wouldn't think twice about breaking the laws of his country, if they crossed with the laws of his Church. I'm sure he appreciates America. I know he does, but it just doesn't come first with him." Diana turned in her seat and looked at Joanne. "You have to understand about the Amish. They don't like systems of any kind much."

A cooling breeze came in through the open windows. They sat for a while longer.

"What are you going to do?" Diana said.

"I don't want to walk in on them at dinnertime."

"It's no big thing. They'll have plenty of food, and they'll probably invite us to share it. But you'll have to be ready for some awkwardness. They may not speak to me, or eat at the same table. We may have to eat somewhere else. Do you mind eating in the barn?"

"Let's go to a restaurant," Joanne said. "We'll come back later, when their dinner hour is done."

They picked up the highway a few miles south and found a long row of restaurants on the way toward Lancaster. Walker bought a paper from a box and carried it to a table. The second-day story was boiling on the front pages everywhere. His piece had hit with a roar late yesterday. They had been somewhere in Ohio when they heard that first newscast. A New Jersey newspaper had reported that Joanne Sayers, longtime fugitive, had taken one of its reporters hostage, and had forced the reporter to drive her to Chicago. The man was Dalton Walker, Pulitzer Prize winner, who had been working on the story for several months. In Chicago, the Sayers woman was believed to have shot an FBI man, Joe Armstrong, in a confrontation late Wednesday. The *Tribune* believed, after talking with Walker, that Sayers was considering surrendering herself, but there had been no further contact since early Thursday.

The story of the assassins was carried sidebar fashion, as an unconfirmed but related development. The newspaper had run a story by Walker, which the Sayers woman had allowed him to dictate, and which was allegedly based on information from documents long believed to be in Sayers' possession. The story charged the nation's top investigative and intelligence agencies with harboring elite hit squads, comprised of professional killers working not only in foreign capitals but in the United States as well. The Director of the FBI had labeled the story nonsense. There had been no comment from the others.

It was the shell of a story, stripped of all its guts. Naturally, no names were mentioned. On the radio, it sounded like the work of a good fiction writer.

It looked a little better in print, though not much. Joanne was despondent. The stories contained a clear suggestion that Walker had been forced to write them, and vivid reminders that Joanne Sayers' involvement in radical causes went back to Berkeley of the mid-1960s.

"They don't believe it," she said. "They don't believe me, and what's worse, they don't believe you either. They think I'm holding a gun to your head."

"To them it's a clear possibility," Walker said. "You've made some pretty big mistakes, Joanne. It's going to take some work to undo them."

"I wonder if that's even possible."

"Anything's possible. You got me to believe you."

"Big deal. No offense, but all that'll get us right now are three coffins instead of one."

In a restaurant near Lancaster, Walker read through each of the second-day stories twice. There were holes big enough to drive a truck through. Where was all the federal flap? There was no question of FBI involvement: burglary of an FBI office, bank robbery, kidnapping, transporting of hostages across state lines, shooting a federal agent. All those great things to sink their federal teeth into, but the FBI was nowhere in the stories. The few comments that reporters had gotten were pried out, word by word. And everything had been cleared through Washington. In two days of listening and reading, Walker had not found a single exception to this. Not a word out of the field office in Chicago. As of this moment, Walker didn't even know if the man Joanne had shot was dead or alive.

* * *

And now Diana faced her own time of truth. Everything else around her was smothered under waves of nostalgia and fear, and she saw Joanne Sayers as just a frightened child. Not a dangerous public enemy, not a rabid animal. Stripped of all her bad press, Joanne was just another creature who needed help. Wasn't that what her father had always said? *We are all our brother's keeper.* They were coming up to the farmhouse slowly, riding under the perfectly even trees that lined the road. Behind them, the paved road slipped from sight behind the trees and underbrush. Just ahead was the house, tree-shaded and recently painted. Behind the house stood a new barn.

"I'll have to introduce you as friends of mine. As husband and wife. That's the only way this can work."

"Okay with me," Joanne said.

Several buckboards stood in the clearing ahead. The horses had been unhitched and led around to a small paddock adjoining the barn. Two little boys had come outside and were sitting together on the front steps, watching. They wore the plain clothes of all Amish kids. Their wide-brimmed black hats almost dwarfed them.

Walker parked the car. Diana took a deep breath and opened the door. "Let's do it, people," she said. Her voice was flat, the voice of someone talking to herself. She was a novice again, about to audition for her most important part. In the eyes of her parents, she would be found lacking. She knew that in advance. The only question was one of degree.

Walker and Joanne followed her across the grassy brown lawn. They came together, as husband and wife might. As they reached the edge of the porch, Walker noticed that Joanne had left the bag, along with the gun, inside the car.

Diana stopped at the foot of the steps. "Hello," she said to the boys. "What are your names?"

"Aaron Yoder, ma'am. This is my brother Daniel."

"I see. Then Daniel Yoder Sr. is your father."

"Yes, ma'am."

"Then I'm your aunt Diana. I'm your father's sister."

The boys looked at each other curiously and said nothing more.

"Would you please go inside and tell your grandpa I'm here?"

The older boy jumped up and disappeared into the house. Diana looked at Walker and again her eyes were full of sadness and fear. Walker smiled at her and tears started down her cheeks.

The door opened and a graying woman, perhaps sixty years old, stood before them. For a full minute, Walker didn't know what to expect. The older woman gave nothing until, quite suddenly, she hurried down the five wooden steps and embraced her daughter. Diana cried against her mother's breast. When she could talk, she said, "Mama, these are my friends. Mr. Walker. His . . . wife. Joanne." She looked guilty as the lie passed her lips. Walker wondered if the old woman could see it. To Walker, Diana said, "My mother, Rachel Yoder."

Mrs. Yoder offered a thin, dry hand and no expression at all. She led them into a warm, dark house. Diana was almost overcome by the look of it, by its feel and smells and tiny, dark corners. There were five rooms, with no frills in any. The floors were bare hardwood, each with a small oval rug in its center. They squeaked when you walked on them. The main part of the house consisted of a single room, almost like a meeting room in a community center. Chairs ringed it, as though it had been set up for a prayer meeting. The chairs were straight-backed and hard.

The kitchen area was against the far wall. There was a wood-burning stove of black iron, and a pile of logs beside it, and nearby was a handmade table that extended or contracted to whatever degree of intimacy you wanted. Now it was pulled out, with the appropriate wooden leaves added, to serve perhaps a dozen.

There were three younger women hard at work in the kitchen. Diana knew them, but from very long ago, before they had married into her family. Mrs. Yoder introduced them in a voice that halted, as though suddenly uncertain if they knew each other, and how well. The one nearest the window was Trudy, the wife of Diana's youngest brother Michael. She took Diana's hand warmly and smiled into her eyes, then greeted Walker and Joanne with equal warmth. She was a plain farm girl with freckles. Susan Yoder was lovely and aloof. She was Daniel Yoder's wife, and Walker remembered that Daniel was the eldest, the strictest religiously, and was the man they had seen on the road coming west to Chicago. Susan Yoder didn't speak or offer her hand. Her eyes met Diana's briefly, and she did not look at Walker or Joanne at all. She was perhaps thirty, Diana's age, and her skin was creamy and her hair had a red tint to it. She turned back to the sink at once and went on with her work.

The third wife, now about seven months pregnant, was Abe's wife Elizabeth. She took the middle ground, not nearly as friendly as Trudy, but not as cold and distant as Susan. She spoke an unintelligible word, then, at Mrs. Yoder's direction, began extending the table to include their guests. "You're in time for dinner," Mrs. Yoder said.

She told them that the men had walked over to the next farm to look at Mr. Jenkins' horse, which Daniel was thinking of buying. They would be back shortly.

Joanne told Mrs. Yoder that they had eaten and didn't want to intrude on the dinner hour, but already the woman was helping Elizabeth set three extra plates. Diana was obviously surprised at being asked to join the table. She excused herself and went out back, to the outhouse. Mrs. Yoder looked increasingly uneasy. Joanne offered to help, and Mrs. Yoder didn't know how to react to that. Trudy came over and told them to sit and relax until the men got home.

Diana got back just ahead of the men. She put on an apron and went to work. No one objected. Susan Yoder made room for her near the sink as if she had never been away at all; as if she had always been a good Amish girl, doing for her men. Joanne and Walker sat in the straight-backed chairs, which were even more uncomfortable than they looked. They waited in silence.

It was almost a place out of time, a frontier home moved suddenly into the twentieth century, but unchanged and unchangeable by all of it. The only light came from four oil lamps, which hung by nails in each corner, and from the yellow glow of a fire in the hearth.

"I don't believe this," Joanne said softly.

A moment later, she said, "It's beautiful."

Jacob Yoder was a powerfully built man with piercing eyes. He stood in the doorway and peered into the room, tipped off to the arrival of outsiders by the presence of a car in his yard. Flanking him were his three grown sons. The sight of them, outlined in shadow in the open doorway, gave Walker a momentary chill. Mrs. Yoder crossed to her husband and said in a flat voice, "It's Diana, Jacob. Daughter's come home."

There was no display between them. Jacob Yoder looked past his wife and found the agonized eyes of

199

his daughter. They didn't move toward each other. He withheld his words in a fine display of dramatics, and she simply had no words to withhold. For a moment Walker was certain that she would go to pieces, but she didn't. She didn't look away, either. Her eyes were wide and her face absolutely white.

"So you've come home," the old man said at last. He took a step closer, and Walker saw Diana's lower lip quiver.

"Here to stay, are you?"

Diana didn't answer at once. The question had caught her by surprise. Like so many things that she knew by heart, she had looked beyond it, had overlooked the simplicity and leaped past the narrowness of his thinking. She was prepared for broader talk. She had lived in the city too long, and now the fundamental nature of her people surprised her with its black-and-white directness. She swallowed and said, "I don't know." Her brother Daniel threw his hands up in the air, impatience bursting through the awkwardness of their long estrangement. "God help us all," he said.

Jacob Yoder ignored his son and now stepped past his daughter. "I don't believe I know you, sir." Diana introduced them once more as Mr. and Mrs. Walker. She seemed surprised when her father said, "Will you have some food with us?" Michael came forward and hugged Diana around the shoulders. Her face went red with pleasure. Abe kept his distance, but smiled slightly when their eyes met. Daniel gave not an inch.

"We'll be going, Father," he said.

"As you wish," Jacob Yoder said.

Daniel, unable to conceal his anger, gathered Susan and his boys and hustled them out through the front door. Through a side window, Walker could hear him harnessing his horse. A moment later the buckboard hurried down the dirt road.

"Daniel is impulsive," Jacob Yoder said to Walker. It was an attempt at explanation, not apology. "Daughter here has told you about us?"

"A little," Walker said.

"Good. Then you do understand." He turned to his wife. "Let's eat."

They washed up and ate without further talk. Jacob Yoder rolled up his sleeves and gave thanks, and they passed the steaming plates from hand to hand. The meat was ham, and there were rice and cabbage and cornbread. Diana ate little, having eaten just an hour before, but Joanne ate heartily. Jacob Yoder's eyes darted around, and always came to rest upon his daughter.

"I expect you'll find things changed around here," he said.

Again she forced herself to look at him. "Oh?"

"There's been some letup in the old ways."

"Father's been one of the main movers in that direction," Michael said.

Jacob silenced him with a look. "The Church was too strict for this day and age," he said.

"I never thought I'd hear you say that, Father."

For a while, Jacob said nothing. He ate as he thought, slowly, mechanically. Then he said, "It was driving out the young. Understand, there's been no relaxing of basic beliefs. But some of the old practices weren't in our best interests."

Again she balled up her courage and faced him. "Like shunning, you mean?"

"That's part of it. It makes no sense to shun family. No sense to some of us."

"Daniel's still caught up in the old ways," Michael said.

"Daniel Yoder can be a pig-headed young man," Jacob said.

"That's how he was raised, Father," Diana said.

The old man looked at her sharply.

"I didn't mean he was raised to be pig-headed," she said quickly. "I meant he was raised to be strict and follow the old ways."

"You have to admit that, Father," Michael said. "She's right about that. You made us tow the mark when we were little."

"Something you've sadly forgotten with age," Jacob said. "That's the trouble with change. Don't you think so, Mr. Walker?"

Walker was surprised to be included. He mumbled something noncommittal, about change always being full of danger as well as opportunity.

"That's sure the truth." Jacob Yoder looked at his daughter, and again his eyes were relentless. She seemed to wither before him. Twice he seemed on the verge of words, but he took another bite each time and went on chewing. And Walker thought, this guy would have made a great film director. In another time and place.

"So the Church has changed, and I wanted you to know it, before you go deciding whether you'll go or stay."

"Father, I only came back for a visit. Because I wanted to see you all."

"We'll see. You'll be here at least through the weekend."

"I suppose so."

"Then you'll be here for church Sunday. It'll be at the Jenkins house, and I want you to be there with us."

"I don't know."

Mrs. Yoder looked at her daughter and nodded. Her eyes were full of hope.

"I suppose I could," Diana said.

"Good. Then it's settled."

Michael leaned over the table. "You will find it different, Diana."

She smiled.

"We've split away from the main body," Michael added.

"Really? That's incredible."

"Incredible?" Jacob Yoder seemed offended. "Why do you find it so incredible, miss? Do you think your father is so hidebound and unbending that he can't make up his own mind about things?"

"I didn't say that."

"Well, since Michael here's taken it on himself to tell you, he might as well tell it all. Go ahead."

Michael seemed unperturbed. "About three years after you left, there were a lot of runaways."

"Let's get our facts straight," Jacob Yoder said. "Three children, of which two later came back. Let's not make it worse than it is."

"I thought three was a fair number, when you're as small a group as we are," Michael said. "So Father proposed relaxing some of the Ordnung."

Diana looked at Walker. "The rules of the Church," she said.

"There was a lively debate, which went on for several years," Michael said. "It was a strange situation around here, with Father on one side and Daniel on the other. It got pretty heated, with neither wanting to give much." He looked at his father in apology. "Daniel is a stubborn man."

"You needn't be trying to pacify me at your brother's expense," Jacob said. "I raised Daniel Yoder to be a God-fearing man of the Church, and I have no regrets at anything he's done. Daniel's stuck by his guns. He's stood up for what he believes and I'm proud that he's my son."

"But the end result is that we now go to different

groups," Michael said. "Abe and I decided to go with Father; Daniel remained with the old Church."

"You didn't tell me any of this when you came down to New York," Diana said.

"I didn't see the point."

Again a hush fell over the table. Jacob resumed staring at his daughter. At last he said, "So tell me what you've been doing down in New York City."

"Didn't Michael tell you?"

"If he had, I wouldn't ask you. Do you think I'd have you to my table for the first time in ten years, then lay a trap for you?"

She didn't say anything for a very long time. At last she looked at her father and said, "I'm a dancer at Radio City Music Hall."

Jacob let it lie for just an instant. "Is that supposed to shock me? Is that why you're turning all scarlet in front of me, because you think I'll be shocked? Lady, I might remind you that I'm not a stupid man. Uneducated, yes, and sometimes hard. I'd plead guilty to either of those things, but never to stupidity. I knew where your head was the moment you walked out that door. I knew what you wanted out of life, or thought you did. The thing that really surprised me is how long you rode it out. I kept looking at that front door, thinking you'd walk back in here any minute . . ."

Tears spilled over again, but her eyes held steady with his.

"I don't tell you these things to make you hurt. I just tell you so you'll know. And I regret bringing this up in front of company, but these are words I've waited a long time to say to you. I never wanted you to go, and never God knows wanted you to stay away. But time went by, and more time, and still you didn't come home. After a while, I knew. Somewhere out there you'd found what you wanted, and it gave you more satisfaction than what we had here. And I knew you'd not be coming back, and I'd have to resign myself to it. That's when I decided to make some changes in the Church."

"I'd have come visiting years ago if I'd known that."

"Well, now you do know it." Jacob Yoder reached across the table and covered her hand with his. "Let's have no more talk tonight about visits and things temporary. All I want in my last years is to have my family back together again."

Dusk had fallen on the fields, and in the yellow of the lamps their faces glowed across the table at each other. Crickets had started up. Walker could hear them right through the closed front door. Jacob Yoder threw some more wood on the fire and soon the noise of the blaze drowned out all others, and a cheery warmth spread across the room. They sat talking for a long time after Diana's mother had cleared away the dishes. The old man and his daughter talked as if no one were in the room with them. It was almost eight by the clock on the mantel when Jacob turned to Walker and said, "How long will you be staying with us, sir?"

"I don't know." Walker looked at Diana, as if she should decide, but Jacob took the decision out of her hands.

"You're welcome for as long as you want. Michael will have a room for you. I trust you'll be comfortable."

"I'm sure we will."

Jacob Yoder's eyes moved back to Diana. "You'll stay here with us."

He had taken charge, separated them easily and effectively. It was as if, by cutting them off from each other, he had cemented the bond between himself and his daughter. She got up at once, slipping back into her old role without question or comment. She helped her mother at the sink while Jacob escorted Walker and Joanne to the door with Michael and Trudy.

"You may put your car in the barn," Jacob said. "If people see it in my yard, they're liable to start thinking all kinds of things." He went out with them and opened the barn door. Then he left them in Michael's care. Trudy took Joanne by the hand and they stepped through a gate and into the plowed field. "It's too dark to walk it alone, if you don't know the way," Trudy said. "You might turn an ankle. Here, let me show you."

They found a path that led around the perimeter of the field. They walked under some trees and along a riverbank. Far up the hill, they could see the pale yellow of oil lamps against window frames.

"That's Daniel's place," Michael said. "I'm renting some land from him, and I'm working to buy the farm next door."

"We've got a nice little place," Trudy said. "I hope you'll like it with us."

"I already do," Joanne said. "You're lovely people."

Nineteen

They didn't see much of Diana after that; didn't see her at all the next day. Walker went over to the main house around noon, and was told by Mrs. Yoder that Diana had gone with her father. By three o'clock, the buggy still hadn't returned.

On Sunday, just seven days after they had been taken at gunpoint from his New Jersey apartment, Walker attended church in the Amish farm country of Lancaster County, Pennsylvania. The families gathered in the Jenkins home, about a mile straight across Daniel Yoder's field. Joanne asked if she could go. "In the old Church, it would have been hard," Michael said. "But with us, the question's never come up. Why don't you come along and we'll ask."

So Walker went too. They stood out in the yard until everyone else had arrived. Diana came with her family. She wore a plain dress whose hem touched her ankles, and a bonnet tied delicately under her chin. To Walker she looked like a different person. She looked like Susan Yoder, the perfect, romanticized picture of simple Amish beauty. She smiled at him and her father escorted her in. Mrs. Yoder came along behind them. A few minutes later Michael came out and invited them inside.

There were perhaps forty people in the room, from maybe a dozen families. The room was almost identical to the big room in the Yoder house, with hard wood chairs placed in a semicircle. Walker and Joanne sat in a corner, away from everyone.

A deacon named Carl Miller gave a sermon, which was followed by a long talk from Bishop David Beiler. Neither man used notes. They looked straight into the crowd. The bishop began by welcoming Diana back into their midst. There was no mention of her rejoining the Church. That would come only after a public confession of sin and a vote of the membership. The bishop moved on to other subjects: the coming planting season and its importance in God's framework; some of the intricacies of that framework, and how the various elements interlaced with each other to make a uniform whole. His talk went on for more than two hours. It ended with an indictment of the public school system, which had resulted in more problems for the Amish than the bureaucrats in Washington could ever know or understand. The poisonous influence of the outside had to be stemmed if the Church would survive. And while he talked, his eyes returned again and again to Diana, as the living example of what could happen outside. Her eyes remained in her lap, upon her closed hands.

By the time the service ended, it was midafternoon. In all, it had gone on more than four hours, including the bishop's talk. Next came the social hour, with visiting and talk and piles of food. The men went outside and gathered behind Arnold Jenkins' barn, while the women prepared the meal. Joanne Sayers, feeling part of neither group, took a walk along the riverbank. Walker stood at the end of the barn and watched her until she was out of sight.

Joanne had reacted strangely to the Amish, almost from the beginning. What had seemed stupid and archaic from a distance had become quaint and then lovely at closer view. Walker had seen her growing infatuation that first night, when Michael and Trudy had shown them to their room. The room was small and bare, like the rooms in the main house, and there were lamps for each end table. The house was cold, but Michael didn't light the fire. He turned up the wicks on all three lamps in the living room and it made a respectable light.

Trudy brought them some warm milk and they sat in the large room and talked. Trudy sat under Michael's arm, his chin on her head, and after a while she touched his belt buckle and doodled it with her little finger. To Walker the gesture was wildly sexual, and it took him a moment to figure out why. Back in Jersey, he wouldn't have thought twice if a guy and girl had met at a party and five minutes later they were in a corner somewhere necking. Here, it was so different. There was no demonstration between the sexes, and what may have been a simple gesture looked to an outsider like an invitation to a love feast. As if she just couldn't hustle him off to bed fast enough. That was it. Since his arrival, he had yet to see a man kiss his wife, or touch her hand the way Jacob Yoder had touched Diana's hand at the dinner table. None of them demonstrated any personal feelings at all.

Michael and Trudy were different. And it was such a small thing, but so big in the semidarkness of that farmhouse room. The air in Michael's home was heavy with love. They sat up for perhaps twenty minutes, sipping their milk and talking about the day. Trudy seemed highly progressive for her station in life. Michael nodded, as if deep in thought, and never once corrected her.

"Mr. Walker," he said when a lull had come, "how well do you know my sister?"

"She's a hard person to know really well," Walker said. "Meaning no disrespect."

"No, I know just what you're saying. I'm just wondering if you think she's home for good, and if she'd be happy with that."

"I'm afraid I don't know."

"I hope I'll get a chance to talk to her myself. Wasn't she happy in New York?"

Walker thought about it. "It's just an opinion, but I'd say no. She missed all this."

"And now that she's here, she'll miss all that," Trudy said.

Michael touched her cheek with his finger.

"I hope I'm wrong," she said. "But I'll bet I'm not. I'm a lot younger than Diana, but in a way I think I understand her far better than her family ever can. For a while, I wanted to be like her."

Michael said, "You never told me that."

"I know. I thought I'd wait till I understood it better before sharing it with you." She looked at Walker. "Michael would go off to New York, then he'd come home and tell me about Diana's life there, and for a while after each visit I'd lie awake at night and my soul was full of envy. I wanted what she had, and at the same time I wanted what I had. I went through the crisis in my teens, just like her. Only she went and I stayed, and for all these years I've been contented with my decision. Until Michael started going off to New York. It was hard after that. Diana had a . . . what's the word?"

"Mystique," Walker said. The mystique of the big time.

"It means you've got a certain attraction for another person, or for her way of life," Trudy said. "And now she's come back. I haven't seen her since eighth grade, and I didn't know her then. She was far ahead of me in school, and was already done with all that. I didn't even know Michael then, except to look at. And now here she is, and there's such pain in her that I wouldn't trade places with her for anything. I hope she does the right thing."

"I hope so too, Trudy," Walker said.

The guest bedroom was, if anything, colder than the rest of the house. The double bed dominated it, flanked on either side by handmade end tables. There was no closet. They would hang their clothes, if they undressed at all, on wire hangers that draped from a wooden pole that ran across a corner of the room. They closed the door and sat on the bed.

"Now what?" Joanne said.

Walker could see her breath, and his own as he said, "Now we go to bed, I guess."

"What a strange, wonderful journey this is." She smiled at him. "You start out with Diana and end up with me. Who'd have thought it?"

"Listen, Joanne . . ."

"Oh, Walker, be still. I'm not going to make any demands on you. God forbid."

"You know how it is."

"No, tell me. How is it?"

But he didn't tell her. He didn't tell her that the aura of sex around Michael and Trudy was infectious, that he wanted her too, that she had changed forever in his mind from the gun-toting terrorist to someone much closer and more important. He didn't even tell her that what happened to her mattered very much to him. She watched him with interest born of that primitive hunger that can never be mistaken. Finally she rolled her eyes toward the door.

"What do you think they're doing out there in their room?"

"Sleeping. Wasn't that the idea of the warm milk?"

"Sleeping my eye." She turned down the bed. "Why don't you relax, Walker?"

"I can't."

"Sure you can. Forget about yourself for a while. Think about me."

"I am."

And he was. He was remembering her in the shower, and later, patting her private parts with a heavy towel.

"You are like hell," she said. "You're thinking about yourself, and what'll happen if people find out you screwed Joanne Sayers. What it comes down to is you're a hypocrite, Walker. At the bottom of that tough-guy facade, you're just like all the rest. You want me and I'm here, and what the hell, you're afraid. Scared to death for all the wrong reasons. I'm really disappointed in you."

"I'm sorry you feel like that."

"How am I supposed to feel? What is it, Walker, do I turn you off?"

"No."

"Then what? Is it because I'm your story?"

"Yeah, that's part of it."

"And I'm a fugitive."

He didn't say anything.

"I wonder," she said, "if the simple act of fucking me could be construed in any legal sense as aiding and abetting. Do you think so?"

"I hadn't thought about it."

"You lying son of a bitch. Or maybe it isn't me at

all. Maybe it's your girlfriend, up there in her daddy's house."

"Maybe that's it."

"You're such a goddamned fool. She'll never leave here with you. Even I can see that, and you could put what I know about these people through the head of a needle. And I'll tell you something, I wouldn't blame her if she did stay here. I'd trade places with her in a minute."

"I'm sure you would."

"It's got nothing to do with avoiding jail, so get that look off your face. Take away my so-called crimes, make me a free person and I'd still trade places with her. I'd take her family. Let her go to the big town and fight the traffic and the smog and hunt for a decent job. Let her fight off the phony cocksmen every time you turn around. I'm telling you, Walker, there's something basic and great about life here, and I love it. What do you think about that?"

"I think you're talking to yourself. It's easy to love something when you've only known it a few hours. And when you've got no other choice. It takes a certain kind of person to live like this. Inside of two months you'd be ready for a straitjacket and a padded cell."

"Maybe you're right. At least it'd be interesting to find out. Maybe I will find out. What would you do if I decided to find out, Walker?"

"I don't follow that."

"If I decided to stay here. Become one of them."

"It's a waste of time talking about it."

"So what? What else have you got to do? You won't come to bed with me. But that's your loss."

"I'm sure it is."

"For a little while, I could make you a very happy man."

"You don't make it easy, do you?"

"I sure don't." She stood beside the bed and began to undress.

Walker turned his eyes up toward the window.

"Walker," she said a moment later. "Walker, look at me. I'm goosebumpy all over from the cold. Come on, warm me up. Aid and abet me, Walker."

"I can't. I can't touch you, Joanne, no matter how much I want to."

"Ah, Christ." She threw her clothes into a corner in disgust. "You're just like all men. A grade-A horse's ass. You're so caught up in yourself and your job that you can't see past your own nose."

She stripped off one of the quilts and threw it at him. "Sleep on the goddamned floor, then. And I hope you're sore for a week."

That had happened two nights ago. Now Walker stood apart from the men behind Arnold Jenkins' barn and watched the riverbank for her return. She was gone a long time. The men had already begun filing back into the house for the meal when he saw her appear over the hill. She was wearing plain clothes, like the people here, and she almost seemed to blend into the countryside. It would please her to know that, but he wouldn't tell her, wouldn't encourage her at all. She came to him and smiled almost shyly. They followed the men into the house and ate a delicious supper by lamplight.

After supper, Jacob motioned Walker outside. They went out of the yard and across the field. The sun was low in the west, touching the treetops, and the air around them was purple.

Jacob came quickly to his point. "Young man, may I ask how long you plan to stay with us?"

"Probably not much longer," Walker said.

"I wouldn't want to be inhospitable, but maybe

that's for the best. I want you to know you have my gratitude for bringing my daughter home."

"She came because she wanted to. Has she decided to stay?"

"She will stay," Jacob said. "We've had some talks, but that part of it hasn't been touched on. But she will stay."

"Can I talk to her before we leave?"

"Alone, you mean?"

"If you wouldn't mind."

Jacob shook his head. "I think it'd be best if you'd just pack up and move on. I hope you understand what I'm saying. It's got nothing to do with you . . . or the lady. She's a lovely lady, Mr. Walker. But things aren't what they seem, now are they?"

"No sir. Not quite."

"That's all right. I don't want to know. I'm not asking you anything but to respect my wishes on this. I think it's best you move on."

"All right."

"How about tomorrow? You could get an early start and be home by nightfall."

"If that's what you want."

"Thank you, Mr. Walker."

Jacob turned and left him there. A moment later Joanne came out. They stood by the fence and watched the sun go down. Behind them, people poured out of Arnold Jenkins' house. Buggies began moving off down the long dirt road.

"I saw you leave," she said. "What did the old man want?"

"He wants us to go."

"That figures." Her face was grim. "I guess I knew it the moment I saw you two leave. It almost showed in the old man's face."

Walker didn't say anything.

"So what now? Do we go back on the run?"

"There's no future in that. I think we know what's to be done."

"I know, anyway."

He looked at her strangely.

"The other night I asked you a question, and you never did answer me. I asked what you'd do if I stayed here and became one of them."

"Be serious." He took a deep breath. "It's a silly question."

"Then humor me. Answer it. Say I just give you the diary and the documents and let you fight it out with those people back there. It's a coward's way, so call me a coward. But that's something you do much better than I do. It's what keeps you going. I could just disappear. You could tell everyone I'd walked away in the middle of the night. Who'd ever know? And after you got your story, who'd care?"

"It's a fantasy. They'd find you here, just like they found you before."

"Maybe so, but it's my fantasy. It's the only one I've had in a good long time. So think about it, okay? That's all I ask. I've already asked Michael about it. They'd put me up till I found something to do. And that wouldn't take me long, you know. I'm a survivor, Walker. I'd find a man to take care of me, and I don't give a damn how religious they are. Everyone isn't as noble as you are. Or as silly."

Again he was quiet. The silence stretched between them.

"I'm sorry I said that," she said. "We shouldn't be digging at each other. I really do like you."

"I like you too, Joanne."

"In a way I'm glad you didn't sleep with me. Really glad. Because I do like you, and some of that would have been spoiled." She laughed, but Walker saw only sadness in her face. "Something awful will happen if I go back there. I can feel it. So what I'm saying is, I'm dumping it all on you. It's all yours now, and God knows you asked for it. In the morning you can take the files with you, but you'll be going alone. Take the gun too; I don't want it anymore. I'm staying, Walker. You can tell them where I am, but you'll be signing my death warrant if you do. I'm staying in either case."

There wasn't anything more to say. They walked across the field to Michael's house, and Joanne told Michael that Walker would be leaving in the morning alone. Later they went to bed. She offered to take the floor, but he wouldn't have it. They didn't talk any more. In the morning, Walker was up before dawn, his mind groping with all the problems of his day. Trudy fixed him a breakfast of eggs and bacon and wheat cakes. Neither of the younger Yoders questioned him. Joanne walked with him to the edge of the yard, then leaned over and kissed his cheek.

"So long," she said. "And good luck."

He didn't look back. He walked quickly between the rows until the hill rose up ahead of him. Slowly, as he crossed it, the big house came into view, then the roof of the barn where the car was. He stopped, aware of something strange. A noise somewhere, a car coming toward him. He dropped low in the field as the car turned in from the blacktop road and ran up under the trees toward the house.

It stopped about a hundred yards from where he crouched. The door opened and Al Donovan got out.

Twenty

Donovan knew about the powers of love and hate, but he had never seen hate demonstrated so vividly as that Friday night. He and Lord had been on the phone, double-checking a report that Walker and the Sayers girl had been seen in Tennessee, when Armstrong walked in. Perhaps walked was too strong a word. Armstrong simply came in, less than forty-eight hours out of surgery. He looked pale and ill, but he was on his feet and he didn't stagger. The gods had been with him on both counts. The first bullet had slipped past his throat, just missing the jugular, and exited under his ear. Of the two, that was the lesser. That parting shot she had given him, that goodbye kiss as the elevator door was closing, that was the baby intended to kill. Luckily it had caught him twisting around. It had smashed his lowest rib, then burrowed its way down, snuggling, nestling and finally stopping between folds of intestine. The smashed bone hurt like hell, and would for some time, but it had saved him: slowed the bullet just enough to stop it before any vital organs were punctured. After a four-hour operation in Chicago, Armstrong was placed in a private room and pronounced a very lucky man.

Over the near-violent objections of his doctors, he was gone in the morning. Two FBI men arrived and helped him into a waiting car. He was whisked to O'Hare International for a private flight to New York. Aided by heavy doses of painkiller, he slept on the plane, and was helped off in a wheelchair. That was early Friday. He was taken to a hotel near Prospect Park, and registered there by one o'clock. That gave him time for a few hours' rest before he walked the half block to the FBI resident agency and came in on Donovan and Lord.

It hurt Armstrong to move. Breathing hurt. The heavy bandage around his ribs and gut gave him pain every minute. It especially hurt to talk. His voice had been affected by the bullet's path, though he was assured it was only temporary. His voice came out as a raspy threat. Everything he said was a threat, as if two tiny devils were fighting with flat bastard files deep down in his throat. If Donovan thought he saw hate in the black eyes of Armstrong that afternoon, he didn't know the half of it. Armstrong was running on hate.

For the first hour, he communicated mainly with his hands, eyes, and with short messages passed to Donovan and Lord. When he did speak, his voice carried extra menace and authority. He was especially harsh with Donovan. Some of that was undoubtedly Donovan's fault. He hated guys like Donovan. They played it safe all their lives, then they retired and were pampered till they died. They sucked the federal tit for all it was worth, and their biggest value was in the sheer bulk of their manpower. The FBI could find out about anything in minutes, and for that he could thank the mindless idiots like Donovan, who did the donkey work.

Yes, the FBI could find out anything it wanted to know. Except where that goddamned Sayers girl was.

Whenever he thought about the Sayers girl, his fury began anew. That hurt with a pain all its own. Humiliation was not a crown that Armstrong wore with grace. He could only imagine what they were saying in Chicago. He had let the girl slip through his fingers, and all because he had insisted on playing the Lone Ranger. He actually saw red flashes when he thought about it. He had found the girl all by himself, then he let her shoot him and walk away.

He wouldn't be dumb enough to try it alone again. He hurt too much; his reflexes were too slow. There was simply nothing he could do, no position he could take, to make the hurt any better. Either he would hang tough or give it up and go back to bed. And he would never do that, not as long as he could stand, not as long as he could sit up. His hate was too great. He remembered a saying he had used when he was younger, when he had balls of iron and knew he could lick the world. *When it gets too tough for everybody else, it's just right for me.* The thought bolstered him, made him feel flashes of his adolescent heroism, but the pain was as bad as ever.

He sat in the tiny room that Donovan used for an office, and read for the fifth time the stories that Walker had filed from Chicago. Walker had fired his best shot, and they were still in the game. Essentially it was the toothless part of the story, sensational on its face but proving nothing, identifying nobody, meandering harmlessly around specifics and hinting of more to come. Since then, nothing. The *Tribune* had heard nothing from Walker since that first day, if Donovan's contacts were right. Yes, he had to admit it: sometimes those press contacts did pay off. Surrounding yourself with pricks was the price you paid for it.

Donovan simply hadn't believed Walker's story. He believed that Joanne Sayers was forcing him to write it. Armstrong knew better. He knew that guys like Walker needed no forcing. They enjoyed embarrassing the Bureau, exposing the idiots who had made a slip. What made reporters so unbearable was that they did what they did not out of loyalty or patriotism, not even out of any professional ethic, when you got right to the heart of it. It was glory, plain and simple. The lust for a big story, and fuck anybody who got in the way. He had never known any reporter who would give up a truly big story for *any* reason. That was what they lived on, those coal-black headlines that somehow never really told the truth of anything. They were lice, so dishonest and yet so, so self-righteous when it came to their sacred First Amendment. And guys like this Walker were the worst of the lot.

Again Armstrong went through the file on Walker. Agents in New York had been compiling it all week long. He sifted through the items, and occasionally looked out into the street and thought about the girl.

Not the Sayers girl. That other one, that beauty with the dark hair who had gone to the bank and almost led him to his death. A hostage? That had been his first thought, but as time went on it became more and more unlikely. Lord had done some extensive cross-country checking between New York and Philadelphia, Philadelphia and Chicago, Chicago and New York. Nothing. There were no missing persons of her description during the past week. If not a hostage, then what? A friend of the Sayers woman? Again, possible but unlikely. A friend of Walker's? Armstrong didn't have great hope for that either. He called Lord in and listened again to his report on Joanne Sayers. Everything was negative. She had no friends at work, had associated with no one outside the plant. She did her job, showed up on time, took little sick leave. She worked straight through her coffee breaks and left half an hour early as compensation. Nobody knew her. It was the same story with the neighbors. So he turned his mind again to Walker, and hit pay dirt at once. He called Walker's landlady, a nosy old dame who remembered seeing a woman going up to Walker's flat last Saturday. The description definitely didn't fit Sayers. The girl had worn a raincoat, and the landlady thought her hair was dark. She had been tall, and had come to Walker's in the late afternoon.

Then she had been with Walker from the beginning. A girlfriend maybe, some shack job. A whore Walker had brought in for the night. The file on Walker had indicated a hit-or-miss sex life for the past few years. Nothing really steady, nothing of any duration. The girl might be a one-night stand, which would make it tougher. Some piece of fluff that had walked in out of the night from God knew where, and had planned on walking out again a few hours later. Only Joanne Sayers had shown up. That would explain the tension he had seen in the girl as she came to the bank. It might explain why Sayers had left her a note on the front seat, making her drive around the block in order to expose any tail. What it didn't explain was why the girl didn't just drive away. How about that, Armstrong? If this was just some whore off the street, why didn't she keep on going once she had the car, the keys and no gun against her head? Why would she care what happened to Walker?

Damn good question, and the idea of something casual just didn't wash. The only answer was personal involvement, something the files didn't show. The girl either knew Sayers or Walker well enough that she could be trusted not to run out. Suddenly his chips were on Walker.

He pushed the buzzer and asked the girl to send Donovan in. His words were part gasp, part groan.

"We're working on the theory that Walker has a girl-friend along for the ride. A special girlfriend."

Donovan's face was blank.

"You knew him pretty well," Armstrong said. "Do you know any special girls he went out with?"

"I didn't know him that well."

"Well enough to have him to your house."

"Who told you that?"

"It's in his file. It says he came to your house for dinner a few years ago, when he was working for *Newsday*."

Donovan looked at the file with suspicion and some resentment. "That's a long time ago."

Armstrong nodded and grinned with pain. "I've got to check everything."

Donovan went out. For a full minute Armstrong stared at the door. Then, in a raspy whisper, he said, "You lying son of a bitch." He pushed the red button, Donovan's private line. He looked up the number and called Donovan's home.

Kim answered on the third ring.

"Mrs. Donovan, this is Armstrong. Is your husband there?"

"Why no, Mr. Armstrong. Isn't he with you?"

"No, ma'am. I'm sure he'll be back soon. But right now we're working a new line on the Joanne Sayers case, and I needed to ask him some questions. It's possible that the Sayers woman took Walker's girl-friend along with them."

"Diana?"

"Is that her name?"

"Yes, Diana Yoder."

"Spell that, please." Armstrong wrote it down and said, "This girlfriend. What does she do?"

He took notes while Kim talked. She told him about Radio City and the girl's religious background. "I think she's from Pennsylvania," she said.

"Could you describe her, Mrs. Donovan?"

"Very nice-looking. Tall, maybe five-ten in low heels. I remember her telling me she just made the height limitation for a Rockette. Hundred twenty-five pounds. Very intelligent, lots of interests."

"What about her hair?"

"Black. Or very dark brown. And bluish eyes."

"Have you been in touch with her at all this week?"

"No, not since last week. We had them over to dinner."

"I see. Thank you, Mrs. Donovan."

He called Radio City. Someone there told him that Diana Yoder had quit her job without notice and hadn't been heard from in more than a week. She had called in Monday, the day she was supposed to have reported back after a week off.

He buzzed and asked for Kevin Lord. While Lord waited in the chair facing Donovan's desk, Armstrong got another agent moving on the Diana Yoder development. "Get over to Radio City right away," he said into the telephone. "Find out everything they have on a Diana Yoder." He spelled the last name. "I want everything, where she's from, where she lives, who she sleeps with, what kind of food she likes. Don't say anything to anybody. Just get that information and get it fast. I don't care if you've got to interview those broads in the middle of a show. Call me as soon as you've got anything."

He hung up and faced Kevin Lord. He clenched his hands and hunched forward over Donovan's desk, shifting his weight in an effort to relieve the pain.

"You've come a long way in five years, haven't you, kid?" Armstrong said.

Lord's eyes were cold. "I've done all right."

"You've played your hand right, been careful, stayed out of trouble."

Lord waited, watching him.

"You know how the world works, don't you?" Armstrong said.

"I try to keep my eyes open."

"All right, then." Armstrong sat back, emitting a deep groan. "All right. I need your help."

Lord's mouth twitched in involuntary eagerness.

"You understand what I'm saying?" Armstrong said.

"I think so."

"Let's be very sure," Armstrong said. "This game's liable to get a little messy before it's finished. How far are you willing to go with it?"

Lord smiled. "For what end?"

Armstrong grunted a laugh out. Lord was a cool one. Much cooler than he had thought.

"To help the Bureau get those papers back."

"I'm willing to do whatever it takes."

Now Armstrong smiled. "And to help keep the girl quiet."

Lord hesitated only a few seconds. "Whatever it takes," he said.

"Good," Armstrong said. "Let's talk about that."

They were in conference for a long time when the call came in. Armstrong talked on his private line for ten minutes, then Armstrong and Lord came out and left the office. "You sit tight," Armstrong said to Donovan. "If Walker calls, try to keep him on long enough to get a trace. I'll be calling in."

They went down the hall. Donovan sat there until he heard the faint, unmistakable closing of the elevator door. Suddenly he was full of turmoil. The tension wound tighter inside him. When he was sure they were gone, he went into his office. He felt strangely like a sneak. Even the secretary, he thought, looked at him suspiciously as he closed the door behind him. He sat at his desk, then lifted the telephone and unscrewed

John Dunning

the mouthpiece. The tap was still there, where he had put it months before. It fed by wire into a tiny recorder hidden in a false bottom of his desk.

It was voice-activated. When the phone wasn't in use, it recorded anything that was said in the room. Donovan rewound the tape and played it back. Everything that had happened since Armstrong returned. It took him a while to hear it all. Armstrong's call to Kim. The call to Radio City. The conversation with Kevin Lord, and another call in from an agent at Radio City, less than ten minutes ago. Finally the call to Kennedy, booking flight for two to Lancaster, Pennsylvania.

It was true. Walker's story was true after all.

He turned off the machine and stared out into the darkening street. There was no doubt in his mind what was to happen now. Joanne Sayers would die. So might Walker and the Yoder girl, and anyone else who happened to be there. And the funny thing was that neither Armstrong nor Lord had once mentioned killing. They didn't have to. They spoke the same language, and it was a language that Donovan, for all his shortcomings, understood only too well.

He called Kim and told her he was being sent out of town, and would be home in a day or two.

Then he called the various airlines, until he found one leaving thirty minutes ahead of Armstrong's flight. He fished around in his wallet for his credit cards, and used the personal card, leaving untouched the one he used for Bureau work. He booked passage for one, reading off the digits to the girl at the airport.

When the girl asked, he told her to make it one-way. There was no telling how long this might take.

Almost as an afterthought, he erased the phone calls from the tape.

Twenty-one

Walker squirmed through the deep plowed earth, back down the hill toward the farmhouse he had just left. The hill rose behind him, hiding him from Donovan's eyes. Soon he got to his feet and began to run. A predawn fog was settling in over the land, sealing the houses in a gray shroud. Walker leaped the fence and ran across Michael Yoder's yard. He stopped near the edge of the house and listened. Somewhere he could hear Trudy, humming softly to herself.

He waited, but he didn't hear Joanne and she didn't come. At last he moved up onto the porch and knocked. Trudy came and peered through the glass.

She opened the door. "Mr. Walker, I thought you'd gone."

"Where's Joanne?"

"She went for a walk after you left."

"Which way?"

"Down by the river, I imagine. She said she likes to walk down there." She came out onto the porch. "Is there anything I can do? You look so upset."

"I am upset. I've got to find Joanne."

"I'm sorry . . ."

He walked to the edge of the porch and looked out across the field toward the river, now sealed in with fog. When he turned to her again, she was standing about five feet away, looking pale and anxious.

"Something's wrong, I can feel it," she said. "Mr. Walker, you look like death itself."

"Where's Michael?" he said.

"He went over to Abe's house. The men are raising a barn."

"Where is that?"

"Straight out through the trees." She pointed behind her. "Across the paved road, about a mile down."

"Trudy, do you think you could go over there too?"

"What for? Mr. Walker, you're scaring me."

He came toward her, knowing now that she had to be told. "Some people are looking for us. For Joanne especially. They may come here."

"What people?"

"I don't know. They may say they're police. Maybe FBI agents."

"Are they?"

"I don't know what they are."

She shivered visibly.

"Trudy." Walker spoke slowly now, deliberately. "Joanne's life may be in danger. Did she say anything to you about where she might be going?"

Her eyes went wide. "No, nothing. I wish I could help you."

"You can." He went to the other end of the porch and looked out toward the road. "Go to Abe's. Say you felt like walking. Say anything you want. Only don't tell anyone what I've just told you. Can you do that?"

"I'll get my coat."

He watched her hurry away along the dirt road toward the highway. At the bottom of the porch steps he began searching for Joanne's footprints. He found them in the field, just beyond the fence, and followed them across the endless furrows of earth toward the river. At the riverbank, he began to go double-time. The sun had come up, squatting just above the trees ahead, but the fog was too heavy to burn off and the sun hung behind it like a pale ball. Walker trotted evenly until the land broke away from the water, separated by a series of bogs and marshes. The path ran like a backbone along the river's edge, with the marsh to his left. He had long since lost her trail, and was going now by instinct. The marsh expanded as he went along, separating him from the field by a broadening gulf. Then the fog closed in around him, and he couldn't see the field at all.

He came to a bridge, built, he guessed, the way everything was here: by three dozen hands, all at once. It spanned the river, and the dry path continued through the marsh on the other side. He hurried across, into where the marsh grass grew in thick around his shoulders. For perhaps fifty yards trees grew down close and formed a tunnel over the path. In a pool of soft earth he found a footprint, and it spurred him on. The path meandered in and out, then broke away from the riverbed for a straight run north, away from the water. He emerged into a field, just like Jacob Yoder's. A hill sloped upward gradually, and just over the top he could see the red-and-white roof of a farmhouse.

Smoke poured from the chimney. In the yard was a buggy, all hitched up and ready to travel. Walker skirted the field and picked up her trail again. She had gone carefully, so as not to trample the plowed rows. He followed her tracks in a long arc toward the house. The fog enveloped the house, outlining it like a ghost as he came nearer. One of the windows glowed, with that distinctive yellow that suggested an oil lamp. He broke away from his place at the edge of the trees and ran across the clearing to the corner of the yard.

From there it was a quick sprint to the window. He heard an old woman's voice asking if she could pour more tea. Joanne said, "Yes, thank you." Walker eased along the side of the building until his head was just below the windowsill.

"It's nice of you to invite me in again," Joanne said. "I hadn't intended to stop by this early."

"No bother," the old woman said. "We don't get many people over here anymore. When they were all youngsters, they used to come here all the time, fresh from swimming in the river, the three Yoder boys and their sister. What a joy to see her last Sunday. Now we never see any of them, except at church."

"That's their loss," Joanne said.

"Ours too," the old woman said. "Ours too."

"I love your country. And your Church."

They were quiet for a while. Walker stood for perhaps a minute, and the only sounds were the clinking of teacups.

"I'm thinking of settling here," Joanne said. "Of maybe joining the Church."

"That's nice. Maybe you could persuade some of the children to come visit us again. We never had any of our own."

"You people here have got it made," Joanne said. "You have a simplicity I've never seen anywhere else."

Now a man's voice chimed in. "If it's simplicity you want, you've found it. We don't have much, but we've got that."

"It's enough," Joanne said.

"Except for the young," the old woman said. "That's never enough for the young."

"Maybe they just haven't seen enough of the real world," Joanne said. "When they do, they'll be back."

"She may be right," the man said. "Look at Diana Yoder."

Walker moved forward toward the door. Then a movement far out in the field caught his eye, and he flattened against the house and held still. Something black formed against the gray woods. It solidified, stood up and became . . . a man.

He was too far away yet to be recognizable. He was moving in Walker's trail, skirting the edge of the field where the trees were. He came fast, with confidence, moving as if he belonged here. Walker dropped to the ground and rolled under the house.

He waited, looking out under the wood steps. He heard the man before he saw him: the crisp crunch of feet on autumn underbrush. Something unhooked and a gate swung open, and Walker saw a pair of feet coming toward him. He was dressed in the clothes of a city man, with slacks that could double for work or casual, a dark sports jacket and a pullover sweater under it. The jacket was unbuttoned in spite of the cold and he walked loosely, his hands swinging at his sides. He made no effort to conceal himself, but marched up onto the porch and knocked. Footsteps sounded above Walker's head. A chair scraped and someone—the old man—got up. The door opened and a muffled exchange of dialogue filtered down through the floor.

Sorry to bother you. I was looking for the Yoder place. There was something about the voice. Walker didn't know it well, but he had heard it somewhere.

The old man. *Which one? The county's full of them.*

The man hesitated, as if at a momentary loss. *Michael Yoder, I believe the name is.*

Another pause. Walker could almost see it: the old Amish farmer, staring curiously at the newcomer, unable to understand why some outsider would come looking for Michael Yoder. They had no business with outsiders, none of them. Then Joanne spoke up. *I'm staying with him.* Walker could hardly keep from groaning. She came out onto the porch. "I'll show you where he is," she said.

The stranger said that was kind of her. He didn't offer to find it himself; didn't offer to do anything but let her lead him off into the woods. She got her coat and again thanked her hostess. The old woman asked her to come back.

She came down the steps, and Walker could hear her clearly. "The shortest way is straight out there, through those trees and across the river. Come on."

The stranger lagged a few steps behind her. They went through the gate and started across the field.

They had reached the edge of the woods before Joanne's alarm sensors went off. Suddenly something about the man didn't ring true. Once she grasped that basic fact, everything seemed to go wrong at once. The man's appearance, the strange looks on the faces of Mr. and Mrs. Miller as she left with him. Perhaps most of all, her own instinct. The spell of the land had dulled it. The Amish life-style coaxed, soothed, assured her that everything was all right. Walker's departure had meant the end of all that running, all that hiding, all that fear.

Now she saw the truth of what Walker had told her. There was no escaping the past. She was fooling herself. All she knew at this moment was that she didn't want to go through the woods with this man. She stopped and looked back, hoping to see someone in the Millers' backyard. All she saw was him, coming along about ten yards behind her. She smiled uneasily, but he didn't smile back. His eyes were black and bottomless, his hands fine and delicate as they hung limply at his sides. "It's right through there," she said, pointing. "You follow the path and cross the bridge, then follow the river path on the other side. When it blends into the field, you turn right and go up the hill. You can't miss it."

"But I did miss it. That's the way I came, and the people I talked to said they'd never heard of Michael Yoder."

Now she was alarmed. "That's crazy. Even if you'd gotten the wrong house, everybody around here knows Michael."

"Maybe they just don't want to tell a stranger."

She thought about that. That was feasible. There was so much about these farmers that she didn't know. They might not tell this stranger anything. He might be telling the truth.

"Can I ask you something? Something that's none of my business?"

"If it makes you feel better."

"What's your business with Michael?"

"I'm with Internal Revenue. We've been trying to contact Michael Yoder for months, but he has no phone and doesn't answer our letters. Would you like to see my identification?"

She nodded. "No offense."

He took out his wallet and withdrew a plastic card. It looked official. It identified him as an IRS investigator whose date of employment was March 3, 1973. His birthdate indicated that he was in his mid-twenties. The picture in the upper corner was a good likeness. The name of the bearer was Samuel A. Stoner.

Still she hesitated.

"Your friend isn't in any trouble," he said. "In fact, he's overpaid his taxes for three years running. He's got money coming back. That's why I'm here."

She nodded, but her heart wouldn't calm down. "Yes," she said. Her mouth was dry. "I'll show you."

She hurried into the woods. Behind her, he had to

hurry to keep up. She reached the bridge before she looked back. He was there, about twenty yards behind. She rushed across the bridge and took to the path. The marshes closed in, then the field, stretching away to her right. She started up the hill at a half-run, leaping gingerly across the rows of earth. Slowly, the house appeared on the horizon.

"That's it straight ahead," she said. "You can make it on your own from here."

She had stopped and so had he. His eyes never left her face. She pointed to Michael's house, but he didn't move. Nestled under the trees, just outside Michael's front door, was a black car. One man sat in front, on the rider's side.

"You're not from the IRS."

"No," he said.

"And your name isn't Stoner."

"No, my name isn't Stoner."

The horror of it came over her slowly. The accumulation of years spent running and hiding knotted up inside her, and now at the end she couldn't even cry. "Oh my God," she said. She backed away toward the house. He stepped into the furrowed earth and came toward her.

By the time Walker reached the bridge, they were gone. The vastness of Michael Yoder's rented field stretched out before him, as empty as a great ocean. He had no trouble finding where they had gone. Joanne had taken those long, careful strides, while the stranger had made a mess wherever his feet had come down. He saw the place, about a hundred yards from the house, where they had stood and talked. Then they had gone up the hill, through the gate and into Michael's yard.

There was no one at the house. A faint smell of exhaust hung in the air, as though a car had just left.

So they had her, then, and there was nothing he could do about it. All he could do was jump ahead to the next step, snatch the files and run. As long as he had the files, they all still had a chance.

Trudy had reached the narrow blacktop highway and had gone about a quarter mile west toward Abe's place when the car came. She stood in a thicket and watched the car turn in her driveway. It was just as Walker had said, and it frightened her. She clutched her hand against her throat and waited, but the car didn't come out.

At last the fear got to her. She climbed the rise to the road and set off again toward Abe's, driven now by a new sense of urgency. She wouldn't soon forget that look in Walker's eyes as he told her about Joanne.

She reached a bend in the road. Far ahead, she saw the dirt road that led back to Abe's farm. She began to run. Soon she heard the pounding of a dozen hammers. The sounds intermingled with her racing heart as she came into Abe's yard. A handsaw was biting through wood as she came around the house and beheld Abe Yoder's new barn. The framing was complete, and fifteen Amish men were hard at work on the roof. There wasn't a woman in sight, and suddenly she knew she could never keep Walker's secret, that the need to explain herself would be thrust upon her. Even now, Jacob Yoder had seen her and had stopped sawing. He came toward her, his eyes narrowing to slits.

"Well, miss, what brings you here?"

She opened her mouth, but no sound came out. Jacob put a gentle arm over her shoulder and led her to the water dipper, but even after she had drunk deeply, her voice would not come. Jacob took her over near the house, under a shade tree.

"Take your time," he said. But there was alarm in

his eyes as he waited for his daughter-in-law to speak her piece. She never did get it all out. She made him understand that two men had come and had frightened her. He patted her shoulder in a rare display of affection and told her to go inside and rest.

From the window in Abe's room, she watched as he said something to one of the men, then hitched up his buckboard and drove away alone. She had seen it in his face, that alarm that came and went and came again. He was thinking about Diana, alone at home. He was going to pick Diana up.

She took comfort from his involvement, and she did rest then. She sat in a chair in the cool, dark room and closed her eyes. Jacob had always been like some giant to her, some invulnerable god. Everything would be all right now.

Fog still shrouded Jacob Yoder's house as Walker arrived. He crept along the fence toward the barn, watching for any movement, listening for any noise. There was nothing. Donovan's car was gone, and Walker didn't know if that was a good omen or bad. He hurried across the yard to the barn door and slipped inside. The station wagon was where he had left it. Inside, Joanne's cloth bag rested in the middle of the back seat.

He ripped it open. The gun was gone. He dropped to his knees and looked under the front seat. The files were gone too.

So they had it all, the files, Joanne, all the missing pieces. Everything but Walker. Maybe they didn't care about Walker anymore. Maybe now he could be marked past tense and forgotten. Without the Dawes file, he had no real bite. But that could also be said of Joanne. Even more so of Joanne. Her word alone would have less than zero credibility. It seemed pointless to kill her and leave Walker alive. Far better, from their viewpoint, either to kill them both or leave them both alive. If alive, they could simply destroy the files and deny everything. Stonewall it. Who could prove anything? On the surface, that seemed like the best bet, until Walker stopped to consider the human element. Their hatred for Joanne must be immense. It had colored everything they had done for years.

He remembered something she had said, somewhere along the way. They never kill for revenge. They don't work that way. But really, what did Joanne know?

Just now, Walker wasn't so sure.

He opened the door and stared out at the house. It looked quiet, deserted, in the early morning fog. Nothing moved anywhere.

He hesitated for less than a minute, then he walked out of the barn and up the front porch steps. His soft knocking sounded hollow inside, as if the house had been empty for a long time. Houses were something like people that way. Leave them alone for any length of time and they began to sound different. Then they began to look different. And they began to decay.

But no, he heard something. A single movement, a creak of board as someone moved inside. Someone trying very hard to be quiet. He remembered his first day here, how the floors creaked when he walked on them. There was no way to move in this house without making noise. He backed away toward the steps and saw a curtain flutter, just enough for someone to look out without being seen. He saw a flash of hand and a white cuff. A man's hand.

He moved down the steps, but the door opened before he had reached the bottom.

Donovan.

For much of a minute they stood there like that, looking at each other. Donovan's right hand was partly hidden behind his leg, indicating a weapon of some kind, and Walker's eyes went from that to the old agent's face and back. Donovan didn't move, but there was something in his manner that wouldn't let Walker move either, some vague threat that Walker had never seen in his friend's face. Was that why he had run when he first saw Donovan as he came across the field? He didn't know. He only knew that suddenly, somewhere between Chicago and Pennsylvania, he had begun thinking like Joanne. Everyone was the enemy. Now his pulse ran fast and his face felt flush as they waited for each other to speak.

Donovan broke the silence. "Better come in, Walker. We're liable to have more company."

He went up the steps and inside. Diana sat against the far wall, in one of her father's straight-backed chairs. On the table between them was the Dawes file, opened, its pages sorted and turned back in various places. Walker turned, and saw that Donovan's hand was empty. But his coat hung open, and the gun was in easy reach.

"I'll have to be more careful," Donovan said. He motioned Walker to a chair near Diana. "I thought I'd know if anyone came here, but you snuck up on me."

"You can't look out of every window at once, Al," Walker said. He gestured toward the files. "I see you've been busy."

"Well, you've got to admit it's a fascinating story. What do they call it in the newsroom?"

"A helluva story."

Donovan smiled. "Anyway, I had to see what Armstrong was so rabid about."

"Now you know. So what are you gonna do about it?"

"Take you back. All three of you. And these." He gestured slightly toward the open file.

"Why me?" Diana said. "Why do I have to go back?"

Donovan looked at her for a long moment before replying. When he did speak, his answer was no answer at all.

"I think you know why."

He moved to the window and looked out, then crossed to the side of the room and looked down the road toward the highway. His nerves seemed to be building as he came back to the table and turned a page of Dawes' journal. A moment later he closed the book, unable to concentrate. Walker guessed, from the number of pages turned facedown on the table, that Donovan had read enough. Walker looked at Diana. In the dark room, her features were vague and noncommittal. The light from a far window made the fine hair under her jaw stand out like some silver frame. And Walker found himself wondering what she could possibly be thinking, and how she felt about things now. He wondered if he would ever know.

"Where are your people?" he said.

"My father's at Abe's. They're building a barn. Mother's over at Susan's place. They're working on a quilt."

"Then you're home alone."

"Yes."

Again, Donovan checked the windows. He seemed dissatisfied and did it again, going all around the house. Walker's sudden arrival had unnerved him, and he stepped softly, like a cat, but still leaving those telltale creaks wherever he walked.

"Expecting somebody, Al?"

Donovan looked at him without amusement. "Keep still," he said.

"Oh, sure. You act like I don't have any interest in how things work out. Just keep still and let whatever happens happen. You don't think they're going to let you do what you're planning to do?"

"We'll have to see, won't we?"

"What happened to the Donovan who always played it safe?"

"He's right here, Walker. Still playing by the book."

"I don't see any book."

Donovan tapped his head. "It's in here."

Walker was silent for a moment. "Al," he said. "They've changed the rules on you. Don't look now, but the book doesn't cover this."

"Sure it does. You just don't know it like I do."

"There's no arguing with you," Walker said. "They'll use your goddamn book to bury you. I hope you're ready to retire, old friend."

"Don't worry about me."

Donovan moved to the side window and stood watching the long, empty road.

"You haven't asked me about Sayers," Walker said.

"I assume they've got her."

"You don't seem too excited about it."

Donovan shook his head. "They won't hurt her. Even Armstrong isn't that stupid."

"I'm not convinced."

"Nothing's going to happen until they've got their hands on these papers. You can be damned certain of that, Walker. I know how minds like Armstrong's work."

"If that's true, why don't the three of us split? We can be in New York by early afternoon."

Donovan looked at him, then turned back to the window.

"Better make up your mind soon, Al, before it's too late."

"It already is."

Walker stood and peered through the side window. Far away, he could just see the black car, turning in from the highway.

There were three of them in the car: even from across the room, Walker could see that. He moved toward the window, hoping for a better look, but Donovan waved him back. The car came toward them, and disappeared from Walker's view under the windowsill. A moment later he heard a door slam, and again the sound of those long-striding feet on crisp leaves. Donovan moved back from the window.

"He's coming in," he said. "I want you two to do exactly as I say. Let him in. String him along. Try to get him talking. I'll be in the bedroom, just a few feet away."

"What about the files?" Walker said.

"Leave them right where they are."

"Al, you know what he'll do."

"I want to be sure. I need that, Walker. If you don't understand that, I'm sorry. But for both your sakes, you'd better play by my rules."

Donovan slipped back into the bedroom and closed the door. At the same instant they heard footsteps on the front porch. The young one, Kevin Lord, came in without knocking. He opened the door a crack, then came into the large room. His gun was in his hand, and in one continuous sweep his eyes took in Walker, Diana, the papers on the table and the closed bedroom door. None of them moved for perhaps thirty seconds. Then, so softly that it was almost inaudible, Lord said, "Hello, Walker. You look just like your pictures."

Lord came closer and wet his lips with his tongue. His eyes came to rest again on the files.

"Run out of places to hide?"

Walker didn't say anything.

Lord looked at Diana. His eyes held hers as he said, "And this would be Miss Diana Yoder, of Radio City fame?"

Still they didn't move or talk. Lord again looked around the room.

"Who else is here with you?"

"No one," Diana said, too quickly.

Lord, keeping the gun pointed somewhere between them, eased sideways toward the closed bedroom door.

"Better not go in there," Walker said.

Lord stopped.

"They keep a monster in there," Walker said.

He resumed his slow movement toward the door, reached it, opened it and looked inside for a moment.

"I told you," Diana said, more naturally now.

She didn't falter, and Walker could see it in Lord's eyes as he bought her lie. He moved to the side window and motioned with his hands. A moment later Armstrong arrived, coming awkwardly up the steps with his double burden of Joanne Sayers and constant pain. He pushed in the door and slammed it hard against the inner wall. He thrust Joanne into the room ahead of him, keeping a tight grip on her ponytail with his free hand while holding the gun in his right. Her eyes were wide with fear. Armstrong didn't say anything. He pushed her to the floor and moved to the table. His fingers flipped through the pages, pausing in places. Several minutes passed while he looked through the papers. Then he looked at Malcolm Dawes' diary, satisfied himself that it was intact and put everything into the large brown envelope.

"So much trouble over one crazy agent," Lord said.

It was the only warning they had. The end of something, the beginning of something else. A simple transitory sentence, closing the book on Malcolm Dawes and his little brew of trouble. Only the people lingered now, to be disposed of by jail . . . or something else. There was never any question in Walker's mind which it would be. Just as Joanne knew, had known all along, by now the truth was so obvious that even Diana understood and believed it. In those last few seconds, Walker knew that Donovan had over-played his hand. If he had planned on a grand appearance on cue, there would be no cue. Donovan would arrive too late, and someone would die. Armstrong never spoke. His eyes seemed to change shape, very briefly and only slightly. Walker was already in motion as Armstrong leveled his gun on Joanne. He grabbed Diana around the waist and rolled to the floor. His sudden move distracted Armstrong, who turned and put a bullet through the wall where they had just sat. That was Donovan's cue. He stepped into the room, and his appearance was so unexpected, so stunning that for a full ten seconds neither Lord nor Armstrong could react. They just stood there, and it might have been late one morning in Brooklyn, a brief lull after a day of busywork, three agents stand-ing a room apart, wondering where to go for lunch. Unable to resolve it, they began killing each other. Strangely, it was Lord who moved first. Perhaps in panic, perhaps out of inexperience, he jerked his hand up and Donovan killed him where he stood. Lord twisted and jerked, pumping three shots into the floor while he died.

Donovan was facing his first man with a gun, after forty years in the FBI. The irony that the man was a colleague had long since lost its effect. The man was just a thug, a punk with a gun, and he was Donovan of the FBI. He felt almost invincible as Kevin Lord crumpled at his feet. The feeling dissolved as Arm-strong fired, catching him high in the chest. Donovan didn't feel the second bullet, didn't even hear it, though he knew he had been hit. He dropped to the floor and tried to roll over for another shot, but Armstrong had disappeared. Donovan came to rest on his back, staring up at the dark ceiling, which spun crazily in spite of the dark. He saw faces there. Kim's.

Walker's. That crazy goddamn guy in Nowater, Arizona. Southworth. Barney Southworth. Saw his face now, as clearly as if it had just happened yesterday.

And J. Edgar Hoover. Unchanging, beady eyes staring, pinched mouth walled between two mountainous jowls.

Donovan blinked. With an immense heave, he rolled over and faced the door. They were all gone. Walker. Diana. Sayers. Armstrong. Gone where? Then he remembered. The Yoder girl had grabbed the files and made a run for it. In that final shootout between himself and Armstrong they had all run out, and now Armstrong had gone after them.

The door opened and in the light Donovan saw an immense man wearing the work clothes, black hat and chin whiskers of the Amish farmer. The man said something. Donovan could sense the fear and urgency in the voice, but he couldn't make out the words. Everything seemed so faint, so far away. For a moment the man seemed afraid to touch him, as if death itself might be contagious. Then he kneeled at Donovan's side and looked into his face. *Diana.* The man had said Diana's name.

Donovan tried to look at the door. He tried to tell the man that Diana was gone, but he honestly didn't know if he made it. Some of the words came, some didn't. He knew he said the word *killer,* loud and clear. It seemed to strike the man like a fist. The farmer recoiled as if he had been slapped. Donovan clutched at the pale blue shirt. With a last great heave, he rolled over and put his gun in the big man's hand.

It was a small automatic. Jacob Yoder dropped it to the floor, as he might drop a hot iron. For the first time in his life, he felt an air of evil all around him.

He went out onto the porch. There were no signs or sounds to tell him where they might have gone. He went to the barn, but all was quiet there. Almost quiet. He stopped and listened, and his keen ears picked up the sound of heavy breathing. Unarmed, he moved back into the dark barn, his eyes probing far back beyond the shadows. He saw some movement in a haystack, and as he came closer Joanne Sayers emerged from the dark.

"Where is Diana?"

Either she didn't know or wouldn't say. Jacob left her there. He strolled quickly from the barn and stood by the fence at the edge of his field, his gray eyes trying to penetrate the fog that still covered the bogs. Where would his daughter run, if she wanted to hide away?

He was saved the trouble of figuring it out by the sound of gunfire. Three shots, coming up from the river. He started across the field, then stopped, ran back to the house and picked up the dead man's gun. "Father, forgive me," he said. He stuck the gun into his pants, just under the suspenders, and took off at a frantic run across the field.

Donovan hadn't gone down easy. Armstrong had shot him three times, and Donovan had shot back at least that many. In the heat of the moment, Joanne had made a run for it, then Diana. Walker and Diana had been together under the table, but Diana had rolled out, scooped up the Dawes files and bolted out the front door. By the time Walker reached the porch, she was over the fence and running across the field, a good sixty yards ahead. Walker didn't call to her or try to slow her in any way. The farther away she got, the better. He leaped the fence and tried to keep her in sight as she plunged into the tall grass that grew near the river. Armstrong came out behind him. Walker knew he was there, somewhere back in the yard near the porch. He heard the gun go off and felt the bullet kiss the grass at his feet. He dove to earth and rolled while Armstrong took another shot, and then, in the brief flash of light while he rolled over, he saw Armstrong struggling with the fence. Walker ran the hundred yards to the river path and disappeared in the marsh, running low, hugging his knees as he went. Armstrong would have his work cut out for him now. They could hide in these bogs forever.

But he had failed to reckon with Armstrong's hate. Armstrong came along faster than Walker would have thought possible. Walker heard him, breathing like a bull as he came, laboring with the pain of his two wounds. Periodically he stopped and listened, as Walker did, hoping for some telltale noise as he crept along. The quiet was almost a living thing, and Walker felt certain that Diana, at least, had made it across the bridge and into the woods beyond.

He knew, too, that his own time was limited, that as long as he stayed on this side of the river, Armstrong would surely find him. There was only the one dry path; all Armstrong had to do was keep coming and sooner or later they would meet. He decided to try a run for the other side. At first he ran low. Finally he gave up even that pretense as the path became reinforced with redwood blocks and the cover of marsh fell away. He must have been less than twenty yards from the bridge when he made that last great sprint. Armstrong stood in the grass, holding the gun out at full arm's length. His shot nicked Walker's jaw, and Walker spun and crashed through the railing, flopping headfirst into the water. He swam back against the tide, under the bridge, coming up briefly for air. Through the arch of the bridge he saw Armstrong arrive at the riverbank. He got a good look at the man, perhaps as long as five seconds, before Armstrong saw him and squeezed off two more shots. Armstrong was gaunt and pale. His eyes were wild, and his breathing was raspy. The bandage around his neck had begun coming loose, and Walker saw that blood was soaking through the shirt at beltline.

Then Walker went under again, and Armstrong's two shots tore through the water just above his head. Again he doubled back, swimming toward Armstrong, playing his best chance. If he could get his hands around Armstrong's leg, jerk him off-balance and pull him into the water, it would be all over. He was counting on Armstrong remaining still, a long shot, and on his chance of estimating while swimming under water exactly where that spot was. He wouldn't have a second chance. The tide took him quickly along. His fingers felt the soft mud of the bank. Roots grew out, along with tangles of grass. He pulled himself ahead. Now his lungs demanded relief. The struggle for air almost forced him up too soon. It blunted his judgment, made him more unsure. He stopped and dug in on the bottom of the river. This was it, for better or worse.

He pushed off from the bottom and leaped out of the water. Armstrong was about ten yards back upstream. He had missed. He grabbed some grass and struggled toward the agent, aware that Armstrong's attention had been diverted by something, or someone else. Jacob Yoder had arrived on the riverbank. He stood off from Armstrong, about ten yards away, holding a gun with trembling hands.

"Where's my daughter?" he said. "What have you done with her?"

He never got his answer. Armstrong lifted his gun, and Walker could see Jacob vainly trying to shoot, jerking the trigger, unaware that Donovan, going by the book to the end, had instinctively slipped the safety catch on. Jacob threw down the gun and came at Armstrong unarmed.

The old man wouldn't have had a chance, but Armstrong's first shot was wide. Call it a loss of stamina, a sudden loss of strength, but Walker heard the slug slap into a tree trunk a good ten yards beyond Jacob and to his left. The shot brought Diana to her feet, another few yards away in the marsh. "Stop it!" she screamed. Armstrong whirled, then twisted back for another shot at Jacob. Diana leaped up on his back, tearing at his neck with her hands. By then Walker had worked his way down the riverbank, and had gripped Armstrong by his left ankle. He toppled backward into the river, Diana still clinging to his back. A moment later her dark head broke to the surface.

Armstrong never came up.

Jacob didn't want to talk about it. He threw Donovan's gun into the water before Walker could stop him. Then he took the daughter he had lost once and nearly lost again, and the three of them went back to the house.

Jacob sat on the steps, too stunned to move. In a while, when she was sure Armstrong wasn't with them, Joanne came around the house and joined them on the porch. None of them spoke for a long time, beyond the bare necessity of relating to Joanne what had happened on the riverbank. It must have occurred to Joanne and to Walker at the same time. Armstrong and Lord weren't alone. There were others like them. Malcolm Dawes' diary was full of names, and every name was a threat. But Walker had an answer for that now, as pure and clear-cut as anything he had ever known. Maybe it was inspiration, growing out of shock. Suddenly Dalton Walker knew how to handle this story, and how to make print with it.

He went to the barn, started the station wagon and backed it out into the yard. Joanne waited in the front seat while he went back to the house. He didn't touch Lord. He kneeled beside Donovan and turned his head sideways, padding it with an old quilt. With his thumb and forefinger he fished out Donovan's wallet, and found the airline credit card.

Let the FBI pay for their trip home.

Gently, he put the wallet back in Donovan's coat pocket. He saw the watch, still ticking on Donovan's wrist, and found it strange that the man's watch would still be running while his heart was not. He wanted to strip it off and take it home to Kim, but he left it there. Kim would get it all in time.

It was still early, only quarter to nine. With luck and good connections, they would be home by midafternoon.

A shadow passed over the door. Diana stared down at him.

"We'll be going now," Walker said. "The cops will have to be called."

She nodded absently.

"They'll want me," Walker said. "Tell them I'll be back. I'll do whatever they want, after I've cleared up some things. That won't make them happy, but I can't help it."

"Where are you going?"

"Home. Back to New York."

"Walker . . ." She came toward him. Her eyes were wet and her hand shook. Twice she seemed on the verge of words, and finally she settled for a simple goodbye. She offered her hand and he took it limply.

"You could still come with us," he said.

"Oh, I can't! How can I? Do you think I could just leave him there on the front porch steps with this all around?"

"No, I suppose you couldn't."

"There are other reasons. Don't ask me what they are. I don't know what they are. Dear God, I don't know what's going to happen, so don't ask me anything, okay?"

"Okay."

"At least for now I can breathe again. He's so different . . ." She looked out at the hunched-over form of her father. "When it gets to where I can't breathe, maybe you'll see me back in New York."

That was all they said. Walker put Donovan's credit card in his pocket and went out into the graying sunlight. He got behind the wheel of the blue Plymouth and didn't look back as they drove away toward Lancaster.

Twenty-two

The answer had been there all along, but he had smothered it under his own personality. It meant giving his story away, and that went against everything he was and had been for a dozen years. But Donovan's death and the personal pain Walker felt from that had shown him that he was no longer the reporter, but a participant. It had never been his story, not once he had stripped away the top layer and exposed what lay beneath. His job as a reporter had ended with the burial of a little girl in an unmarked grave. Now that he had accepted that fact, the rest was simple.

He left the Plymouth at the airport and signed in as Al Donovan. Forty minutes later, he and Joanne were on a city-hopping flight to New York, by way of Philadelphia.

They got into Kennedy at two o'clock. Walker rented a car, using the cash in his wallet, and they drove into town. First they went to a photocopy shop, where he ordered a dozen copies of Malcolm Dawes' diary, and the same number of the accompanying file pages. It took more than an hour. In a phone booth a block away, he made his calls. Perhaps out of loyalty,

he called the *Tribune* first. He asked for Jerry Wayne,
swore him to secrecy, then gave him the schedule. He
didn't elaborate; just the bare facts of what was
happening, when and where. He called a friend at the
New York Times and went through the same process.
Then he called the *Post,* the *Daily News* and the
networks. It took him thirty minutes to get them all.

After that there was only the waiting. He and
Joanne went to a drugstore on Seventh Avenue and sat
in a booth drinking Cokes. She was building up to a
good case of nerves. He talked about things far away.
Her childhood. Her little girl Robin. And he kept one
eye on the clock.

At quarter to five, they drove the ten blocks to the
Knickerbocker Hotel. Joanne held the copies in her
lap. He turned a corner and faced a street full of cars.

He hadn't bothered to rent a conference room. He
told the networks to set up right there in the lobby, in
a little circle of chairs that were usually reserved for
guests. They were all there. He could see that already.
Every car parked in the tow-away zone bore press
plates.

"I'm scared," Joanne said.

Walker touched her knee.

He pulled to a stop and left the car running in the
street. Behind him, someone pounded on a horn. He
hurried around and helped Joanne out. He took the
copies out of her hands and held the originals in his
other hand. Far up the street, Jerry Wayne was coming
at a full run.

"Let's get it over with," Walker said.

They pushed through an old-style revolving doorway and walked into chaos. The first person he saw
was Lesley Stahl of CBS. "Hi, Les. I thought you were
in D.C. these days." Her answer was drowned in
voices. Three network cameras were set up facing a
bright wall, and Walker and Joanne were hustled

toward them. A ground swell of print men moved toward them. Walker held them off.

"We have a statement."

He stood in front of the whirring cameras, staring into the smoky eyes of Lesley Stahl of CBS. "Ladies and gentlemen, this is Joanne Sayers."

Then he moved back and let Joanne have the floor. She looked like a child, lost, alone and frightened. Her voice shook as she started to speak. While she talked, Dalton Walker, playing the ultimate flack, drifted around the room and gave the press fresh copies of Malcolm Dawes' diary.

**POCKET BOOKS
PROUDLY PRESENTS**

*THE HOLLAND
SUGGESTIONS*

JOHN DUNNING

**Coming Soon
from
Pocket Books**

The following is a preview of
The Holland Suggestions. . . .

Two separate forces, long since banished from my life and buried, returned that fall to put the nightmare in motion. Naturally, at first I tried to push it away, but once it started, there was no stopping it. Judy brought her pressures to the conscious element; my subconscious did the rest. Before I could begin to understand it I was drawn in and found no way to go but straight ahead to the end of it.

Judy's part, limited as it was, provided the initial impetus. It was Judy who first began to ease my mind—then jolted it—into that early critical examination of my past. Though she never asked specifically about the Holland experiments, her interest in her mother was tied directly to the time when Robert Holland and I were taking those long dips into my id. Either I was too blind to see it in its early stages, or my subconscious had screened it out the way psychologists say it sometimes does for self-protection. Later it became too obvious to ignore. The beginning was probably sometime after Judy's fourteenth birthday, and I began to notice it the following year. Suddenly I saw that she was experimenting, and learning many things about her mother from my reactions to her experiments. She's quite a kid, Judy. She looks so much like her mother that I am still startled when she enters a room without warning. Judy has always looked more like Vivian than me; I guess that's her blessing, but it leaves me a strange feeling of sadness and discontent to carry into my middle life. Dull pain, bone deep, that you can never find and snuff out completely. Judy helped bring part of that to the surface.

Teenage girls are a joy. They seem to develop overnight: Now they're kids, and soon there are breasts and curves, and they're testing the old man's reaction to all the artificial lures of womanhood. Judy tried them all, and I let her do it, with one exception, until it had run its course. The exception was orange lipstick. I just hated that, and I told her so. But Judy has always been a sane kid, and I know she would have abandoned it in a week or so anyway. She settled on a subdued makeup that was almost a replica of Vivian's. How she arrived at it I couldn't then guess, but she was developing an amazing instinct for her mother's taste. I thought it had to be instinct, because I knew—wrongly—that she never got any clue to Vivian's character from me. We never talked of Vivian beyond the fact that she had lived and had once been my wife and was Judy's mother. I didn't know where Vivian was and I had no interest in knowing.

I should pause a minute. I've just caught myself in a lie, and if this is to have any value, I guess it should be done without all the little ego-saving games that people always play. In fact, Vivian has always been the most fascinating woman in my life. I would have suppressed my interest in her then, but deep inside me it has never waned. Vivian has affected my relationships with other women through the years, the most recent being my secretary, Sharon Welles. Sharon blames Judy for that, perhaps with good reason, but Judy was merely the manifestation of Vivian. Vivian has always been my millstone. I still do not feel at ease talking about her or even thinking about her beyond those flashes that have passed through my mind several times a day for fifteen years. So when I first noticed Judy's strong resemblance to her mother, when it became so strong that I could not ignore it any more, I began to watch her growth with a morbid brand of depressed fascination. I was eager to write it off as simple mother-to-daughter physical heredity. Now I find my lack of insight into the needs of my growing daughter terrifying. Early in her life, Judy sensed my inhibitions about Vivian and constructed inhibitions of her own. My hang-up fed her fantasies, and, in a different way, Vivian became the most fascinating woman in Judy's life too. With her only weapon, her looks, she fought my reluctance to discuss it. With an utter lack of material to go on, Judy reconstructed her mother's image for me. It was a slow process of trial and error. But when I first saw her in one of those 1950s sweaters with her lips touched a pale pink and the hair that she always wore in a bun flowing out behind her, my reaction must have gratified her. I dropped my drink down the front of my shirt.

She refined the image slowly, adding and subtracting touches here and there, but never again did she catch me so unprepared as she had that first time. Gradually I learned to live with the fact that Vivian, in the person of our daughter, whom I also loved very much, had come back to me.

When she wasn't being Vivian, Judy was going through all the perils of adolescence. Boys flocked around, and she was in and out of love more times than I thought possible in a school year. We had some very frank talks that year, the kind that most girls have with their mothers, but I think I handled them well. I strived for an open, honest relationship built on mutual respect, and it seemed complete in every aspect except where Vivian was concerned. Judy's spirit is strong, but her mind is reasonable. I could always guide her, but never boss her, and I think she knew that, though she never put it to a test. My strongest influence over her will always be the value she places on my respect. I hope I can keep that forever, though I have to admit I have occasionally abused it. The Vivian problem seemed to be our only serious hang-up. I saw to it that Judy understood about sex at an early age, yet I never failed to marvel at how much solid information she picked up on her own. Street-level sex education in action. When she turned sixteen I suspected that she was going deeper into sexual experimentation than I wanted her to be, and the object of my suspicion—a pimply right guard on the football team—was hardly the man you always hope your daughter will someday bring home. I suspected he was into pot, a rumor I picked up third-hand through the parental grapevine. But I found out how reliable the grapevine was when half the varsity football team was arrested for marijuana possession and Judy's pizza-faced hero was *not* among them. When the cops came crashing through the door, he and Judy were at the movies.

Naturally, she dropped him just as my doubts were beginning to subside.

The second element in the Holland story began on the same day that the first came to a head.

I awoke that morning two hours before the alarm went off. Beyond my bedroom window there was not even a hint of light, yet instantly I was awake and peering through the darkness for some explanation of what had awakened me. I lay there for several minutes, then turned back my blanket and sat on the edge of the bed. Some noise had done it; I was certain of that, because normally, when the house is quiet, I am a sound sleeper. I did hear a noise; sharp, clicking, like the closing of a door in the lower part of the house. I got up and moved to the door, then peeped out into the hall. At the end of the hallway Judy's door stood open, and the small nightlamp at the head of her bed was on. I moved quietly to the head of the stairs, looked into her room and, satisfied that she was not there, went downstairs. A light was on in the kitchen, and there was a half-finished glass of milk on the table. The back door stood open a crack; it does that unless you slam it hard. I stood just inside the doorway and looked outside. Judy was sitting alone in my backyard workshop. The inside of the workshop was dark, but I could clearly see the round whiteness of her face as she sat at my work table and looked out through the window. I stepped outside and felt the cold night air penetrate my pajamas. The walk across the back lawn was short, less than twenty yards, and I knew that she would see me approach and would already be deciding whether to tell me what was troubling her.

But she didn't see me at all. She was so engrossed in thought that I came right up to the toolshed door without revealing my presence. I was about to speak to her when something held me back: some instinct perhaps, a feeling that my voice would be a gross violation of her privacy. I stopped then and took a step backward. My mind filled with conflicting thoughts. Later I could ask her about it, if that was the proper thing to do. Then I heard her say the word *mother*. My heart beat faster. She said her mother's name, Vivian, and, in a whisper, words that sounded like "somehow he's got to realize . . ." I took two more involuntary steps backward, turned, and walked quickly back to the house.

It was disturbing as hell. I waited for her in the kitchen, watching her intermittently from the window. For more than an hour she did not move. When at last she did come out of the shed I hurried upstairs to avoid embarrassment for both of us. I fell into my bed and lay there until the alarm went off, then got up to shower and shave. As always, she had breakfast ready when I came down, but she did not eat with me.

"I've got to run," she said. "I've got an early test and I need the library time for studying."

She kissed my cheek as she brushed past, and the door slammed as she went out. I walked to the front door and watched her walk away, briskly, as though she were racing the first bell. I went back to the kitchen and thought it through over a second cup of coffee. The conclusion was inescapable: Judy was going through an identity crisis, Vivian was at the root of it, and I had promoted it by making Vivian our household Mata Hari.

The question was, what should be done about it

now? Without doubt it would all have to come out, but how and when? *Soon.* Movement and action always helped relieve emotional logjams; I had seen it work many times. I went upstairs. She had closed the door to her room, as always, but I turned the knob and pushed it open. The bed was unmade, and several copies of teen magazines were scattered across the floor. Just as I had seen it three hours ago. I stepped into the room, feeling immediately guilty for violating her sanctuary. But never mind that; I justified it under the righteous cloak of parental concern. I did not touch anything; I did not pry, unless just being there was prying, as I suspect it was. I just walked through the room, stepping carefully around the magazines, and had myself a good look. It was the first time I had ever gone into her room without an invitation, and rightfully, I felt like a prowler.

Since I was a prowler, then, I let my eyes prowl across the top of her bureau. There were lipsticks and a cologne bottle and a few snapshots of Judy and her boyfriends, and one of me. At the end of her bureau lay her lock-up diary, apparently locked, but if she had left without putting it away, perhaps she had neglected to lock it as well. All the answers to my sudden questions would be there, just the turn of a hairpin away; but under no circumstances could I do that. I did not touch it, did not even go near it. In fact, I had just decided that I had already overstepped the rights of parental concern and was turning to leave when I saw, in a corner, the small stack of canvas paintings she had done for art class. Something about that first one caught my eye; it was not one I had seen before, though I had assumed that she always showed me her work. I moved up for a closer look. Yes, it was a new one: a faceless woman standing in a fog, with a deeper blue that might have been a river running behind her. The painting had a ghostly, morbid quality that I hated at once. Her signature was in the lower right corner, with the date below it. The painting was two years old, and I had never seen it.

I flipped back the canvas to look at the painting behind it. This one I knew well; it was the seascape that had won first prize in the freshman competition two years ago. Behind that was another new one, a full-face portrait of Vivian. It was so real and so good that I was truly shocked. It was called *Self-Portrait by J. Ryan.* That was a relief, but when I looked at it again, the relief dissolved. She had painted a small mole over the right cheekbone, where Vivian had always had a mole but where she, Judy, never had. I stood there looking at it for a long time, remembering small things about Vivian that I had put out of my mind years before. In almost every respect the portrait more closely resembled Vivian, just twenty-one years old the last time I had seen her, than it did her sixteen-year-old daughter. I studied it for so long that I had to rush to work; only as I was backing my car out of the garage did I remember my morning schedule of the vital meeting with the boss and an important new contract.

Harper Brothers Construction Company is located in the valley, on the far side of town. The company actually is owned by Al Harper, who bought out his brothers Joe and Vic more than twenty years ago, when all were struggling young builders. Nobody is struggling anymore. Al has grown fat and prosperous, and he pays his employees well. At least, I've got no kick. For a contractor located in a medium-sized semi-Southern town, Al Harper has done all right. He's still a hustler, and he gets plenty of jobs away from the big outfits in Richmond and even in Washington, D.C. But I'll write Al's success story some other time. After my initial reaction to the lateness of the hour, my thoughts came back to personal matters. Before I was halfway across town I had made a decision: The time had come, was long overdue, to get everything about Vivian out in the open. By now I had no doubt that what I was observing was an early symptom of something unhealthy, and it bothered me more the longer I thought about it. *Tonight;* I would start it tonight: throw out the subject myself and see where it led us. Perhaps that was all that was needed; maybe it would resolve itself. Judy's reaction would tell me everything. If she accepted it, we were still on solid ground. If she withdrew, we might be in trouble. That might mean that what I was observing was not an early symptom, but some advanced indication of her identity involvement with her mother. It was not a thought to start a big day with.

I pulled into the Harper parking lot just behind Sharon Welles. Sharon had parked near the door and was walking briskly into the office before my car had even stopped. Her aloofness was almost part of my life; after all, our little cold war had been going on for almost a year, and there was no reason for her to change tactics now. I shrugged it off, got out and went through the main office. The working offices at Harper are along a narrow corridor that leads from the showroom to the shop; mine was at the end of the corridor, a two-room job that allowed me to keep a door between Sharon and me. These days, that had to be a plus. I walked through without speaking. She was turned away from me, as always, this time ostensibly looking through the filing cabinet for some document, so there was no need for any morning greeting between us. She would fake it like that until we got through the unpleasant business of beginning the day; then the momentum of the job would carry us through to the end. Sharon played an excellent woman scorned.

With the door closed between us I loosened my tie, hung up my coat, and sat down at my desk. The phone rang immediately.

"Jim? Al Harper."

"Al. You been trying to reach me?"

"Just once; no sweat. Look, we'll have to postpone our meeting this morning. I've got to fly to Richmond."

"If you want to, but I can handle it."

"I'd like to be there. I've already called them and moved it back to next week, okay? So just hang tough till I get back."

That was that. I had blocked out the whole morning for the meeting, and now I had nothing on my agenda until one. I sat at my desk, doodling on my notepad, for about half an hour. Then Sharon came in with the morning mail and the coffee. As usual, we had nothing to say. She poured my coffee, then put a stack of mail on my desk and left, with a malignant glare at the portrait of Judy in my bookcase. That annoyed me; it always had, but there was no way I could thin the bad blood between Judy and Sharon now. So I would have to live with it or find myself a new secretary. Often I thought that that might be the best answer for both of us.

There followed more doodling and a superficial examination of the mail. Sharon had opened and thinned it for me, handling by herself the kiss-off letters and passing on the rest, in order of importance as she judged it. I sifted through it quickly. There wasn't much; there never was on Monday: the usual engineering crap, sales pitches from field agents. Nothing even mildly interesting until, at the bottom of the stack, I found a thick, padded manila envelope. I turned the package over and examined it. The postmark was New York, two days ago, and on both sides someone had stamped the word PERSONAL. Naturally, Sharon had not opened it. I tore it open and pulled out a large photograph, wrapped twice around with a long rubber band and protected on both sides by corrugated cardboard panels. I slipped off the rubber band, pushed away the cardboard, and turned the picture face-up. I expected it to be some technical shot of one of Harper's big jobs, but instead I saw a primitive mountain trail that dead-ended at the base of a wall of rock. The trail seemed to drop away into a canyon. The drop was sheer and I knew it was deep. There was a cave among the rocks at the end of the trail, and as I looked at it a strange sensation passed over me; the feeling that everyone has at some time in his life of knowing a place where he's never been. In this case it was nonsense. I have a slight problem with heights, and I knew I would never go out on a ledge like that.

I looked inside the envelope for some explanatory note, but there was nothing. There was no writing, other than my name and HARPER BROTHERS CONSTRUCTION COMPANY and the address. I examined the cardboard and the back of the print. Nothing. The picture was intriguing in a vague sort of way. I looked at it again, carefully this time. It was not a particularly good shot. The sun had probably been behind the mountains; at any rate, there was too much darkness. But it was clear enough. The trail looked treacherous. Scattered along its length were many loose rocks; any of them might send a careless climber plunging into the canyon. The thought gave me the shivers. It was difficult to get a perspective from the print, especially since there were no people in it, but I guessed that the trail was no more than three feet wide. Again I felt a wave of distinct familiarity. Absurd.

The buzzer. "It's your daughter," Sharon said coldly.

"Put her on, please."

I had time for just a brief reaction; mixed surprise and apprehension. There was a click and a loud background noise; a shuffling of feet and the hollow sounds of hallway talk.

"Judy?"

"Hi."

"Something wrong?"

"No, everything's fine."

"Well, then, what's the occasion?"

"I just wanted to apologize for running out like that."

"I didn't even notice."

"Look, I know you're busy and all."

"As a matter of fact, my whole morning's suddenly free. What's on your mind?"

"Nothing really. Just what I said."

There was a long pause while I gathered my thoughts. Obviously she was fishing, groping for an opening to discuss whatever was bothering her. Just as obviously, she wasn't finding it.

"Listen, I'll be late for class," she said.

I pondered it. It would have to be done, but not now and certainly not by phone. "Okay, you run on then. But don't cook anything tonight. I just might be in the mood for a night out. How about dinner at the Roadhouse?"

"Really?"

"Sure. Just the two of us, okay?"

"Great."

That little gesture, I told myself as I hung up, was a stroke of genius. I felt confident again, and I decided to work the Vivian thing out in my mind now, as long as I had a free morning. But then Sharon came in, dropped some drawings on my desk, and went out without a word. I made a mental note to get her replaced, absolutely and irrevocably; to have her shifted into someone else's office, even if I had to answer the goddamn phones myself. With that decided, my mind wandered and settled, strangely, on Robert Holland.

Actually, some of the things I had learned long ago from Robert might be of help in my little family crisis. Hypnosis had always scared the hell out of me, and now, considering it half seriously, I felt like a kid about to make a wild dash through a cemetery at night. I had not done it in fifteen years, yet there was not the slightest doubt in my mind that it would be as easy now as it had been then. I fought with it for another minute, then got up and turned off the lights. My fingers tingled with the excitement of it, and I sank back in the comfort of my chair, still too nervous to try anything. Gradually I relaxed, staring at the opaque window, and I went into a light trance immediately the first time I tried. I went deeper. The room darkened around me, and the window became a point of light in the darkness. I deepened the trance again, and Vivian's face came into focus. Or Judy's. At first I couldn't be sure. Then I saw the tiny black mole and knew it was

Vivian. I heard her voice, though I could not yet make out the words. I had almost forgotten the soft quality of her voice. Such effective camouflage for deadly poison. One level deeper and I would have her. I would see her and hear her, and if I wanted to I could reach out and touch her. Robert Holland had said that *you can relive any experience in all five senses under hypnosis,* and I knew the truth of it. I'd done it.

In the outer office I heard a filing cabinet drawer slam shut and Sharon swore, but the image of Vivian did not fade. My mind wrestled with both worlds at once and handled them with ease. I went deeper and the image sharpened; now I could see the little red lines above her green eyes, and the holes in her earlobes where the earrings went through. Behind her, the apartment where we had lived then, with the battered red sofa and the picture on the wall never hanging quite straight. She said, *Hello, Jim;* it was letter perfect, precise, like a videotape replay fifteen years later. I wanted to go closer, to step into the apartment with her, but instead I backed away from it. That cold, unreasonable fear forced me back, the apartment faded to an obscure black and white, and Vivian melted and became part of the blur. I came out of it very fast. The window focused in my eyes, and I saw that in the few minutes I had been under, it had started to rain. I sat there for a long time, just listening to the rain falling on the pavement outside. My mind was all a mixture of Robert and Judy and Vivian. Sharon pushed her way in by slamming another filing cabinet and saying "goddammit" just loud enough for me to hear.

All right. Enough.

I barked into the intercom: "Sharon."

"Yes."

"Get the hell in here."

I was surprised at the tough guy sound of my own voice, but the scene itself was carried through without emotion, as I knew it would be. We had come to a point where we could no longer communicate, and I wanted another secretary as soon as possible. She could handle it any way she liked: with a request to Al Harper for a transfer or with a resignation. I didn't care what she did. She took it without a word and left me alone. Finished, and it felt like scratching a sore that had itched for a long time. Done. After simmering for a year, the matter of Sharon Welles was settled and disposed of in thirty seconds. Vivian might be as easy, once the preliminaries were out of the way. My eyes fell on the mountain photograph, and in a quick flush of impatience I swept it lightly, wrappings and all, off the desk and into the wastebasket. Then I picked up my coat and walked out, asking Sharon to *please* cancel my afternoon appointments.

I did a lot of driving and thinking that day. When I got home Judy was already dressed for the Roadhouse. She waited for me in the living room, reading her new *Seventeen* while I showered and changed. Then we were off. The restaurant was an old favorite, located ten miles out of town on a hill overlooking the valley. We sat at a window table with a view of the patio. I was calm and confident right up to the moment when I had to face it. A bad case of nerves set in, and I ordered a strong Scotch to help get me started. I was halfway through my second drink before I decided to bite the bullet and do it.

"I know you've been wondering about your . . . mother . . . for a long time." My voice cracked and the words seemed to stick. I looked at her, but she was staring down at her water glass and would not meet my eyes. "Look at me, Judy," I said.

"I can't."

"Sure you can."

With that she did look up, and I saw that her eyes were filling with tears.

"Isn't this what you want?" I said.

"Yes."

"Then we'll do it together. I'll tell you about Vivian, anything you want to know."

"When?"

"Soon. I want to go through some papers first. I've got some stuff filed away that might help. Sometime in the next few days we'll get it all out and go through it together, okay?"

She nodded. Both of us were relieved to have that initial thrust behind us, and we looked for a new topic of conversation. We unwound slowly through the night and got home sometime before midnight. It was after two when I went up to bed; I fell asleep immediately.

I awoke in a panic. I jumped up and ran to the bedroom door, stumbling over a chair that blocked my way. The hallway was dark. Judy's door was closed, and there were no sounds or lights from the lower part of the house. I went back and sat down on the bed. *Now what the hell?* I looked at my bedside clock; the luminous dials said three-thirty. I had not slept two hours. *The dream.* I had been dreaming, not about Judy or Vivian, but about Robert Holland and that mountain trail in the photograph. A strange, screwy dream, but coming with it was one of the strongest impulses of my life, an overpowering need to save that picture from the janitor's fire. Morning would be too late; the janitor would have come and gone by the time I got there. I dressed, crept quietly downstairs, opened the garage, started the car, and drove to the office. I let myself in with my side-door key and went straight to my desk. The picture and all its wrappings were still in my basket, just as I had left them. I gathered up everything, cardboard, envelope, even the rubber band. By the time I got home it was almost five o'clock. I went into my den, unlocked the filing cabinet, and filed the photograph in the drawer marked ROBERT HOLLAND. Then I pulled the drawer handle to be sure it was locked and retired to my room for what little remained of the sleepless night.